TAILINGS
OF WARREN
PEACE

TAILINGS
OF WARREN
PEACE

STEPHEN LAW

Roseway Publishing
an imprint of Fernwood Publishing

Editing: Stephanie Domet
Design: John van der Woude
Printed and bound in Canada

This book is a work of fiction. Any resemblance to actual events
or persons, either living or dead, is entirely coincidental.

Published in Canada by Roseway Publishing
an imprint of Fernwood Publishing
32 Oceanvista Lane, Black Point, Nova Scotia, B0J 1B0
and 748 Broadway Avenue, Winnipeg, Manitoba, R3G 0X3
www.fernwoodpublishing.ca/roseway

Fernwood Publishing Company Limited gratefully acknowledges the financial support of the
Government of Canada through the Canada Book Fund, the Canada Council for the Arts, the
Nova Scotia Department of Tourism and Culture and the Province of Manitoba, through the
Book Publishing Tax Credit, for our publishing program.

Library and Archives Canada Cataloguing in Publication

Law, Stephen, 1969-
Tailings of Warren Peace / Stephen Law.

ISBN 978-1-55266-515-2

I. Title.

PS8623.A922T34 2013   C813'.6   C2012-908104-3

CHAPTER 1

Imix *(water)*

"Although this story is linear,
time in my culture is not.
So while it may have happened
not quite two decades ago,
it is part of my tomorrow,
remains in my yesterday
and informs the history of
my grandchildren
and the future of my great-grandparents."
–Celina

There were multiple shades of green. Pine needles in the early spring, while they are still vital, new, fresh. There was the green of avocados, light, almost yellow. There were emeralds and olives, the greens of Kentucky Blue grass, and shades of Crayola. But the trees were not like ones he'd seen before. They were tropical, with broad sweeping leaves like surfboards, and tall canopies that stretched with layers along spindly branches.

He felt as if he could see everything, skimming over the landscape as it panned the horizon. The air was moist, humid, the humus of composted earth with a whiff of sweet decay.

The girl beckoned to him, with large brown eyes and a grin that suggested games and mischief. She skipped along a path that led through the green curtains, her bare feet kicking up the dirt of the well-worn trail. He ran, chasing her as if they were in a game of tag. They passed over rocks and he felt the uneven terrain beneath his feet as they scrambled around boulders. His hand gripped the layered skin of a palm tree, pulling it off like birch bark.

She kept her distance, giving him glances and glimpses of her brightly coloured skirt disappearing behind a tree or across a brook. He ran as if breath held no meaning, and he could traverse the world without the need for oxygen. He heard her laugh, teasing him with the possibility of capture, only to emerge outside his grasp, just on the edge of sight.

He felt joy, the kind of pure joy spoken of by mystics and seekers. He could play this game for a lifetime.

The landscape changed, from green to browns, as if the trees had been airbrushed by the scatter-splash of mud from wayward ATVs. The jades made way for ashen browns and grey. He struggled for breath and his lungs ripped from exertion. The little girl was no longer laughing, it was if she was pleading for him to catch her, but she kept up the pace as if to escape pursuing wolves or demons. Her face was stricken, her tortured gasps imploring him to get closer, to move faster. The density of the forest gave way to bush and brush, then boulders and rocks. She got further away, and her calls became higher pitched. He strained to hear her, to see her. She was moving out of sight, and he kept running. He watched her sail over a barren hill, and he scampered up a carpet of shale in pursuit.

The sky was scorched red and lit up before him. He looked down upon a scene he had run from before.

Warren awoke. Each time he awoke, and each time he was unable to reach her.

· · ·

A single sentence centred on a piece of pink paper on a random power pole in his Annex neighbourhood.

She was my favourite sister, even from a young age.

The colour caught his eye. He had gone to Steven's Local Mart for a cool drink and began walking with beverage in one hand and a book in the other, to one of the big elm trees that billowed out from Palmerston

Park. The elm offered the perfect mid-summer canopy. The pink paper was on the first hydro-electric pole he passed as he strolled by Manny's Fresh and Fold Laundromat, a simple notice, like those advertising lost dogs or garage band gigs.

Warren wondered who the writer was and why he or she felt compelled to declare a sibling preference to a public of strangers. He shrugged and continued on.

He enjoyed Sunday afternoons. He was off work, as the cemeteries were busy places on the Sabbath, crowded with folks cruising the trails, more to promenade than in remembrance. Sunday night the church-attired and spandex-jacketed made way for the hooded and long-robed—pasty white-skinned Goths with dyed-black hair, skull and crossbones types, and their Pagan counterparts, the post-modern witches. Lots of running, picnics, rituals and dancing, and from what Warren could gather there was no harm done. Besides, a gravestone repossessor ought not to throw stones.

The next pole contained another pink notice and Warren's curiosity was piqued.

As the oldest of the young girls I had to look after the new babies— and to look after her was always a challenge.

Each pole contained a new line—a fragment, or a full sentence.

She was feisty,

He looked up the street and saw a string of pink, the colour linking one pole to the next. He continued past the park, his original destination.

like she didn't know she wasn't supposed to do certain things

At first he hurried, quickening his pace from one pole to the next. But as the story unravelled, he slowed, savouring the rhythm of each piece as it was discovered. It was meditative and he drank in the words and then moved off to the next light standard.

And she could scream

Oh, she could sure scream as a child

*great wailing bursts that would shudder
throughout the whole village*

Warren followed the story until the previous pole and the one in front of which he found himself were mirrors—reflections of the same.

It's the reverberations that still haunt me.

He continued walking, following the story in reverse this time, beginning with the reverberations and ending with the favourite sister. It was a palindrome writ large, filling the space of his neighbourhood. He emerged at Christie Street—a crossroads and an ending. Only a series of free-yourself-from-fat notices remained. It was over.

Warren was disappointed. He wasn't a fan of cliff hangers or set-ups for sequels. So, he hopped off the curb heading to the other side of the road trailing after the story as if it were a severed snake bisected by traffic. The blast of horns and Portuguese screams followed his frantic leap back to the sidewalk. He shrugged off the near miss and went up to Dupont Street and down towards Bloor. Nothing on either end.

He returned to Christie Street, reading from one beginning to the other, stopping when the story spun upon itself.

He was surprised when he looked up to see the blinds from his own apartment. The story stopped outside his door.

. . .

That night he sat on the porch and drank a Keith's Pale Ale. He was mesmerized by the pole, the last pole, on the left, below his balcony. He constructed his own story, about a favourite sister he never had. He left out the unsettling screams and created an alternative ending that had the little girl running into his arms as he came home from war or perhaps a dramatic naval expedition.

He stayed his hand on the third beer though, the alcohol had feathered the edges and he wanted the taste of the day to linger as he made his way to bed.

Sleep brought him oblivion on most nights—except when it didn't. He was startled when he awoke, confused, slow. His eyes darted around the room, noting the futon, kitchen, bookshelf, his black cat Vamp, white walls. Familiar.

His brother used to do that when they were growing up, awaken and not know where he was, as though he'd just been ripped through time from a dream. It was discombobulating, and truth be told, Warren felt a twinge of regret to find himself in his own room, in his own bed.

A coffee and a croissant were an early breakfast for him in the late afternoon. With CBC Two as the white noise in the background he descended to the neighbour's recycling box to grab the previous day's *Globe and Mail*. Since the day was already half over the paper was two days behind for him. He didn't mind, given it was already old news by the time it made the paper.

It was during his ascent up the stairs that he recollected the story on the lamp post. Curious, he backed down the stairs to check.

There was a new ending. In his haste—in the oppressive heat of the summer—he headed to Bathurst Street in his boxers and bare feet, wanting to read the story in sequence. A funny glance and then a shrug from a young, stern, dog-walking woman, alerted him to his state of undress. "Never you mind," he thought, "this is Toronto, at least I have shorts on."

The pink papers still lit up the lamp posts, but from start to finish, it was a new chapter.

The older sister is supposed to be the hero

He walked on.

But I idolized her

5

And continued.

At first it was kind of maternal—when you carry someone on your back for a year, you get attached

But later

with the other kids watching her make up games and getting everyone to play them

me included

I should have known better

I was older, I had work to do

But I was hooked

He passed a couple with a stroller, oblivious.

We all were

I sometimes gave her a little more of my food

It was the chain

My father, the boys, the girls, the youngest, then my mother

She was always a bit of a runt though

The food only went so far some days

"Maybe it's poetry," Curtis ventured as they drove around that night. "Kind of performance art sort of stuff. You know, like a gallery that has a big piece of meat with maggots burrowing through it—or those one -streak-of-paint canvas-type things."

Warren let that hang. They were coming up Albion Road to Glendale Memorial Gardens in Etobicoke. The heat didn't dissipate at night. It hung in the air, a grungy goo of decay and pollution coughed out by the millions of cars, people, and factories. It left a layer of stick. Open windows in a moving vehicle offered a reprieve.

"We've got a stash and dash." Curtis read the evenings details as they passed through the gates. "File says they buried and bailed. No payment since the dirt cracked the casket."

It was one of the things Warren liked about Curtis, his dispassionate irreverence for the task at hand. They repossessed gravestones, but Curtis kept it light.

They crept through the maze of monuments towards Glendale plot C-46.

IN LOVING MEMORY
ROGER DAVIES
1943–2011
PEACE, PERFECT PEACE

DAVIES, ROGER

68, passed away peacefully in his sleep on February 16, 2011. Roger was born in Saskatoon, the son of the late Phillip Davies and Beth (Steeles). Roger was predeceased by his wife Agnes (Klupper). Surviving son Jamie. Funeral service to be held Saturday at Mortimer's Funeral Home in Etobicoke at 2 pm. Donations can be made to the Canadian Mental Health Association.

Warren touched the name—probing, sensing, listening. He knew it was a game—a conjuring trick—to while away the time. Like his night dreams, a way to create a world from a stranger, even for a moment.

His hand on the stone evoked an image of Roger. He saw him as a miniature-ship builder in his spare time and pegged him as a pay clerk for a large factory. He had a family, a small one. Warren saw him in his home, where the attic was his refuge from the life he'd fallen into. It was a cosy place, warm and quiet, for Warren heard no sounds, other than the turning of pages of books. He stood over him, like a spirit wanderer. Roger read stories of mariners and shipwrecks, journals of seafarers who travelled around the world. He read about the world in which other people lived, and Warren felt a kind of kinship in this.

Warren liked to believe the images were real, for they offered a clarity to his thoughts and were presented in full colour as if he had been abducted from his own life and plunked into theirs. The immersion experience never lasted more then a few moments, though the taste would remain. And though it only happened when he touched stone, it didn't happen with every stone he touched.

Warren would let some musings take him through one day to the next, embellishing the scene he'd viewed, recreating people's circumstances, imagining their troubles, picturing their lives with their foibles, their tragedies. He wondered which was better: the life he imagined for them, or the one they'd had.

It had been a quiet night, and there were no new notices on the light poles when he went to bed early that morning, and fell asleep with Vamp purring at his feet.

· · ·

Curtis and Warren surveyed the damage as they made their way past the wrought iron gates. Some of the stones had been pushed over, others cracked with what must have been the vindictive blows of sledgehammers, bouquets had been trampled and ripped apart, petals and stems flung about, and epitaphs defaced with repugnant slurs.

Curtis parked the truck and they sat for a moment, looking over the destruction. Warren's mouth was dry and his stomach churned when he jumped out of the truck.

Cemeteries pride themselves on the pristine: ordered lawns, pruned bushes, majestic oak trees, and abundant blooming flowers; becoming known as much as locations for wedding photos as for burials. Warren savoured that order.

The scene that lay before them spoke of something different.

The police had removed their evidence and the media had captured their images and it was up to Curtis and Warren to clean up the mess.

Curtis ducked under the yellow tape with the wheelbarrow, shovels, and brooms. He moved to the nearest grave, and set upright a plastic flowerpot of yellow-centred daisies.

The air felt as though it had been weeping and he had trespassed into its midst. He envisaged the spirits risen above their graves swirling the way ants would scatter when their nest was destroyed. He was reluctant to touch anything.

Curtis knelt on the ground and raked the stone chips and floral pieces into a bucket and the cloud of images that had transfixed Warren swirled away. Forcing himself to get started, Warren went to the nearest grave marker and brushed away the loose stones scattered around it.

"Hey, careful with those," Curtis admonished him. Warren looked at his hands and the stones they'd cast aside.

Warren had forgotten it was a Jewish custom to leave stones on the markers. He bent down and gathered the rocks and pebbles together, re-forming a heap beside the daisies. He looked at the other memorials discerning the stones that looked like they'd been placed there with intention and those that had been strewn about in the destruction. Each mound signified a continuance, that by never finishing to build the monument, they never forgot the deceased.

It was Curtis who'd first told Warren the significance of the little piles of stones. Warren had asked where he'd learned it.

"The army."

"Part of basic training?" he asked.

"My buddy died."

Warren wondered if Curtis thought about his friend when he went through the sections of Jewish graves. He didn't speak much about that time and Warren didn't ask.

Now, Curtis moved to the next grave. The stone had been spray-painted with a swastika. They'd have to remove it to clean up the markings.

Warren looked at the epitaph of the monument that had been attacked. It was in Hebrew and English and read, "First Book of Samuel 25:29. 'May his soul be bound up in the bond of eternal life.'"

Curtis patted down the earth that had lifted with the gravestone and moved on.

Warren picked up a pebble that had slipped and rolled down from the small pile. He held it in his hand and then slipped it into his pocket and followed Curtis to clean up the rest of the desecration, working the rest of the day in silence.

Warren kept the pebble in his pocket. The dead man didn't speak to him or appear in any of his dreams, but Warren held the stone to ensure Abel wasn't forgotten and the vandals would be unable to obliterate his memory.

• • •

A new segment of the pink pages story appeared every few days, sometimes once a week. With a flush of anticipation, when he saw a new ending, he would bound down the street to pick up the story.

It was mysterious and exciting, like the discovery of chocolate bunnies at Easter. And with each new element, he would replay it in his mind, words morphing into images that would infiltrate his dreams where he saw an exuberant young girl and the older sister watching over her. He imagined them playing, talking, working; watching their lives as they grew and shared pieces with him on the papers.

My sister was the first to stand up

She was just fourteen years old

I couldn't have done that at nineteen, she who could barely
stand tall, did it for us all

We came together—all the families gathered at the church

The elders spoke first—the men of course

I remember waving the flies away from my face

It was hot outside, but a cool breeze blew in
through the open pillars

My whole family was there that day to listen

Most of us didn't know what to think

The men were inside, and us women and children

On the margins, outside, but present

To tell you the truth, I was a little intimidated and scared

You'd laugh at that knowing me now

The story had become personal, as if it were written just for him. And he felt as he read every line that he was cocooned away from the bustle of the streets, the slamming doors, knocked-over garbage cans, harried commands of parent to child, braying kittens. Not a sound entered his head. He had gone—the body still, grounded in place, the imagination soaring.

Yet, he had seen others reading. He knew he was not alone. He saw three teenage boys with hockey sticks using them to gesticulate and emphasize—pointing from one pole to another. This was a story his neighbourhood was beginning to learn.

Meena, his next door neighbour, a woman he saw rarely, but was pleased when he did, stopped him and asked about the posters when he was returning from work. She'd come back home to study, her father had bragged to Warren one day as he'd been hopping up the stairs careful to hide their newspaper under his armpit. They shared a semi-detached house: Warren lived upstairs on the other side of the multi-level duplex, their houses separated by a banister on the porch.

"Who do you think is writing and posting them?" Meena asked as he was heading up to his apartment and off to bed.

"The sister I suppose."

"Yeah, but who is she?" Meena was sitting on her side of the porch, in a chair reading a book. She got up and leaned against the rail that separated them.

"She's the writer."

"I know that, but what is she doing? Who is she? What's the point, what is she trying to say?"

Warren shifted his gaze away toward the light posts. He didn't want to guess at people's motivations. He shrugged.

Meena fixed Warren with a look and a grin. "Want to get a coffee?"

"Uh, no, sorry…" Warren turned to go upstairs, flustered. "Maybe later."

"Okay." Meena pulled a yellow sticky note from her law text and handed it to him. "Just in case you change your mind," she said. Its edges were crinkled and bent, and her phone number, neatly printed on the note, was worn. She smiled again.

Warren bounded up the stairs to his apartment. He put the newspaper on the table and fingered the sticky note. He could feel the tips of his ears burning, though no one was there to see his embarrassment but Vamp. He stuck the note with Meena's number on the refrigerator, and tried not to think about her invitation.

Later, allowed time for sleep. He didn't. He couldn't. He was restless. He played quiet music, read about string theory, moving from one layered cosmos to another. But the parallel universe premise kept him thinking that one of his personalities was having a better time than he was. He stepped out on his veranda to breathe in the city, to connect himself to the world.

A woman with a paint can, a brush, and a sheaf of papers she was struggling to control in the wind was beside the electric pole below him. She glanced up when a car door banged shut. So he was only glimpsing, seeing fractions of shadow. She had a red bandanna tied around her long dark hair, a black shirt, dark pants, Doc Martens. He caught her gaze, and held it for a moment. He saw fear, or panic, or maybe even defiance. Warren raced down the stairs to catch her, but she was gone. The pink page was the only evidence of her having been there.

. . .

They came in army trucks—the company and government representatives

Distinguished and differentiated in form

But not substance

Business dress or camouflage

They were totally foreign to us

They didn't look like us or speak our language

A man translated and presented to us their words

Or what he said were their words

The words they used then

That were spoken

Aloud

Turned out to be different from the

words we would use

To describe

What happened

• • •

"No pay, nowhere to lay," Curtis rapped his fingers on the side of the cab as they eased their way along the cemetery road to Daniel Black's headstone. It was a clear night, with the lights of the city reflecting back off the sky.

"Coast's clear," Curtis said, glancing around. "Let's go." Repossessing gravestones was fraught with hazards. Stones would be removed because they had cracked or were disintegrating, or because someone had defaulted on the payment. Though they were meant to act as everlasting monuments, they could be sanded, shaved, glazed and re-engraved for someone else who could meet the required payments. Many people would prepay their funeral and burial costs the same way they would buy insurance or pay a mortgage. But not everyone, and not always. And therein lay the opportunity.

Because someone couldn't make the payments for a loved one or family member, didn't mean they wanted the stone removed. But cemeteries were businesses and stones were for sale.

Still it was a tricky business. Warren and Curtis would spend the late afternoon hours doing maintenance and repair. They would remove the stones at night, when the sun went down, and visiting hours were over, so as not to disturb daytime patrons who might be paying their respects, attending a burial or visiting their departed loved ones. The night time extractions also tended to ensure distraught family members wouldn't be found standing guard over tombstones they were late making payments on and feared losing to Curtis and Warren's work-order sheets.

To begin a removal process, Curtis and Warren would manoeuvre their truck, which was fixed with a winch, over the grave. They would affix rubber-padded crampons and hoist the rock onto the truck. Depending on the size of the stone and the ornate nature of the engravings or design, memorials could range anywhere from a few hundred to a few thousand pounds.

Warren always felt a touch of coldness akin to delimbing a tree or pulling the wings off butterflies when they moved the stone. The depression left in the ground appeared as a scorched branding upon the earth, marking territory that was now being abandoned, particularly so for those stones that weren't coming back. Stones that were going off to be repaired were minor surgeries, abrupt removals were more like amputations.

Curtis and Warren eased out of the truck, leaving it running and the doors open, and walked toward the black marble marker. Cinching the stone onto the hitch, they eased it back and forth, careful not to bang or scratch it, nor drop it on either the manicured lawn or a vulnerable toe.

Warren felt a shock when he touched the rock as if he had been rubbing his feet on a carpet and touched his hand to metal. He interpreted it as penance for removing someone's testament from the land in which they were buried. He didn't want to imagine Daniel, and he had the pink drama rolling around in his mind, so he visualized the young girl carrying a basket of mangoes on her head.

A booming sound from the street exploded toward them scattering the vision of fruit. Curtis ducked on instinct and Warren whipped his head back and forth, searching around. It was a graveyard, after dark, it was hard not to be twitchy. Just the week before, Warren's heart was stopped when a figure rose up from the ground. It was a grief-stricken man, who'd slept out by his mother's grave. Rising bodies from sleeping bags in cemeteries in the middle of the night were not easy on the nerves. Nor were sudden and violent noises in the silence of a graveyard. Warren looked at Curtis, who was already half-turned back toward the truck. There was another loud bang and lights blinked toward them, then veered into the distance. They worked as fast as they could and made for the exit. Warren's mouth had gone dry and he wished he'd brought along some water. Road crews were repairing a sewage break on the other side of the cemetery gates as they hurried out with their cargo safely stowed.

"And to think, I'm scared of rollercoasters." Curtis said and they looked at each other and laughed.

Curtis dropped him off at Jane and Bloor. Warren wanted to walk home as the dawn approached. Walking gave him an opportunity to fill his head with random thoughts. He turned to make his way up Dundas Street and Warren noticed the long spider web patterns that hung over the city and cut across the major intersections, crisscrossing wires and streetcar grids. Each web shot tendrils out along the side streets, silk vines connecting one to another.

The pink pages had the overall effect of making Warren more attuned to his surroundings. The hovering spider webs made way for green canopies of sugar maple, ash and white oak trees along the side streets. The trees stretched out on one side of the neighbourhood and greeted their counterparts on the other, embraces that shaded the roads and yards. Houses in this part of Toronto were made from brick, which Warren figured must have come from the nearby clay deposits and been supplemented from the sand and water from Mud Creek. The remnants of the Don Valley Brick Works company were still visible from the highway that brought the commuters into the downtown core.

Back home the houses were all clapboard shingles and you could tell the state of the economy according to whether someone's home received a new slap of paint or not. The salt air played havoc on the shingles and they would peel from year to year. It was Warren and his brother's job to strip the boards and touch-up and reapply the paint. Even during the strikes or when the meal tickets were sparse, Warren's dad insisted on painting the house every year, so that no one could call them poor.

In Toronto, it would be hard to tell. The brick didn't seem to fade and the paint didn't seem to curl in response to the elements.

The thought of his old house brought to mind the cobwebs in the cellar. Cobwebs were different from spider webs, cobwebs are spider webs covered with dust and abandoned.

Warren noticed light had filtered through the canopy shining on the dew caught in the silk of an actual spider's web on the lawn. The light bounced off the water droplets illuminating the trap that would otherwise have been hard to see between his house and Meena's.

Warren skirted around and thought of the sticky note on his fridge.

• • •

Warren was sleeping when the knocking on his door took him out of his slumber. He was inclined to wait till the person went away, but in his semi-comatose state imagined it might be Daniel Black coming to collect.

"I'll be there in a minute," he called out as he pulled on his jeans and slipped a t-shirt over his head.

"Good morning," Meena said, pushing past him into the apartment with two coffees in hand. "I took a guess, one is black and the other has one cream and two sugars."

"Uh, sugar's good," Warren said. He took one of her mugs. His feet were cold against the floor; in his haste, he'd neglected to put on socks.

"So this is the hovel of a recluse?" Meena said. She looked around at the shelves crammed with books, the bare walls and sparse decorations. He squirmed at the strangeness of someone in his space.

"Look at these titles," Meena said, her voice rich and teasing. "*Life of Pi, Staying Alive, Such a Long Journey*? Not only a reader, but a man with taste. I like a man with taste." She looked at him appraisingly and he noticed her eyes, brown and clear and looking at him with warmth.

"Ah, yeah, um, hey thanks for the coffee." Warren raised his mug in salute breaking the contact.

"I saw you when I came home from university for Devali and I knew then and there I needed to make a visit to meet the neighbours," Meena said. "I had a feeling about you."

Warren squirmed a little harder.

"And now that I'm back home, and going to law school, I figured it was only polite to introduce myself properly." She gave him another look, all melting eyes.

Warren smiled and then tried to cover it up. "Do you want a cookie with that?" he asked, not sure of the etiquette.

"Great."

She liked his smile. She recalled seeing it for the first time, she'd been running up the porch, knapsack full of dirty clothes, anxious for a taste of her mom's dhosa. She was startled to see a guy's hand reaching between the slats of the banister between their verandahs. He'd been reaching for the newspaper, but when she appeared, he'd retracted empty-handed. She said "hi," and grabbed the paper out of the recycling and handed it to him, and he'd smiled, the kind of hello that moves from acknowledgment to eye contact.

On her next return home, during the holiday season, she'd been up till dawn watching Alastair Sim's metamorphosis in *A Christmas Carol*, when she'd heard scraping at their door. She glanced out the window and saw Warren in his winter attire shovelling snow off their porch and sidewalk. By the time she finished a cup of tea he had moved on to the elderly and incapacitated neighbours. When the lights went on across the road, Warren skittered back to his apartment, like a little house elf leaving a gift for the community. He didn't know she'd been watching him, but he'd gotten her attention. He was a neighbour worth getting to know.

Warren came back wearing a pair of socks and carrying a plastic tray of store-bought ginger cookies. "Here you go."

Meena took one and sat down on his couch.

It had been hard to tell what he was like. He'd seemed mysterious, she'd test-flirted with him with glances, subtle references, a few bold invitations. As he seemed to grow shyer, she became bolder, and the shyness intrigued her, made it a challenge.

She'd coaxed bits of conversations out of him, trying sports, politics, literature, world affairs. She knew he had opinions, but they were guarded. She took in his lean frame, grey eyes and dark hair. He was far more attractive than the people she'd eyed at university. He was different, she thought, though she'd never been able to move him beyond a minute or two of an exchange. So her efforts remained a series of flirtatious moments that had failed to be strung into anything robust, until the pink story opened up their conversations.

"I see you like books," she said, admiring the collection on shelves and the pile on the table in front of her. She had to move some aside so she could put down her coffee. "And what do you think about that book we've both been reading downstairs—the one on the lamp posts?" Meena asked.

"Oh, shit, I almost forgot." Warren jumped up and and threw on his shoes. "I haven't checked for it today."

Meena finished her cookie and then took a long sip of her coffee. "Sure, let's take a look." She smiled as they headed downstairs.

· · ·

I must be more careful

To be heard is what's important

to be seen

Immaterial

"I think she's referring to you, Warren," Meena teased.

"Doubt it," he said. "Let's see what the rest says." They scampered to the next pole.

To be seen and heard?

Well that can be deadly

They headed to the next one. Nothing. Then to the next and back again, checking in both directions just to be sure. There were no more pink notices dotting the neighbourhood. "Is it finished do you think?" Meena asked as they walked back to the duplex.

"I don't know, I guess we'll have to wait and see."

They paused at the foot of the verandah steps. Meena seemed to be waiting for something.

"Uh, thanks for the coffee." Warren gulped down the contents and handed back her mug.

"You're welcome." She smiled, and headed into her house and Warren ran back up the stairs to his.

• • •

For days there were no new postings.

Warren circuited the apartment the way seniors exercise in empty malls. To try settle his mind he grabbed Foucault's *History of Madness*, which he'd left unread at the top of the pile of books on his coffee table. He'd been hoping for some insight and some advice on all sorts of crazy.

But he couldn't concentrate on the book, he was drawn to the wall that separated his home from Meena's. He wondered if a glass held to the drywall, as he may have done as a child trying to overhear his brother's conversation with a girlfriend in the family's living room, would work to overhear Meena on the other side.

He shrugged it off, trying to dig into Foucault's dialectic challenging the states of madness and reason. To no avail.

He found himself standing near the corner, with his hands touching the wall, trying to garner information, to get the walls to speak to him the way the stones would.

She intrigued him. He liked that she had pursued him, come to his apartment. The feeling of being wanted was gratifying and filled derelict spaces in his ego.

Warren retreated to the kitchen, poured himself an espresso and sat down on his rocking chair which faced out the window. Coffee and a rocking chair were his most important comforts.

The Boston rocker he had spied near Lansdowne Avenue in a furniture store that restored antiques. His grandfather had sat in one for years, beside the woodstove near the door in the kitchen, with a quilt his grandmother made draped over his legs. His grandfather did crosswords and surveyed the activities of the home from his perch. It was one of the few reminders of home Warren permitted.

The caffeine was a crutch and three shots from his cherished espresso machine in an hour made him jittery. He felt caged in his apartment. He was anxious about going outside and running into Meena. He calculated he could make his escape later that night; when the lights were out he could dart for the street. If he packed a bag, he could flee, leaving his stuff to gather dust and unopened letters to accumulate for his landlady. That way he could skip out on both the possibility of hooking up with Meena and the likelihood of its failure.

But Warren was made inert by his inability to take both the espresso machine and the rocking chair—he couldn't manage both, and even to take one was impractical.

Meena came to his apartment on Saturday to tell him the writing had returned.

Warren smiled upon seeing her at his door. "There's more?" he asked.

"Yeah, a whole new chapter."

"What, no coffee?" He noted her hands were empty.

"No, but my parents want you to come for dinner tomorrow night," Meena said with a grin.

. . .

Sorry to make you wait

That's what they told us—as if we were the ones
anxious for the mine to be

developed

They split us up

Some in favour, some opposed

Lalita sparked the opposition

She stood up at the meeting

Came in from outside to where the men were speaking

She interrupted them, felt what they were saying wasn't true

while we all remained silent

She didn't believe them

She didn't trust them

She'd felt the scorn behind their tales and moved to tell them

We were surprised

They were surprised

But she was right

They were not happy and they were not friendly

That night they came to visit us

. . .

"So I'll see you tomorrow night?" Meena asked as they parted ways on the porch. Warren would have preferred coffee. The invitation for dinner had thrown him off. He had been trying to come up with a good reason to deny the invitation.

"I've noticed you don't work on Sundays, so I thought it might be a good time to ask," Meena said.

"I don't know..." The work excuse was the one he had been leaning toward.

"She'll keep asking. My mom is like that. If you come over Sunday, you'll get it over with sooner and you won't have to think about it."

"Uhh..."

"Come over around 7 pm. No need to bring anything, my mom will take care of everything."

Warren thought he was going to have to put something with a little more kick into his next drink.

. . .

There were five men

One was from the village down the river

I remembered him. We'd done the catechist together

I think he forgot that

They read us the new rules—broke our table and

22

grabbed Lalita by the neck

I screamed and they shouted at us

They were louder

It was hard not to listen

But Lalita tried

Screaming over a meal was something Warren could handle, it was the polite awkwardness he felt as he sampled the aromatic dishes of aloo pilau, sambar, and lemon dahl, that was troubling.

More than that, Warren was confused. He didn't know quite where he stood with Meena. They'd never so much as kissed, and now here he was, facing down her family. Surely this was out of order. He'd never been in such a formal situation with someone whose hand he hadn't even held yet. Wasn't even sure if he wanted to hold yet, he told himself sternly. This was all moving too fast. And while his head was swimming and his senses were reeling at the unfamiliar tastes and scents, Meena and her mother, Raita, kept up a cheerful banter. Her father, Vatu, wasn't sullen, Warren didn't even think he was indifferent. He was just silent, which Warren took for disapproval.

"Why did you leave Nova Scotia?" Raita asked in her gentle accent. "I hear it is so beautiful." Warren wasn't schooled in table etiquette, he'd never learned what spoon went with what dish and which body parts were allowed approximation to which section of the table. His family dinners had been rambling affairs, free-for-alls, TV or radio blaring, people bustling in and out and a whiskey bottle as the only condiment kept on the table. Witty repartee, though, that he could do. "I'm neither a miner nor a fisherman be," he said.

"Aye," Meena broke in, threatening to out-repartee him, "but Nova Scotia is not a mere medley redoubt of the Men of the Deep nor Barrett's Privateers."

Warren had looked for the cutlery when they'd sat down for dinner, the whole family, together. Raita had taken his hand and showed him how to scoop up the rice with his three fingers. He struggled now to keep up the banter and balance the lentils on the way to his mouth. "I see you've been doing some research and have managed to unearth references to some of our Maritime treasures," he managed.

"So evasive ," Raita chipped in.

"Your mother has an innate ability in jurisprudence," he said, wiping away some stray lentils that had dropped onto his lap.

"It appears we have a hostile witness." Meena raised an eyebrow and the corners of her mouth glided into a smile. "So, answer the question Mr. Peace."

"Could you repeat the question your honour?" Warren was uncertain whether to disclose or retreat. He wore a button-up shirt with trousers that had been pressed in the humidity of his shower. He was conscious of his presentation. Raita had welcomed him, Vatu had offered a nod, but kept his eyes at a distance. They had spoken more as neighbours on the porch than they had inside his home. And Meena was both beautiful and relentless—a combination that was slowly unhinging him.

"Why did you come to Toronto?" Meena asked.

The disaster of the dinner was overwhelming him. He didn't know how to eat the food, what cultural norms he was violating, what to say to Vatu, and whether Meena regarded him as a putz. He abandoned the battle "My brother died," he exhaled in exasperation.

Vatu looked at him for the first time since Warren had crossed the threshold into the Awinyolans' home.

"Vatu's brother died too, not too long ago; they were close." Raita filled the silence.

"What happened?" Meena's voice was soft. The veneer of lawyer in training evaporated.

"He was drinking, drove home, hit a car, hit a tree, and died." He kept it simple.

"I'm sorry Warren." Meena grabbed his hand from across the table.

PEACE, DILLON

21, East Cove, was killed in a car accident on Thursday. Dillon was a diligent worker for the Mugawash mine. He was predeceased by his father, Rick, and survived by his mother, Georgia (Georgie), and his brother Warren. Funeral services to be held on Saturday at St. Matthew's Catholic Church at 11 am. Interment will take

"Yeah, me too." He was sorry he'd let it slip.

"Were you close?"

"No." He put his head down and tried to concentrate on clearing his plate and keeping his fingers clean.

• • •

"Do you want to talk about your brother?" Meena asked when they were alone doing the dishes in the kitchen after supper.

"No, I'm good," he said, letting the water drain.

Warren and his brother had not been close, in fact he could think of few times when they liked one another. He thought that when they got older, they would be afforded an opportunity for reconciliation, but he was misled.

Dillon died before either of them matured into their adult selves. They were different: sloven strength ruled over studious rigidity, tall towered over taller, green eyes to grey, athletic to average, drunk to sober.

His brother kept his own counsel, younger sibling be damned. When their dad returned from the mines and began his real working day, labouring over the condiments, Dillon would disappear and Warren would be left to comfort or protect his mother.

He helped finish cleaning up and then thanked Raita and Vatu for dinner. "Thanks Meena, for supper," he said, slipping out the door before the goodbye scene became awkward. He closed the door and ran up to his apartment for a drink.

• • •

Warren thought about his brother as he and Curtis circled the graveyard the next night. Curtis was humming to himself, a funked out rap song. Warren was lost in his own melody.

They opened the extra gate that protected the Jewish graves, looked around and found Rocovsky. A stone had been placed with neither designation for husband or wife: no first name. No dates. A premature marking; a stone set in anticipation, yet defaulted on. It meant less an escape from death than a change in other fortunes: a cremation and scattering, a bankruptcy, or any multitude of possibilities. Warren reflected on the options of demise and the possibilities for memorializing. But he could conjure no images, no personalities emerged. No games to distract the mind. The stones had nothing to tell him.

So he thought back to the girl. Her name was Lalita. The little girl's name on the pink pages was Lalita.

. . .

They hit my big brother

Hard

The screams were my own

They told us to shut up

And we stifled our shouts inside

"Shut up—Stop talking about the mines or

you'll die

They left

The table and front door shattered, my brother bruised,
all of us shaking

My brother went to the mountains the next morning

And joined the guerrillas

Meena waited for Warren on his doorstep with a mug in hand, draped in a blanket. The steam from her breath and the hot chocolate mingled together, dancing up to the sky.

Warren almost ran her over on his way up the stairs. "Oh, sorry, I didn't see you." He'd been remembering being back home and scrounging through the earth as the dawn seeped up the horizon, collecting red wrigglers for his brother who was going to be fishing that morning. Warren always held out hope his brother might invite him along.

"What about the new instalment?" Meena asked. "Did you notice it?" Warren looked over his shoulder, and then back at Meena.

"Come on," she said. "Let's see what it says." She let the blanket fall to the floor, and put her hot chocolate to the side.

They stood in front of the last pole. "What do you think?" Meena asked. Warren was quiet. "Is it a story? Is it real?"

Warren looked up and down the street. He was a long way from a fishing hole. "It's kind of like poetry," he replied. "Fiction, I think. Why display your life story for others to critique and dissect?" Personal stories were territories to divulge to only the most trusted confidences, and only in small fragments, allowing no opportunities for analysis and interpretation.

Meena considered this. "I think it's biographical," she said. "A opportunity for catharsis. Why else would she share?"

. . .

It didn't stop, some people went underground, people who weren't happy with the officials' stories

Which is ironic really, for a group fighting a mine

Columbus had come up empty

These guys came with the same avarice and malice in their eyes

Gold,

for five hundred years they've been searching and raping our land

For gold

"It's a gold mine." Warren sent a text message to Meena. She was spending most of her time at the library, studying and preparing for her impending articling interviews, but she anticipated each chapter like the next episode of a popular serial. She told him to let her know the second he saw a new posting. He was compelled to respond, she was a force of nature he wasn't sure how to control.

So he wasn't surprised when she knocked on his door a few hours later, then burst into his apartment and threw her knapsack on the rocking chair.

He was at the stove, stirring cod, kale and rice. The house he grew up in had a revolving door, people moved easily in and out. He'd grown unused to it in Toronto, but he pretended this was no different.

"Smells good," Meena said. "Can I have some, I'm famished." She peeked into the pot and slipped him a kiss on his cheek in greeting. "Just the kale and rice though."

Warren was conscious of the touch of her fingers on his shoulder and her lips on his skin. "What, you don't like my Atlantic staple? It's gone from Newfoundland, but not the world you know."

"It's 'cause I'm vegetarian." She poked him in the ribs. "You know, no meat."

"No fish?"

"Vegetarian, you know, vegetables, meathead."

"I didn't know that."

"You weren't paying attention."

She took a plate and loaded it with kale and rice, ground pepper over it and sat down at the table to tell him about her discoveries, while Warren fixed his own plate.

"I started looking in to resource-extracting corporations, especially gold mining companies," she said.

"As part of your studying?" Warren asked, ladling cod onto a mound of rice and kale.

Meena rolled her eyes. "No, dummy, instead of that. The new instalment? It's like being on a treasure hunt," she said. And it was, for her. She loved research; she was most interested in case law, trying to find the connections around precedent and interpretation, and to see where and how she could make the links. Researching the mining company was a diversion from her studies, to be sure, but she couldn't resist the chance to play detective and get a reward at the end, if for nothing more than the satisfaction that she'd discovered the best hiding places.

"Harder than I thought," she said between bites. Warren took the chair opposite and picked at the bones from his fish. "Either they're private companies and not subject to public disclosure, or you have to look at each company's financial report and there are hundreds of them. They've got numbered companies, publicly traded companies, fly-by-night companies listed on the TSX Venture Exchange—if it's even a Canadian company for that matter. Then we don't even know where or when it happened. So I have to look back at the last twenty-five years of annual reports."

"Did you try Magma International?" Warren ventured.

MAGMA INTERNATIONAL INC   G

Exchange	TSX, CAN	Trading Currency	CA dollars

Figures displayed on this page are dollars except where noted.

Last Price	Open Price	Day Change	Change	Daily Volume
28.41	28.63	0.01	0.04%	3,873,766

Day High	Day Low	52-week High	52-week Low	Below High
28.77	28.21	45.99	22.97	37.70%

"Magma, no… why?"

"Just try it."

He'd seen Lalita before.

CHAPTER 2

Ik' (*waterlily*)

"*Events in our lives happen in a sequence in time, but in
their significance to ourselves they find their own order in
the continuous thread of revelation.*"
—Eudora Welty, author, 1909-2001

"It's like playing repo man with corpses," Curtis told him. "Taking a
grave stone in the middle of the day is bad luck."

"Says who?"

"It just is, that's all I'm saying."

Warren glanced around. Two cyclists cruised the trails of Mount
Pleasant Cemetery, a woman sat drawing under a tree. A crowd of
mourners gathered far off on a hillock. The final bites exacted by winter's
breath gave the early spring air a crisp crunch, yet there was a short man
in a grey suit sweating and waving them toward a gravesite.

The man wielded the authority that comes only from privilege,
ordering others about as if he had every right. Warren had seen it before.

His father had been a union man, the one and only conviction he
had in his life. Neither the sweet nor the strong arm tactics of the company fazed him. The manager had come to the house, to speak with his
dad, looking for a back door deal to an ugly strike. He'd come into their
kitchen, and Warren felt the man's distaste masked in cologne as he sat
at their table. His veneer was pleasant, taking a cup of tea, and dropping
in a few cubes of sugar, but not deigning to let the cup touch his lips.
When it was clear the only price his dad would agree to was the one that
included all the other union brothers, the man brought in tough guys

from outside to close the deal. His dad reached for a tire iron and swung at them. They backed off, but the strike lasted another four months.

The man in the suit had the same demeanour, and Warren recalled that same sense of anger, shame, pride, and fear.

"Get this the fuck out of here," he screamed as they drove up.

Warren had neither tire iron nor the convictions of his father. But he and Curtis did have the ability to be obstinate, and to use the time honoured tradition of pretending to be slow and stupid. They told him they had to wait for the manager. He tried to argue, cajole, get them moving, but they waited till they had the okay from the cemetery manager to remove the stone.

A hearse drove up from the office and the manager came out and spoke to Grey Suit.

"I'm sorry Mr. Brownley," he apologized in practised tones. "Go ahead guys, move it out." He motioned to Warren and Curtis.

As they went to move the stone into their truck, Warren glanced at the epitaph, and then ran his fingers over the letters, as if he were blind and reading Braille. With his hand on the stone, he felt an electric shock curl up his arm. Out of the corner of his mind he caught a glimpse of a young girl skipping, an apparition behind the curtains on a stage. He recoiled as if branded by the rock.

As Warren rubbed his fingers and searched the horizon for the little girl, he noticed Curtis staring at the stone.

LALITA ARAYO
1981 – 1996
"LEST THE BROWNLEY FAMILY FORGET
KILLED BY MAGMA INT'L"

"Not your typical last hurrah," Curtis said, nodding his head, more bemused then bewildered by what lay before them.

Warren shivered, trying not to imagine what had passed through him. He drew his finger forward to touch the stone again, unable to resist, the way an electrical shock is both addictive and repulsive. He was prepared to draw back if he encountered another surge. But he felt nothing, his finger felt fine, and the image was gone. He rubbed his hand with his thumb as if he were removing chalk, and then brought it to his tongue to see if it left a taste. There was nothing but the gritty residue of the stone.

So Warren shook out his arm and shook his head from the image that had gone through him and went back to doing their work.

The headstone bore all the signs and weight of an authentic memorial. They oriented the small operating crane over it and Curtis attached the crampons, while Warren shifted the levers to glide the rock on to the truck.

The stone had stood in front of another one, covering it, replacing it, almost as if they'd made a mistake the first time and needed to put up another one to conceal the error. They were set together like a row of dominoes, requiring one easy push to make them both fall down.

"I don't know how it got there," the manager was saying to the man in the suit. The man glared at Warren and Curtis.

"We're here for 2 pm," he glanced at his watch. "If there is a fuss, or any other mischief, you know the hell you'll pay." His voice was steady and menacing. With a final look of disgust, he turned and strode off, jumped into a silver Jaguar and sped away.

Warren and Curtis finished removing the illicit stone. Warren wondered why someone would have gone to all the trouble to put a fake stone in front of the real one. He knew back home that where you were placed when you were dead had a good lot to do with how you were viewed by the rest of the family. The girl referred to on the stone was only fifteen, so Warren wondered whether there was a family squabble.

Curtis seemed not to have paid it much more attention. He often said, "I'm too busy stepping on all the white men's graves," when Warren would notice some aberration or intriguing epitaph. Curtis enjoyed describing his job as payback for white folks desecrating Indian burial grounds for five hundred years.

The images of stone and permanence played in Warren's head as he climbed up to his apartment, ripped off his shirt and left food for Vamp. He stripped to his boxers and turned his ceiling light off.

• • •

The crash woke him. Or maybe it was Vamp screeching—either way he leapt out of his bed and peered from his apartment to the street below. The dawn had just begun to touch the corners of the horizon and he could see the door to his truck open to the breeze and the interior light illuminating the cab. He looked down the street in each direction. The other houses were dark. He went downstairs, in his bare feet, and deked around the broken glass of a beer bottle to inspect the damage.

"Dumb punks," he muttered. "Fuck," he blurted as his big toe picked up a glass shard. He struck his arm out onto the truck in an attempt to balance, as his toe started to bleed over on the sidewalk. He removed the chunk of glass and then wiped his foot on the grass to stem the flow of blood. He checked the cab of the truck, it was empty. None of his tapes were stolen; the crappy stereo was still in place. Nothing. "That's weird," he thought, "maybe the noise scared them off."

He closed and locked the door, and raced back upstairs, avoiding further glass shards, and trying to avoid painting the entire sidewalk with crimson droplets. He was bandaging his toe when he remembered Lalita. He ran back down, retracing his steps, and looked for the gravestone they'd left lying on the bed of the truck. Gone. He looked in the shadows, jumped in the back and felt around: nothing. There was no Lalita Arayo stone, just the red toe prints from his scamper up to the apartment.

"Who the fuck cares; the guy told us—just get rid of it." Curtis mocked the funeral director's voice when Warren picked him up for their deadhead run. "No record of it, no one paid for it, no one owes on it, just forget about it," Curtis shrugged, gazing out the window as they drove up Parliament Street heading for the cemetery.

And he hadn't spoken of it again.

• • •

They wanted us to move—our house was in the way of the mine development

Lalita said no. She didn't want to move, nor did

She understand why we had to

She was just a kid remember

It didn't matter to them

*They weren't asking us, but then we weren't sure
if we understood*

We didn't speak Spanish

not in the beginning

My brother was gone

It was now just me, my parents and my younger siblings

We didn't really think they'd move us

Till they killed my father

. . .

"What's wrong?" Warren asked as he climbed up the porch with a stash of library books. Meena was curled up in the Adirondack chair on her deck, drinking tea.

"It's sad."

"What is?"

"The story, it's sad now. The undertones were always there, but now—I don't know, I just read it coming home and it made me sad."

Warren put his books down and moved over to her side of the porch. He sat down on the steps in front of her chair facing out and looking at the light pole and the string of pink pages that ran down their street.

"Why are you a gravestone repo-guy?" Meena asked as she huddled into her chair.

"Why are you studying law?" Warren responded.

"Okay, Warren, anytime I ask a question you don't want to answer, you do a little dance. Come on now—give it up—what's a nice guy like you doing going around repossessing monuments people put up for their loved ones?"

"And why do you want to defend rapists and corporate crooks?" Warren countered

"Oh, that's fair; we can return to the lawyer quips later. So?" Meena was interested. She hadn't believed Warren when he told her what he did for a living. She hadn't imagined that anyone would do that, or would want to. It seemed cruel that a gravestone could get taken away, and that Warren would participate in it.

"It's a job."

"Warren, working at Timmie's is a job, being a traffic cop is a job, but taking away people's headstones in the middle of the night, that's a little weird." She tried to say it lightly, by shaving off the edge.

"Every job has its perqs."

"Come on, I'm looking deeper, how come you take away people's gravestones?"

Warren was aware it was not a typical profession, the way foot models or elevator engineers would be considered out of the norm. And it bordered, but didn't descend quite to the level of port-a-potty maintainer or crime scene cleaner. But it worked for him. He and Curtis were independent, they worked outside, and it was steady employment. Because of the paths and the green spaces, and flowers and trees, it was like a walk in the park. He enjoyed it. And in part it was true, but it wasn't everything, and not what she was looking for.

"Redemption."

"Whose?"

"Mine."

"Why?"

"It's complicated."

"So's tort law, gimme a chance."

"Well…"

"This related to your brother?" Meena prodded him.

Warren held his breath for a moment, then let it out. "My brother, my father and that ever-long line of cursed Peaces."

"Because they died?"

"And killed."

Meena shifted, swallowing her surprise. But Warren noticed, recognizing the reaction from his Nova Scotia days where anonymity was impossible and the reaction was second nature when people heard his name.

"What do you mean, Warren?"

"My brother killed a nice young family of four before he careened off the road and smashed into a tree. My dad blew up his liver because of his taste for the bottle, and my mom lives with the consequences, pretending she never had a family. And me, well, I learned that life bites, and when you bite back, you get bit even harder."

"I'm so sorry Warren."

There was more, sounds and smells etched in his memory he had been unable to disinfect or obliterate. But he swallowed his own role in maintaining the family tradition, kept it from spilling and staining those who weren't familiar with his past.

Five Killed in Fiery Two-Car Collision

East Cove — A young family of four were among the victims of a fiery crash along Sweet's Corner yesterday afternoon. Names of the

"And so I work taking away headstones, searching graveyards, contemplating the afterlife and re-writing people's histories in my head, wondering about mortality and living and thinking that maybe someone will explain it all to me." He picked up his bag before Meena had a chance to respond and went up to his apartment.

He threw his bag of books onto the couch, then stripped off his clothes, turned the shower on hot and grabbed the loofah scrub that hung there.

Meena stayed on the porch cupping her tea.

• • •

Yet still, we did not leave

My mother, I realized later, did not know what to do,
or where to go

She was paralysed by fear and uncertainty

She'd lived there all her life

My father had come courting her and moved to her village as

she could not be persuaded to move to his

He got teased about it, but he shrugged it off and pointed to all

of his children as proof of his decision,
proscribing the river and the mountains

as witness to the prolific nature of his coupling, his progeny

My mother blamed my sister and brother for his death

She couldn't see how the company, the government,
and the army were responsible

Marriage didn't make my mother leave her village, the death of it did

· · ·

Warren spied Meena doing yoga in the backyard from his kitchen window. He doubted she could see him, as the glare of the sun shone from the roof overhead. He'd gone out of his way to avoid her, feeling bad about their last conversation.

He observed as she moved from one pose and held it, bending her body as if in worship to the sky, balanced on one knee with her other leg extended behind her and her arms slicing upwards into the air. It was like watching honey as it descended from a spoon.

Her motions were slow, leading his eyes to take in her calves which gave definition to her legs, her biceps, supple, yet strong. He watched transfixed as she arched her back and brought her arms forward pulling the air and the world toward her in an embrace.

He was drawn to her. Little tendrils that she had sent out had affixed themselves to his skin and despite his efforts, he couldn't resist her pull.

He decided he could learn yoga. He knocked on the gate to the backyard. He'd never been back there, as the upstairs tenant on the other side of the duplex he didn't have access. He opened the gate to the small herb and flower garden maintained by her father, and found Meena sitting erect with one leg folded under the other, facing him in front of the calendula.

"You warming up for soccer?" Warren said by way of greeting. He smiled so she'd know he was being friendly.

"My people call it yoga. Do you wanna try?"

"Sure." Warren found himself bent at the knees like a human chair, his quads screaming their resistance. "I think soccer's easier," he said pulling himself up to stretch his legs.

"Like anything, it takes practice. I've been doing it a little bit longer than you have."

"I can see that," he replied in admiration.

Meena took Warren through various postures, being careful to move slowly and provide him with plenty of description. She kept up a conversation as they moved from one position to the next. "My father fancies himself an agnostic yogi or sage, with all the wisdom, but none of the religion," Meena noted as she came out of the cobra posture. "So, if you get caught up in one of his stories, go with it," she said moving to downward dog.

"My father was a bit of a storyteller," Warren responded, trailing behind in the movements as he stood erect moving out of the triangle, to a standing position. He found it hard to talk and learn yoga at the same time.

His father could regale a crowd. While there were ceilidhs going on in the kitchen, Warren's dad would be in the living room, entertaining those who'd gathered to listen. With the fiddles in the background, Warren would be scrunched up under his chair enraptured by tales of family lore, of nearly drowned sailors from swamped fishing boats, old Scottish ballads detailing battles with the British, and the heroic resistance of the settlers to the Clearing of the Highlands, when his fore-family was first put off the land. It was nice to remember his father in this way.

Meena was surprised, first at his appearance, and then by how forthcoming he seemed to be. Maybe the yoga was opening up his heart more than he intended. She sat on the ground and brought her knees to her chest. "What do you remember?"

Warren would sit out in the orchard telling the same stories he'd heard the night before to an audience of squirrels. He had only resurrected the practice with Curtis's family, as a goodnight tonic for his kids.

"Well…" Warren was gauging whether to stay in the safety of the veil or whether he should try his hand at the family raconteuring. He looked at Meena again, and sat down beside her, leaning against the trunk of a cherry tree.

"Alright. Well, he used to tell the story of the Halifax Explosion."

Warren loved the smell that permeates the air from a lit match. He would watch his father's yellowed fingers delicately line up the dried tobacco leaves, rolling the paper into a cylinder and licking the edge to seal it tight. Warren could picture him using his knuckle to clear an errant flake from his tongue before wiping his hands on his jeans.

Meena picked at the grass like a pupil listening to a teacher in a village. "What about it?"

Warren remembered his father would tease out the start of the story by lighting the cigarette, and taking a deep drag and then exhaling the smoke into the air as a dramatic device to heighten the suspense before embarking on the tale.

Warren took a breath. "This happened in the First World War, when the *Mont Blanc* munitions ship in the harbour blew up, taking half of Halifax with it." He could see his father with a drink in one hand and cigarette in the other. Warren recalled the flush of anticipation not knowing where his dad was going to take them. He could hear his dad's voice becoming his own.

"Well, it's a bit of a story about the never-do-wells and their whiskey. My folks, and theirs before them, and I imagine as far back to Scotland, Ireland, and Rome as you can get, my people have worked hard at living and drinking. My great-grandfather, my dad's granddad, Stewart, was much the same and no different. He, like far too many of them, worked in the mines. But a cart took a spill on his leg one day, cracking it up one side and crushing it on the other. It ended his days underground and as fate would have it, gave him a clear medical discharge from the army. This was 1917 of course, the height of the war in Europe against the 'Huns' as my dad would say."

Warren would collect the matchsticks, sometimes making forts, or train tracks where he would lie them end to end. Other times he'd use the black soot to write on the road, to draw pictures that could be erased by the rain.

"Stewart was supposed to go to Halifax with a coal shipment. After his accident in the mines, he became a kind of porter travelling back and forth on the rails, moving the coal from the ground to the ports."

His father's eyes would be bright, his gestures grand. He was theatrical, on stage, it was what made him a good union leader, when he had an audience.

"He and his buddies got on the train that day, same as lots of others. They'd started drinking the night before, and hadn't slowed much or quit despite the inconvenience of working. The train made a stop in Truro, as it used to do, and him and his two buddies jumped off to get a bite to eat and slow the flow if you will. Or to keep it going as the case may be. So, they found themselves in a pub by the station sharing the drafts and the time with a young redheaded waitress by the name of Lizzie." His mom hung in the background, but she'd have curled her hair, and pressed her dress. Warren thought she looked pretty.

"The way Dad tells it, they thought the train was to be stopped for a few hours, having some cars pulled off and others put on. But, it was a mail run, a grab and go kind of thing."

The parties would last the night, and sometimes the whole weekend.

"So, while he was downing his second beer and catcalling the girl, the train whistle sounded and the big engine began its departure. Now those old trains were pulling a lot of weight, and it would take them a fair time to get going: long enough for the lads to down their beers and make a run for the caboose to haul themselves up. Except, the thing was,

Stewart had this bum leg. Now, truth be told, those trains were laboured, and if he'd put his mind to it, he could have hopped and hobbled quick enough to grab a rung and not be left behind. As it were, there were other things on his mind." Warren remembered watching his brother finishing off the dregs of the drinks, telling their mom he was clearing the bottles to keep things tidy. When Warren followed suit, he ended up spitting it out, much to his brother's entertainment.

"While his buddies threw their coins and ran, Stewart called Lizzie over for another beer."

His brother had learned to enjoy the taste.

"It was when Lizzie awoke him the next morning in the room in her boarding house, that he found out the harbour had got shot up and blown all to hell, the boys, the coal, and the train car with it."

Warren finished and emerged out of the nostalgic haze with Meena's eyes upon him. "My father told that story when anyone told him it was time to finish his beer and get going. He figured his granddaddy always gave him a reason to stick around to have another drink, and in fact, he felt there was more harm in leaving."

He looked at Meena. "You have to understand that story fit well into my dad's worldview, not only was it the story of his dad's conception, but it was his great rationalization as to why whiskey was better for you than work."

Meena didn't speak for a moment, and Warren realized that maybe he had revealed too much about his own background. "There's also a lewd part of the story involving Lizzie becoming his grandmother and both the ship and Stewart getting blown at the same time."

"You can spare me, thanks. Good story though." She marvelled at the tale, picturing Warren as a small boy absorbing the stories in his family's kitchen. Stories that seeped into him and shaped his being. She saw him as a blank canvas that with the right incantation could reveal a rich tapestry. It made her want to find the clues that could keep the curtains open.

"Was it true?"

"Does it matter?"

"Not really."

"Like I say, it was a good rationalization for Dad; he also told it to illustrate the Peace family luck. The line would have ended there according to my dad. It was a powerful intoxicant to him."

The story times were always good times.

"My father likes to believe there's a lesson in every story, and it may not be the same lesson for everyone, in fact you may not interpret it the same way the teller is trying to give it, but there's always a lesson there if you look for it," Meena said.

"Well, my dad figured out his lesson."

"And you? What do you take from the story?"

"Luck has an awful lot to do with circumstance. My great-grandfather could as easily have ended up on that train as off," he said, his mind lingering on the smoky room back home.

Meena was beginning to draw lines between their histories, seeing how invisible threads could link and entangle one soul with another. "That story would fit well as a Hindu fable—a reflection of his karma, where deeds in past lives or previous actions dictated his present circumstance."

"How do you figure that?"

"There's good and bad in everything. Your great-grandfather's leg getting crushed was a bad thing at the time I imagine, the pain, wondering what work he could do. But, then along comes the war, and he doesn't have to fight because of his leg, which might have saved his life. Or, he gets reprimanded for not being on the train, and then the train blows up because he's not on it."

"That's a kind of sad way to look at the world, as an accounting of sorts."

Warren wondered about the ledger of his dad's tale-making, and if the storytelling filled up the credit column that had been depleted by what happened on the debit side.

"Depends on your perspective I suppose," Meena said. "Let me tell you a story my father told me. It's from the Ramayana, one of the Hindu epics. My dad always uses these kinds of stories to emphasize his points as part of his amateur theology and advice columnist pretensions."

· · ·

Why Rama Went Into Exile

Dasharatha is the father of Rama, and he had a number of wives, including Kaikeya. In the midst of one of the epic battles waged during these times, Kaikeya saves Dasharatha's life. In recognition and gratitude, Dasharatha grants her three wishes.

Kaikeya knew that she was not the first wife, and therefore her son would not be able to become king. So, realizing her great fortune, she proclaims that she wishes that her son Bharata take the throne, even though she knew it was her stepson, Rama, who was to become king. In an attempt to further entrench her son's dominion, she also wished that Rama be banished to the forest and spend fourteen years as a hermit, allowing Bharata to rule unhindered. So, Rama took his leave, off to the forest.

Alas, as in many Hindu tales, all actions have karma. So, while Kaikeya loved Dasharatha very much, she did not realize that banishing Rama to the forest would also result in the death of Dasharatha.

You see, when Dasharatha was a young, impetuous man, he was on a hunting trip in the forest. While looking for game, he shot an arrow into the air and it struck and killed a young man. This was the only son and provider of a poor couple who lived in the woods, who were both blind. Upon finding out about the loss of their son to the indiscriminate activities of Dasharatha, who was a mere prince at the time, they put upon him a great curse. This curse declared that Dasharatha would die when he was separated from his son.

• • •

Even after what happened we still stayed near the old community

We moved further up the mountain

To my aunts.

We stood on the hill and we watched them bulldoze our home

As if it were a tower of cards made by children.

I'd grown up there. It's where I had played

With my siblings

It's where we would grind the corn from the milpa

And make tortillas

Everyday

We had a garden, with chilli, avocado, oranges, cilantro, flowers

My abuela

My grandmother, would weave

I could picture her in the corner

Chattering to us, telling us stories

As her fingers would thread and pull

Placing colours on a loom, following the intricate patterns

Of our people

It was our home

. . .

"AT LEAST I TRIED—FOREVER IN OUR HEARTS"
AMOS HUTCHINSON
DECEMBER 18, 2010

"Guess he didn't try hard enough," Curtis mumbled as they edged the casing into the truck. Warren had run his fingers over the engraved words—evoking an image, an inkling of a face. He saw an old man, an eccentric, an inventor. All around in his workshop were trinkets, discarded metal, ends of wood pieces, and rubberized tips. Creaking machinery whirring as the old man worked a lathe— wood chips spewing, arching in the air like a wooden rainbow. Set to baroque music, the scene played in repetition. As he saw the man and focused on his eyes and crackled face, it melted and contorted and merged into another, with a darker complexion, black hair, striking cheekbones, an assortment of teeth. He wore a yellowed shirt,

pants like slacks but worn and worked. Laid against his shoulder was an oversized wooden hoe, the metal blade reaching almost two-handspans wide. The handle glistened and shone from oiled sweated palms, the shape of the handle wavy and warped, hewn at home, no factory lines. Amos was Pablo.

My father Pablo was a good man

The pink pages of earlier in the day stuck with him. One life turned into another, unclear what was fiction and whether it mattered. Pablo had become as real as Amos. Amos's life was validated by the gravestone, he was marked, he lived, died and was remembered. Pablo lived through the story on the poles, just as real and imagined.

He was a campesino all his life

A farmer

His tools were a hoe and a machete

As a child, I imagined my father who worked the land

Was made from the earth

Wizened, cracked, and hardened in the dry season. Full of

Humour and generosity during the rainy season

His body nourishes the soil now

Hung

He was hung to dry with his own machete swinging from an

Avocado tree

That's how we found him

It was a warning, to everyone, the whole community

He became the example they would make of all of us if we

Continued to resist

We're lucky. His body we had to bury, offer blessings

We have nothing for my sister

. . .

Warren's first burial had been his grandfather's.

He had looked at peace in the living room in a way he never had while sleeping in the bedroom. The coughing and phlegm would wrack his body convulsing him out of a dream. Warren was curious to see his face in repose, knowing the convulsions had ceased. He was glad of that.

He had a sneak peak when everyone else had left. His dad was passed out in the bedroom, his mom was tidying the kitchen and his brother was sneaking a cigarette and a grope out behind the stoop with their second cousin.

His grandfather was dressed in the same suit he wore to weddings, funerals and church on holiday Sundays. It was the suit he wore when he and Warren skipped out during the sacraments and toddled towards the shore. His grandfather would take off his shoes and socks and roll up his pant legs as they'd skip rocks out over the water. They'd competed to see who could collect the most and skip the fastest, the farthest, the most times.

Even then, his grandfather's breathing was laboured. Warren had gone slow, passing up good specimens to make it a fair fight.

Warren had slipped out during the service, this time alone. His dad called him back, but he heard his mom respond, "let him go, it might be too much for the boy."

He'd left the funeral because he wanted to get a good rock, one his grandfather would appreciate, that had heft, yet was smooth. Something he could use to skip over the clouds with.

While everyone was gone, Warren took the rock and picked up his grandfather's hand. It was cold and stiff, like a store mannequin. He placed the rock between his grandfather's fingers, so he could hold it and take it with him wherever he went.

• • •

Curtis and Warren eased through the cemetery.

"Hey, can you stop a minute?" Warren said, "so I can take a leak."

"Be quick, I gotta get back before Shirley's gone to work."

Curtis's wife was a nurse who did the occasional night shift, but more often than not worked during the day. That's what they preferred; then they didn't have to rely on others to babysit. Curtis looked after the kids during the day and studied part-time and Shirley looked after them when he was at work at night. Curtis was studying his masters in cultural anthropology. He told people it was to rile up the taxpayers so he could access the free tuition available to Aboriginals, but Warren noticed he pushed his kids to study. Curtis would interrogate Warren after he babysat whether they had done their homework. Warren always lied. Babysitters by nature told parents what they wanted to hear.

Warren jumped out of the truck and moved out of sight of the red beam from the taillight, it cast an eerie shade on the grounds that made him uncomfortable. He preferred the pitch darkness, there was less commentary. He headed for William Brownley's grave and pulled out his penlight and shone it upon the stone. Under William's name, in a childlike hand, was etched another name, visible in the right light: Pablo.

BROWNLEY WILLIAM
1926 –2011
LOVING HUSBAND, FATHER, GRANDFATHER
FOREVER GOLDEN

Warren made as if he was doing up his pants and jumped back into the truck and they headed home with the last of their headstones.

"Why did you go back and check?" Meena asked. He'd knocked on her door upon arriving home from work that morning, inviting her to breakfast. She'd showered and dressed and joined him in his apartment.

"I don't know, I just felt I needed to look," he said. Like kids communicating with strings and styrofoam cups he'd been drawn there, one grave taking him to the next. Though he'd been slow to receive the message, it was effective. Still, he edited himself. He told Meena about the name, but not the visions.

Meena shivered as she thought about the writer who posted the pink pages in the neighbourhood. "She must know it's you."

"Why do you say that?"

"She must have seen you at the cemetery, or followed the truck one day. Have you ever wondered why the pages are on the poles outside this house? Why after you read them, they disappear? Someone's putting them up—and taking them down—for you."

Warren shrugged. "They have a short shelf life. Besides, the woman, the writer, could live on this street and these are the only poles that will publish her."

The truth was, he had considered it. It was clear it was a message, someone was communicating something to him. Who it was, and what they were trying to say, he wasn't sure. But he had no doubt that the message was intended for him. As a young child he recalled how his grandfather had told him about his late wife's ability to "see." Warren had never known his grandmother, but he'd heard the story many times. She envisioned the collapse of the mine one night and forbade Warren's grandfather from work that day. When the alarm sounded after the dust had billowed from the shaft, his grandfather was never again in doubt. The community shunned his grandmother though, out of fear. Warren had learned that lesson at home, he kept those things to himself.

Meena watched as Warren cooked eggs and fixed espresso. As they had uncovered the layers of the story, Warren had drawn more into himself, as if he were conserving his energy and strength for a battle.

"I found out some more about Magma," she said with hesitation.

"What did you find out?" Warren was distracted by the eggs. He was ravenous, hungry in the way the body can get after an exertion, when it hasn't been nourished.

"It's not good."

"Well, do tell." Warren flipped breakfast onto their plates and poured the coffee at the formica table with its chrome-plated chairs.

"They're a gold mining company."

"Yeah?" He popped the toast out of the toaster and buttered the multi-grain bread, covering the whole area, right to the edge but not over.

"They're large, they've got hundreds of millions of dollars in assets, run six existing mines, have specs on fifteen exploratory ones and their head office is located here in Toronto."

"So, what else?" Warren loved marmalade. He spread a thick layer onto his toast and gulped it into his mouth, grateful for the taste of bitter sweet.

"They have a mine in Guatemala. Or, at least they had one."

"Guatemala, that's in Central America right?"

Meena hesitated, watching him put a piece of toast in his mouth, chewing. A drip of marmalade clung to the corner of his lip. "Yeah, and Magma was cited in the deaths of fifteen people there."

He'd been waiting for this, trying to have breakfast as if it were a normal day, and they were having a normal conversation. He left the eggs on his fork.

Meena told Warren about the company that was responsible. He knew Magma, he was familiar with companies that left strings of corpses. Images of the dead flooded his brain, those the companies had been responsible for, and those he had a hand in. Warren saw Pablo, he knew him, and Lalita too. He'd dreamt of them, as if they were living people who continued to exist if you kept pushing play on the recorder. He could still taste the ashes of an explosion on his tongue.

"Cyanide poisoning in the local river.

Poison. In a river, a body.

A father, a grandfather.

Warren's grandfather had told him the snakes weren't poisonous, that they were good for the garden. His grandfather had kept a small plot at the back of the company house when they'd moved in with him. It's where Warren learned about vegetables, where he developed an appreciation and wonder about food. When his grandfather became unable, and they no longer could do it together, Warren would scoot up the crabapple tree and drop apples down into his basket, and then his mom would make them into jelly. One day he'd been playing nearby, gathering the apple drops into little mounds to use in backyard golf games or as baseballs. He saw something sneak under a rock, and pulled up the stone to find a nest underneath, little wiggly snakes. His grandfather called them garden-variety, there was no harm in them.

"A tailings pond broke."

There was a brook just near their property. He'd taken Warren there many times. They watched tadpoles, listened for the cicadas, he showed Warren the tree holes where the pileated woodpecker would burrow for insects.

"They use cyanide in the process of the extraction of gold. The pond was filled with cyanide."

Warren flashed onto the bedroom, the smell of the bedroom. His grandfather lying on the bed, propped up under the family's quilts, the ones made by the women who stayed above ground, keeping their hands moving while they waited for the bump to tell them about seismic shifts that covered and buried those who would lay under them. He coughed and coughed, night or day, he'd cough. You couldn't drown out the sound, even when Warren stuffed pillows on his head, he couldn't drown out the sound. It was raspy. He could hear his grandfather try to clear his throat, as if somehow that would be enough, and the phlegm would be dispelled and allow him to breathe air free of particles that came up from his lungs.

The air was poison to his grandfather. When Warren's mom told him what was wrong, that his body had inhaled too much dust, Warren had taken to wearing a mask around the house and when he went to play outside. He thought breathing would kill him, so he would hold his breath as long as he could, because he thought if he did it would help him to live longer. He thought his grandfather had extinguished his allocation, as each person was allotted only so many breaths in their life.

"The company denies it, the connection to the mine was never proven and the bodies disappeared."

Warren had to clean up the bloody black spit that came out of his grandfather's mouth. He was scared to touch it, like it was an infection that would grab him. He'd heard from older boys in school you could get diseases from a toilet seat. He used a rag and then washed his hands in hot water, sometimes with bleach from the laundry.

Meena kept talking, presenting information as if she were developing a case for the prosecution. Warren tried to focus, but knew they were a part of him, that Pablo was his

Amnesty Cites Canadian Company in Death of Guatemalans

Dan Fairmen
Associated Press

Amnesty International accused the Canadian gold mining company Magma International of responsibility in the deaths of fifteen peasants in the highlands of Guatemala

grandfather, his grandfather could have been Amos, that it was all connected, and that they were all protagonists in the pink notices.

. . .

Her name was Lalita Arayo

She came from San Jacinto del Quiche in Guatemala

She was my sister. Pablo was my father

They killed my father, and took away my sister

My village died

They poisoned it, and they poisoned us

I will not forget

• • •

Warren noticed her right away. She had long dark hair, was wearing a white t-shirt, black pants and Doc Martens.

It was a poster at the campus that had caught Meena's attention, a poster advertising a fundraiser for the Lalita Arayo Solidarity Association to be held at the Bloor St. United Church. It was a pink poster. She brought it home and posted it on his door with a note saying "I'll pick you up at 7."

"That's her."

They walked into the church and the woman with the Doc Martens approached them.

The woman smiled at Warren, like she knew him.

Warren felt there was a hand guiding them to the church, leading up to this moment, where they would meet and confront the pink pages woman. It would be a time when the grand plan would be revealed and they would discover the purpose of the story, and why they had been invited into the drama. He had no question whether he would attend.

There was a big space in the sanctuary, like a gymnasium, and the party was being held there. Overhead was a theatre-style balcony, like something out of Shakespeare's time.

The woman in the white shirt placed her hand on Warren's arm and leaned up to kiss him on the cheek.

"Thanks for coming." She had an accent, Spanish. Warren stared. "And you too." The woman smiled warmly at Meena.

For weeks they had read this woman's story on a lamp post, following it like a daytime soap, lurching from one tragedy to the next. Now, here in front of them was the author, yet neither knew why they were there nor what to say.

"My name is Celina Arayo. We have a lot to talk about. After the fiesta, we'll talk."

She grabbed Warren's other hand and squeezed. They watched her walk away to the canteen where she spoke with a group of women in the corner.

They hadn't shared a word with her, asked her why she'd put the posts outside his door, what she wanted from them, why they were there.

"Let's sit," Meena said. She led Warren to a table on the fringes, wanting a vantage point on the entire room.

"She seems fine," Warren said, raising his voice so Meena could hear him over the band that had taken the stage and was playing traditional Latin-style country and western. He realized as he spoke that he'd been half expecting the author of the pink pages to be unhinged, a bit crazy. But he recognized her. She shared the features of Pablo and Lalita, people he had seen in his mind.

"Appearances may be deceiving," Meena kept her eye on Celina, following her movements. She took note of Celina's long black hair, similar to her own, but Celina's was wavy with a kind of curl that might have come with assistance. It accentuated her features, her face was round, where her own was thin.

A tall man approached their table. "Hi, I'm Bill," he said. He held out his hand and Meena grasped it. He was fair with short-cropped hair, cut military-style. "Haven't seen you folks around before," he said, extending his hand to Warren. "You one of Celina's projects?" He pulled up a grey plastic chair and sat down.

"What do you mean projects?" Warren was wary, he didn't like to be toyed with.

"I mean to say, did Celina invite you here?"

"Not exactly." Meena was guarded.

"Well, whatever, we're happy you made it." He twisted in his chair at the sound of raised voices. "Oh, excuse me for a minute." Bill jumped up and headed to the door, where a number of people were gathered.

The hall was full—university students marked by their glasses and mismatched outfits, professionals who wore dress coats, a woman with a clerical collar. Small groups of families, likely Guatemalan, Warren thought, wore clothes made of bright and colourful fabric.

He realized he and Meena had spiralled up a cloak and dagger elaboration of what they thought was happening, and yet these people were innocuous, ordinary. The extraordinary story they had followed on pink pages appeared to be about people they passed every day on the street.

The noise at the entrance to the hall escalated and shouts could be heard over the sounds of the band. Warren and Meena exchanged looks. "Get ready to run, Hemingway, the bulls are coming," Meena murmured. A circle of people had formed around the disturbance like kids gathered to watch a playground punch-up. Warren was drawn to the crowd, but Meena said, through lips that barely moved, "sit, we're staying right here."

Bill burst through the crowd, dragging a man by the arm to the door. He threw a menacing glare over his shoulder, and two more men quickly followed.

It looked like a bouncer bar toss, Warren thought, not unlike what he had experienced himself when he tried to follow family tradition.

Bill returned alone, did a quick scan of the hall and then directed a stocky young man and a woman with Michelle Obama arms to secure the door. Warren figured if Bill wasn't a drill sergeant already, he certainly could be one now. The spectator ring disintegrated, having flared like a match leaving just the smoke and a stench. The band upped the volume on stage, and soon people were dancing again.

"What was that all about?" Warren asked Bill when he walked by headed to the kitchen.

"Nothing to worry about," he said with a glance at the door. "Just a few folks who wanted to create a fuss, and put a dent in the festivities. We don't shut things down that easily though." He chuckled. "Now I have to go and fix the tap on the beer keg." He smiled at Warren, then at Meena. "Enjoy the night." And he continued on.

"Not much chance of that," Meena said.

Warren nodded. "Strange party." He had his eyes fixed on Celina as she moved about the hall. Meena's head was ever in motion, from the door to the dance floor to the kitchen. But no one else seemed bothered by the earlier disturbance. The fundraiser settled into an evening of music, dancing, and people gathered in clusters socializing.

After a fashion, they both began to relax. "What do you think?" Meena asked.

"I think I should get us something to eat," Warren had spied the canteen toward the corner.

"Good idea, I'll watch your back," Meena replied with a smile.

Warren made his way across the crowded dance floor as the band switched from twangy Latin western to grooving salsa.

"Not bad." He'd returned to the table with a sampling of dishes he was unfamiliar with and two beers. He dug into a tamale, a thick stuffed dumpling with spicy insides. He picked out chicken and made apologies to Meena for not getting the vegetarian.

She wasn't paying attention, she was looking past him, out into the crowd that was dancing in front of the band. He turned his head, and saw Celina approach.

"*Quieres bailar?* Would you like to dance?" She held her hand out to Warren. He looked at Meena who nodded her head once.

He was anticipating a shock. He wondered if he was to be an electric conduit between Celina and her family, transferring their spirits back to her hand.

She led him to the dance floor. Her hand was soft.

"I don't really know how to dance to this stuff," Warren began to say as she placed his right hand on her lower back. His left she held at shoulder height in the air.

"It's okay, I'll show you. Just feel the music, it's all in the hips." Celina moved her lower body, side to side to the beat. He would have preferred to watch the musicians, the bellowed reed of the accordion player was accompanied by drums and smooth guitar rhythms, he could feel it reverberating on the floor, pulsing up his legs into his body. The music was syncopated, tick a tack, tick a tack.

"It's like you are shifting your weight from one foot to the other and pushing your hip out. See how my hip goes out." Warren saw. "Grab my hip, do you feel it?" He felt Meena's eyes on them, but moved his hands to Celina's hips.

"We'll just do it slowly," she told him as he tried to make the wood in his limbs into liquid. As he became more practiced, he fixed on Celina.

"Why me?" he asked.

"Why not you?" she came back at him.

Why indeed, why not anyone? But Warren wasn't just anyone. He was below the radar, he'd constructed his life to bear no account, to require limited commitment to only those things which he chose, was interested in, or connected to. He wasn't supposed to have been noticed.

The music stopped and someone else approached her to dance. He was left alone on the floor, surrounded by salsa swingers, with no more insight than he had before.

He returned to their chairs. Others had sat down at the long table, but Meena made no effort to engage with them.

"What did she say?" Meena rushed to ask, before he'd been seated.

"Nothing," he replied. "She didn't tell me anything."

So they sat at the fundraiser and tried to fit in. People were laughing and dancing, others were getting drunk and louder, but Celina remained out of their reach. "This is crazy," Meena said. She stood up, pushing her chair back decisively. "I'm going to talk to her." But as Meena approached, someone whisked Celina away into the kitchen, and when she tried to follow, Meena was met by stern volunteers, tiny women, their arms folded across their chests like bodyguards. Thwarted, Meena bought two more beers instead and returned to Warren's side.

Warren drank both beers, and they waited. They tried to dance a few times, dancing apart where others moved in pairs. Neither felt very good at it, and it was easier for Warren to sit and take it in. Meena remained on the dance floor, not suffering from suitors interested in touring her around the floor. She was glad to be moving, but was conscious to keep both Celina and Warren in sight.

Gradually the crowd thinned. Some of the Guatemalan families left, with crying kids in tow. Then Warren noticed the seniors were gone, and eventually the students too. The band stopped playing and the lights went up and Warren went to approach Celina. She stood near the door, counting coupons people were given when they arrived.

Warren moved towards her. His patience was worn. He took Celina by the arm, swinging her towards him, "What is this about?"

Warren didn't notice Bill come up behind him and place a warning hand on his shoulder. "Is everything okay?" he asked. Celina waved him off.

"It's fine, thanks Bill. I'm okay." Celina beckoned Warren to join her at a table in the corner, while a small group of people continued clearing away chairs and sweeping the floor. Meena sprang up from her seat where she'd been rubbing her feet and went over to join them.

"Do you want some tea?" Celina asked

"I'm looking for something a little harder," Warren decided.

"Eduardo, *un botella de Flor de Cana por favor*," Celina called out, and one of the men who was clearing up nearby dropped what he was doing and rummaged behind the bar. He returned with a large bottle of Nicaraguan rum and poured them all a generous shot of the amber liquid. "This is my friend Eduardo," Celina said while he poured the shots. "And I know you met Bill, and over there is Chantel, by the canteen. They are all friends of mine."

Meena brought her chair closer to Warren, and took the shawl she had been wearing and laid it around his shoulders.

"So, what the fuck is this all about?" He glowered at Celina.

"Thank you for coming," she began.

CHAPTER 3
Ak'bal *(night)*

...if one can go forward in imaginary time, one ought to be able to turn around and go backward... where does this difference between the past and the future come from? Why do we remember the past but not the future?
—Stephen W. Hawking, A Brief History of Time

They were greeted by the humidity at the door of the airplane, enveloping them with a blast of hot air, pregnant with moisture, a welcome to the tropics. After the drone of the aircraft, Warren's senses took a moment to adjust to the cacophony of valets in burgundy vests pushing trolley-carts, and brightly attired Guatemalans pacing all around. He realized he couldn't understand anything. There were displays of products that were familiar in logo, but not in text, and his ears strove to hear something he could hold onto, that would ground him in the knowledge of his surroundings. Celina took his arm and directed him toward a taxi, and he was able to let his sense of sight and smell catch up with the distance his body had travelled.

The airport was in the centre of the city. Discarded plastic bags, banana leaves, palm fronds lay strewn on the street, on pavement and sidewalks and mingling with the constant beeps of horns used as a form of dialogue to negotiate the traffic. A whiff of garbage, urine, and cooking oils mixed with dust and diesel permeated the air.

The houses were pastel, colonial style with large shuttered windows, and with paint that dripped off in flakes from the twin pressures of piercing sun followed by torrential rains. There were yellows and blues and greens, all faded into the wood or concrete vestibules. Those windows that were open had their views dissected by steel bars, enough to reach in a hand, but not fit the arm, to protect those within from those without. And he saw vendors everywhere, selling mangoes, oranges, pineapples, papaya, belts and keychains and plastic bits, potato chips or coloured drinks in plastic bags, batteries and cigarettes. Some pushed carts with two wooden wheels, and others threw woven blankets to the ground with products arranged on the street.

Warren pivoted from his reference point, his head still in Canada, he catalogued the sights by what he already knew, transposing the scenes before him with Chinatown, along Spadina and Queen Street, where the vibrancy of trade on a Saturday required the same careful negotiation of the crowds. He often didn't understand the language spoken there either.

"What's with all the English names and security guards everywhere?" Warren asked, curious as they passed by a variety of places with names like Biggest, Pizza Hut, and Mr. Donut.

Celina glanced at the guards in white shirts who carried heavy-duty, sawed-off shotguns or semi-automatic machine guns, part of her ordinary, but anomalous to the visitor. "Imitation and poverty. Can't have one here without the other."

They were moving into a neighbourhood with narrower streets, lined with forty-year-old apartment buildings with balconies running the length of each floor and metal staircases at each end. Warren noticed graffiti everywhere, not just tags, but elaborate murals and paintings like the ones on bridges and overpasses in Toronto or along the factory walls heading out to Scarborough on the Rapid Transit lines.

They got out of the cab, headed towards a faded, salmon-coloured building and climbed to the second floor. Travelling from one end to the other, they passed a number of apartments adorned with small religious stickers of Mary and Jesus affixed to the doors, which Warren figured indicated to the Jehovahs and Mormons to either pass on by or try harder. They stopped at number 22.

"*Hola querida, bienvenida.*" The man who came to the door kissed Celina on both cheeks and clasped Warren's hand.

Marcos, Celina explained, was an old friend. He'd kindly offered them a place to stay when Celina returned to a city she had been away from for many years. The two fell into easy conversation, belying their many years apart. After several minutes of lively chatter, Celina remembered herself and offered to translate, but Warren waved her off. He was wary of drawing attention to himself. He preferred the quiet of limited interaction. He knew Celina would tell him if there was something he really needed to know, and so he smiled and sat back, immersed in acclimatization through observation. Before long, a small woman wearing an apron, with her hair tied back, came into the room with coffee.

Warren sipped the strong drink and looked around, drinking in the details of this new place. He noted the cross and coloured paintings of Jesus hanging from the concrete walls. Walls that were grey, though they looked as though they'd been painted white at one time but couldn't retain the purity of colour given the pollution hanging in the air. He thought about the buses they'd passed coming in from the airport, and imagined the black exhaust fumes clinging to the concrete. Sparse furniture and a black and white television completed the room. The windows, which opened like cut-glass fans, also had bars on the outside.

They had dinner that night in the kitchen, prepared by Doña Beatriz, the woman who'd served them coffee when they'd first arrived; rice, beans, fried eggs, plantain, and small, fat tortillas, and a kind of homemade lemonade sweetened way past sour.

While he ate and watched, Celina and Marcos spoke together, gesturing and laughing. Marcos made efforts to engage Warren at first, each stumbling through an unfamiliar language.

"He thinks you're a farmer," Celina said.

Marcos had asked about Warren's profession and Warren had mimed digging. Repossessing items from a graveyard was on the elaborate side of his acting abilities.

"You could tell him my harvest requires a crane, can't be composted, and has very little decay." A language barrier and limited charades manoeuvres kept their interaction on the surface . Warren resorted to a constant grin, with eyes stretched out to other distances, indicating he was content to listen.

The talking flowed over and around him, engulfing the room with the sounds of comfort. Celina seemed at ease here, in a way he hadn't observed in Canada. It was like she had shucked a heavy cloak from her shoulders, the weight of an alien culture. She was home.

Warren found himself jerking his head up from the table, in response to the meal, travel, the sights and sounds, and the constant buzz of unintelligible conversation. He wished for a shower, to clean off the threads of home still clinging to his clothes, to clean off, and start afresh. And he longed for a bed to close his eyes and absorb all that had soaked through his senses.

Celina spoke to Marcos who looked Warren's way and nodded. He stood and shook Warren's hand.

"He says we can use his sister's bedroom and that he's arranged a driver, *de confianza*, to pick us up in the morning."

Warren nodded.

"I told him we're married. It's easier that way," Celina added.

Easier seemed an interesting choice of words. He began to wonder if he should have been paying closer attention.

Marcos led them to a starkly decorated room that had a double bed and dresser overseen by a large crucifix adorning the wall.

"I'll sleep on the floor," Warren offered when they'd brought in their packs, settled into the small room, and closed the door.

"Don't be silly, it's a concrete floor, it's cold and you'll wreck your back. Besides, I trust you." She said the last statement looking straight into his eyes and holding his gaze.

· · ·

He hadn't thought about what to wear to bed. He had mosquito netting, a hat, sunscreen, and malaria pills, but no pyjamas. Instead of slipping under the blankets in his jeans, with a modest shrug and his back to Celina—for his sake, not hers—he stripped to his boxers, then climbed between the coarse sheets.

Celina came into the room with him, went through her bags and removed assorted articles. She didn't look his way, but sat on the bed, and began combing her hair, humming to herself. Then she pulled off her pants and facing away from Warren she unstrapped her bra and snaked it through her shirt and out one sleeve. Warren tried not to notice.

Celina turned the light off and moved to crawl in beside him. There was a glare through the window from a streetlight, or maybe the moon, he wasn't sure. He held himself still, awkward, he wasn't sure if this had been an invitation, and whether he should accept, or lie like a fool, which depending on his actions, he would have to do in one context or another. He turned his head and looked at Celina. Her eyes were open, soft, looking at the ceiling.

"*Buenas noches* Warren." She leaned toward him to kiss his cheek, and then turned her back to go to sleep. Warren lay in bed and thought about trust.

• • •

Celina wasn't sleeping, he could tell: she didn't move, her breathing hadn't become regular or rhythmic.

Years of remaining on the sliver between wakefulness and dreaming had taught him sleeping patterns. He had shared a room with his grandfather and could differentiate the breaths that were laboured from those that asphyxiated. After his grandfather died, he shared a room with his brother, and he slept with his eye cocked in case of a knee drop. It was there he developed his understanding of parenting modelled on the shouts from his parents' bedroom, learning to grasp sleep in blocks of time bookended by slammed doors and squeaky bedsprings. He knew when someone had drifted and he could tell when they were in a full and deep unconsciousness, when the whole house was still and quiet, when he could finally let go.

Celina was awake.

"Can't sleep?"

She rolled to face him and searched his face. "No" she whispered.

It felt intimate, close. He felt the proximity of her body, the heat rose above the wool blanket they had stretched over them. He could feel her breath on his neck.

"So, how do you know Marcos?" he asked, to draw a boundary between their bodies.

He brought Meena to mind, as she had first appeared to him at his apartment. He thought of her skin, as the tiny black hairs on her arm rose when cold. She had a dimple on her right cheek that only surfaced when she smiled.

Celina told him that Marcos had been her lover. She said it to Warren as they lay together in the small bed in a room with concrete walls and adorned with a wooden Jesus crucifix hanging over their heads, keeping them in check.

He hadn't picked up on the obvious clues, the hesitations, the looks Marcos had flashed towards Celina while they were talking. He thought of them now, put them into context. She told him that Marcos had been a student leader from El Salvador, from the seminary, who'd had to flee to Guatemala after six priests had been killed by the army at the university.

Marcos had been a priest, or was a priest, and a lover. Warren knew priests did all sorts of things back home, some of them good, some of them unmentionable. He wondered how Celina had felt about being with him.

"He was conflicted in many ways; that was just one of them," she told Warren. Marcos had joined the guerrillas, had fought in the mountains. Warren didn't know what that might mean. He found it hard to reconcile the picture of Marcos now, short with a receding hairline, with Marcos then, Rambo decked out with headband and ammunition clips across his chest.

It made sense now, given their history, that Warren was presented as her husband. It avoided complications and closed off the possibility of misunderstandings; and as he looked at Celina, lying so close to him that by moving his head, he could kiss her lips, he realized it perhaps also created some as well.

"Anything else I should know about him?"

"He's a good man Warren. I trust him. We should sleep." And she turned away from him again and closed her eyes. Warren lay still, awake. He had come a long way.

CHAPTER 4
K'an *(corn)*

"What matters in life is not what happens to you but what you remember and how you remember it."
—Gabriel Garcia Marquez

The church was empty of all but Celina's friends, plus Warren and Meena. Celina pulled a stack of pink papers from her knapsack and laid them across a table wiped clean of church suppers.

"This is the rest of my story," she said. "Do you want to finish it?" Warren wondered where it was going to end. The invitation suggested at something more than just reading the rest of the story.

Meena placed her arm around his shoulder, a deliberate touch, the first they had exchanged. He wondered if she placed it there for comfort or protection.

He wasn't sure he wanted to read the rest of the story inside the empty church, under the overhead lights, in front of everyone. He relished the gift of each street offering, the uncertainty about when it would arrive, what each new section would contain, layers added to those he'd already read. It was anticipation, meaning, mystery. But now, sitting in front of him on display in its entirety, to read in his own hand, the grandeur went out of it. It meant that a novel he had loved to read was about to come to an end, and he wasn't ready.

But Meena had no such illusions. She was eager to consume the story so she could place it in context, put an end to what had at first seemed an innocuous game. Meena grabbed the sheet on top and handed it to Warren.

My sister stayed in the community after we left

My aunt, my mother's sister, had a new baby and needed
help taking care of the other children

Lalita didn't want to go

She loved the land and she missed my father

For awhile, everything was fine

I went to school

sponsored by the Sisters of the Precious Blood

My family,

My mother mostly

Put her hopes in me

The dutiful daughter

The quiet one

The smart one

I went to school

I learned the language

I learned everything I could

Warren picked up each new sheet as he finished the one before. He
passed them on to Meena, who read separately at first and then glanced

over his shoulder as he moved through the stack, his objections forgotten as he plummeted back into Celina's life.

My siblings went back to the village on holidays

We all worked

Some were street vendors,

Maria cleaned the houses of the well-to-do

Carlos joined the military

It pains me still

To think

He didn't understand

He never could

I stopped going back after awhile

To the village

There were other things that had become important to me

I met men

Boys really

They were ladinos

And I am indigenous

I was exotic to them

Even though our origins were mere hours apart

Indian women wearing traditional clothes

Were discounted, ignored

Like we were stupid

Thought less of

I wanted more

It was as though

if I wore jeans and a t-shirt

I could be different

So, I learned to dress like them

Talk like them

I didn't see it as shame

I saw it as opportunity

But now,

Maybe as survival

I was able to go to university and study

This was not common for an indigenous woman

But

I'd been transformed

I had a new language

New friends

Maybe I could hide

So I did not have to be afraid

My sister saw this

She came to visit us in the city

She saw my change

She challenged me

She yelled at me and called Carlos and me traitors

I yelled at her and called her many things

I think I hated her

I told her I hated her

She knew I hated myself

She hugged me when she left and whispered

She loved me

I was still so angry

I turned away

Didn't even watch her go

Warren looked up at the end of the page and noticed the busy work to restore the church to clean and tidy had ceased. He watched Eduardo wring out a mop in a bucket, while Chantel tucked a broom and dustpan into a cupboard. With the church spotless, the pair moved toward the last remaining table, its surface a riot of pink pages.

"We're heading out," Eduardo said.

"It was nice to meet you both," Chantel said, smiling at Warren and Meena. She leaned down and kissed Meena on one cheek and then the other, and then did the same to Warren. "Bill will get you home safely," she said to Celina. She held out her arms and Celina stood. They hugged warmly.

"See you tomorrow," Eduardo called as he and Chantel headed for the door.

"Goodnight," Meena called after them.

Warren remained stiff.

Celina filled their glasses and without another word, they resumed the story.

It was ironic of course

Carlos came to tell us

He heard because he was in the military

Someone knew he was from our village

Someone who'd been ordered to hide and bury the bodies

fifteen people, mostly children had died

My sister Lalita

was with them

The mine had been operating for a few months

It was a few hundred metres

From where our house used to be

They tore it down when they built the road

My aunt's house was much further away

Up the hill

We found out later

Lalita and many of the kids

From the families who stayed and moved further away from the
mine

They'd gone down to the river

It was Lalita's idea

That's what my cousin said who'd stayed behind

They were playing in the river

They didn't know

The company didn't tell them

Cyanide

They use it to extract gold

It's poison

They didn't know

They were playing in the river

The company dumped it into the water

They didn't know

To drain the tailings pond

The leftovers

The refuse extracted from the earth

The kids noticed the fish floating dead in the water

But they didn't understand

There is no smell to cyanide

Lalita knew

Not about the poison, but that something was wrong

She yelled to them to get out of the water

But the kids didn't understand

She ran into the water

And tripped and fell trying to pull the kids out

They thought it was a game

It didn't matter

It was too late for all of them

Most of them

Died that night

It doesn't take much

They must have poured hundreds of litres

Of the stuff into the water

One entire family

Whose daughter had brought water from the river to cook with

Died

They all died

There were eight in that family

There was Lalita

And six other children

Two of whom were my cousins

Lalita died last

She made the kids eat dirt

To get them to throw up

It may have saved some kids

If there had been more time

But

There wasn't

And

It was all over them

They couldn't drink the water

To flush it out

They couldn't wash themselves

To clean it off

There was no health clinic for the villagers

Only for the miners

They asked for help,

Begged them

And they were turned away

Until they were dead

Warren felt the empty echo of the hall around them as they read a few words or sentences and then flipped the page onto the mound that was piling up on the table.

Officials came and took the bodies away

Saying they needed to find out what went wrong

To help us, help us all

But they never brought them back

And said they never had them in the first place

As if they had never died

Nor lived

Cyanide poisoning is an awful way to die

The mine killed my father and my sister

And eventually killed my mother

And tore the rest of the family apart

My mother died two months later

She sold watermelon and fruit on the streets

After my sister died

She stopped working

She stopped eating and drinking

She gave up

I nearly did too

It's maybe hard to contemplate

All of this

It seems unreal

as I put it to paper

But when they killed my sister

I stopped being afraid

I loved her

With all of my heart

My sister was everything I wanted to be

She was strong and funny

And cared what happened to our family

The company never apologized

In fact, they never admitted to doing anything wrong

They told people the polluted water was

an Act of God

They never said

Whose god?

We were poor indigenous people who didn't matter

It mattered

It matters to me.

Que Viva, Lalita, cariño

Que viva!

Celina sat back, behind them, out of sight as they read the story. She moved back into their line of vision when it was finished. Warren held the last page in his hand, reluctant to let it go. Meena moved on instinct, she embraced Celina, drawing a link to her story and sharing it through her body. Warren stayed in his chair.

It was finished, the story that had shaken him out of complacency as he'd gone walking out to the park was finished. A story that wasn't a story, that wasn't fiction.

Warren was struck silent by how sad it was, what a great and tragic loss. It was something he understood. He knew what loss meant, what happened in communities like this, like his own.

"The mine was closed a few months later," Celina added an epilogue, "but the company has the lease for two more years. If they reopen the mine, they get another fifteen-year option. If they don't, they lose the concession. And they've started preparations to re-open the mine."

"Magma International?" Meena felt the need to be definitive, to know where she should direct her anger. Celina nodded.

"And tonight?" Warren asked. Because the events at the fundraiser spoke to something that transcended the story, that brought the story closer to home, to their home and not some forgotten part of a small country in a place that was so small and orbiting so far from the big picture as to be obscured and discarded into complete and total irrelevance.

Celina explained the company didn't want to lose the concession, it was worth hundreds of millions of dollars, perhaps billions even, and the sheer scale, the sheer number of those dollars outweighed recognition for the unfortunate incident that happened over a decade ago.

"And you're such a threat?" Warren looked at her, this small Guatemalan woman in this church in downtown Toronto.

"Apparently so."

"And where do we fit in?"

"I want to hold them to account, to acknowledge what they've done, and I want to find my sister, where they buried her." Celina trained her gaze on Warren, like she could see through him, like she was holding him to a pact he wasn't aware he had signed.

His mind echoed with traces of her sister, entrapping his spirit in their ordeal. If she thought he could be of assistance, she was wrong.

"I'm hoping, given your history, you might help," she said.

That was what he was afraid of.

Warren felt his skin creep. The church sanctuary at night, the intensity of Celina's gaze, the things she was saying were all more frightening to him than any graveyard at night. Even the pressure of Meena's arm on his shoulder wasn't enough to calm him as the reality of what Celina was saying sank in. Still, he fought it.

"What are you talking about?" he asked, as if he didn't know. He picked up the stack of pink pages on the table in front of him, tapped them against the table, trying to align their edges, and continued tapping them while Celina spoke.

"Nova Scotia," Celina said. "I did my research on Magma, looked at mining in Canada, practises, mishaps, accidents, came across what happened in your town. I found out about your brother, and I found out about you."

Warren went cold. "You're referring to something that happened a long time ago. I don't talk about the past."

Warren looked at Meena, who was almost out of her chair with consternation. "This is bullshit," he said, looking at her hard, hoping she would somehow intervene. He drained the last of his rum.

Meena took her arm from Warren's back. She turned her gaze from Celina to Warren as though he were revealing a treacherous affair. There was a truth he'd kept from her that had been circling around them, like an omen looking for a perch. And there was a woman in the room they had just met who knew more about it than she did. She wasn't going anywhere and she wasn't about to try and stop the proceedings.

Warren stared at Celina. She held it, her face remaining neutral, passive. He looked back at Meena. She held his gaze too, till he looked away.

He squeezed the empty glass in his hand. The bottle wasn't going to help. He had been running for so long and so hard, perhaps it was time to stop. He could tell them, be judged accordingly, and then go remake himself again somewhere else.

"I was young, and angry."

He could see his house, a bungalow, built in the fifties by the company for the staff. It was white with blue trim. His mom always planted petunias and geraniums out front and they had orange and red nasturtiums climbing up the windows. No one used the front entrance, everyone came in the back door, into the kitchen.

He saw his brother's size eleven shoes, converse cross-trainers always left right in the middle of the door. Dillon never learned to move them out of the way.

"He killed a young family, he was drinking and driving and he hit the other car dead centre. The father and daughter died instantly, the mother and youngest son lingered."

There was a picture of the family on the front page of the paper he'd seen when he'd gone to get milk for the coffee and tea for the visitation. The family had used the same country backdrop his mom had chosen for their own family portrait the year before.

"Six months before that my dad died." They had told him his father had aspirated, a word Warren hadn't been familiar with. He'd fallen down drunk on his back and the vomit had been sucked into his lungs, leaving him with only bile to breathe.

Warren let Meena and Celina imagine what it was like to have a brother responsible for the death of a young family. Of how in a small town, everyone knows everyone else's business, and there was no hiding and no pretending. He was shunned, his mother too. As if alcohol was an infectious disease. He'd been popular in school. He told them that, that he'd had friends, played sports, been like any other kid in the community who held secrets at home.

He gave them morsels, pieces, crumbs, and seeds spread on the lawn for the birds to peck. He fed them enough to satisfy, but not enough to engorge. Meena and Celina sat listening.

He'd been beaten by his drunken father at home, and later for the sins of his brother at school. His family was tainted, they all knew it, and no one ventured a look to see how the survivors were managing. His mother retreated, embarrassed to go out, go shopping, hang laundry, to show her face to the town that knew her now as the mother of the one who killed the McCluskeys.

And he had to retreat too, to hide away into his own cocoon, where he wouldn't feel shame and no one could see his pain. And it was in his room, alone, where he put it all together, where he figured out the locus of the problems with his family. It didn't lie with his family, but with where they lived, what they were forced to do, with a mine that was at the centre of their misfortune.

The mine employed his dad and brother, his grandfather. The mine caused his grandfather's laboured death, and all the adults to drink, from fear, boredom, the blackness of the coal, and the weight that lay over their heads. The mine was ubiquitous in their lives, with its gaping holes and clockwork sirens announcing the end of shifts, day and night. With its dreaded bells that would clang and clang and a collapse would cause them to review the work details and pray it was someone else's father or brother, stuck below.

Warren knew that those who came out of the mines, day after day, left something down there. They'd made a deal with the earth, that if they were able to take out the coal, the earth could keep a little piece of them in turn, and the overflowing pubs and blackened spittle were reminders there were debts unpaid.

Warren was in his kitchen with the yellow linoleum floor and the chrome chairs with beige plastic padding. He was with his grandfather, who'd withered into an old dried-up apple figure who only had space in his lungs to rattle out a call to the bathroom. Warren would have to sit him on the toilet and clean his messes, drag him on his chair to the table for supper. The kitchen was the centre of their family, it was where they came together, and were driven apart. No one stepped into the breach, he'd been in high school, a time that can pain any kid into acts of depression. But in his school, there was no one to help. There were no guidance counsellors, all the careers, other than joining the army, were connected to coal, which called out from the abyss, like the mouthpiece of the devil. It whispered to young guys about new cars and fat wallets and the young girls would swoon, eyes glittering, reflected back from the blackened glint, hopeful for a family and a guy with a steady job, because that was the pinnacle, and alternate dreams were whimsical fantasy obliterated by the dust that swirled up from the mine. But it was the one thing Warren was clear about. He wasn't going down the hole, and he wasn't going to sling a single load of coal for anyone, anywhere.

His home and his head had come together again, all the emotions of rage and anger and pain threatened to burst out of him.

Meena asked, "What happened Warren?"

His hands flexed into fists and he brushed through the pages of Celina's story, oblivious, they spread across the table, some floated to the floor. He didn't notice and he didn't stop.

He cracked, fought back. His rum glass felt like the tire iron he'd held in his hands. It was cool and hard. He remembered holding the pipe and the power it gave him when he smashed the windows. It was glorious, watching the pieces of glass crumble into shards. He saw himself pushing the machinery down the shafts like they were toys and the earth was their keeper and he was feeding back to it the metal they'd stolen.

"I started trashing the machinery. I snuck in and spray-painted the windows black. Blind them to what was around. It was minor vandalism. Nothing serious. But it didn't have an effect. It wasn't enough."

It was momentary, because as soon as he smashed one window, he looked up and there were thirty, fifty, a hundred more. He knew they replicated, as soon as one piece of machinery was destroyed, another was brought in to replace it. There was no end to the cycle. It was the level of Dante's Hell that formed into an endless assembly line, leaving him to smash metal for an eternity. But the mine went on working, people went on with their lives, their whispers.

No one spoke. Warren replayed it in his head, till he found the narrative string and was able to hold on tight enough to continue. He sucked in air. "So I snuck in gasoline, bottles, some rags. No one was supposed to be around. I wasn't stupid."

But he knew he was stupid, he was forever stupid for that one act, an act born out of vengeance and grief, driven by the need to burn, to feed the red fire he saw every day getting out of bed and seeing his mom still asleep on the couch, where the rats scampered through the kitchen, and the gifted casseroles had long since stopped appearing. His brother's bedroom door was kept shut, so they could pretend he was still there. But the decay ran through them all, it was passed on through the generations.

"Things blew up alright." He grimaced. "I felt a sweet vengeance, like somehow I'd fought back against those bastards." He shook his fist and his head as he relived the moment.

He could still bring it to mind, if the sunset had been at his back, rather than glaring into his sight, it might have been picturesque. He'd replayed it so many times in his head that he was surprised there was room for another thought. He could feel it still, the funnel of wind that sucked him back towards the flame. He didn't see it blow up, he'd wanted to remember the sound of the blast, a kind of trumpets call to arms. He wished he'd watched. He forever wished he watched, because he knew that his mind made it worse in the re-enactment.

"I didn't know though. The old guy was there. He wasn't supposed to be. I didn't know."

His teeth were clenched. He felt shame, he wanted to scream at Meena and Celina to stop looking at him, to look away, to stay away from him. Pity punctured further, he knew he deserved none of it. He wished they'd hit him, that he'd been whipped for his sins, he would have welcomed the pain and then he would have been able to continue reopening the wounds till they festered with gangrene.

"What happened to him Warren?" Meena was horrified.

"He didn't die," he said this looking at Meena, or past her, she couldn't tell which. "Not right away, he had no hair, his face had started to melt when they pulled him out. The first layer of blackened skin came off. I know this, they talked about it in court.

"He was in a coma for six weeks, and then he wished they'd killed him. Skin grafts. I offered my own, like somehow they could peel it off me and cover him in a cloak, like somehow he would want to walk around in my skin.

"But you know, he didn't blame me. Said he felt sorry for me. Can you believe it? He felt sorry for me?"

"Did you turn yourself in?" It was all Meena could think to ask.

He hadn't. He made them investigate, put the pieces together, to notice abnormal behaviour in the mine workers, the townspeople. He made them notice him. He'd gone to the old man, visited him in the hospital, to apologize. But the guy was unconscious and the RCMP were suspicious.

There were crimes that were punishable and crimes that were acceptable, and he hadn't been clear on the difference as a teen. He told them about being picked up, getting charged, pleading guilty. He realized the mine would never be held responsible for its instigator actions, even if his own were precipitated by their particular context.

He went to Juvie, as a Young Offender. He told them the guy lived for eight months, in a kind of agony that caused Warren to shudder. He did the remainder of his schooling in the lock-up, housed in a facility that gave him regular meals, told him when to go to bed, when to wake up, when to shower. He kept to himself, a new kind of protection he practiced wearing. He found it suited his need to introvert his life, unconnected to others.

"Got out, got my stuff and got on a bus to Toronto. That's the story." As if a story like that could end.

Warren became aware of his surroundings, brought his head back from the scorched recollections. He still felt the sharp edge of anger that he'd had to share this part of himself, this part of his story. "You couldn't have known that, not from the start." He said. looking over the scattered pink papers right to Celina.

"No, not all of it."

"When did you know?" He wanted to know how much she'd surveyed and calculated him for her uses. Because he felt manipulated, an instrument, used by Celina just like he'd been used by the coal company, forced to reveal his innards, let them be rooted through to find that which suited, then squeezed and drained till the blood was dry.

"I had been doing research, trying to find a way to get the mine to make reparations," Celina said. "I found an article that described what happened in Nova Scotia. I was curious. You have to understand, we have tried so many different things. I was looking for new insights, new tactics. Anything that would help us." Celina sat back, her eyes softened. "Then I found you were here."

Warren was horrified. He had carefully constructed a life with nothing to connect him to the past, so that no one would know where he had come from.

"These things are easy to find out now, with the Internet" Celina explained. "But whether you would care, want to help, whether you would listen, I didn't know that till later."

"When?" Warren asked.

"In the cemetery. When you took my sister's grave marker away."

'You were there?" He searched his memory to take him to that place. That moment. Yet, somehow, he already knew it was true.

"I was under a tree, pretending to sketch."

He remembered, a young woman with black hair beside her bike, the same bike he saw her take off on six weeks later. She said she saw him touch her sister's name on the grave at the cemetery, like he was brushing her cheek. She told him she and the others had followed him and Curtis, after they'd removed the stone. They'd waited outside his apartment until the blinds were shut, the lights were dimmed. Then they broke into the truck, moved the stone away.

"Why not go to him?" Meena didn't understand.

"Would you have listened?" Celina turned to Warren.

Warren was apt to have packed up and vanished. He and Vamp, his cat, were skittish. He knew he would have run if he'd been confronted on the street.

"I wrote the story to try to direct my actions, to understand my own motivations. It occurred to me it might be a way to reach you, to compel you to at least listen to what I had to say," Celina explained. "We put up the stone as an action against the company. To remind them that we would never forget. If you hadn't worked there, we wouldn't have thought of it."

Celina reached down and grabbed the pages that Warren had knocked to the floor. "And these," she said, holding them up and adding them back to the stack, arranging them carefully. "These are for me, so I don't forget."

Celina spoke of wishing to receive the bodies so they could bury them properly, and he saw coffins, and funerals, and wished he'd been able to mourn.

She described the struggle for recognition, to assign blame, culpability, and the company's refusal to acknowledge or accept, and he understood how that could feel. He had spent hours around a table at home, sitting at their feet, climbing a counter, or seated at a chair, where they would describe, over tea or tonics, injuries to neighbours from disregarded safety standards, docked pay from questioning superiors, families put to the streets when they'd had enough, and wearied workers forced to go down the pit again and again, with the expectation of blind devotion. Warren knew about refusing to acknowledge or accept.

Celina told him that she didn't want certain crimes to be acceptable anymore, that it was the least she could do for Lalita. Invoking her name brought her forth to his mind, allowing her memories to become his, with a mine in Guatemala as real as the one he knew back home. Warren knew there was no leaving the mine behind, it followed him, everywhere.

CHAPTER 5

Chik'chan *(serpent)*

"Truly, it is in darkness, when one finds the light."
—Meister Eckhart

J ames looked out from his desk onto his front yard and circular drive. The stirring harmonies of the Three Tenors filled the room, the only other voices in the house. There were neighbours to either side of him, but the construction of his Rosedale home was such that he couldn't see even a sign of anyone else. He liked to be alone, though he played music all the time, ensuring there were sounds even while he was sleeping. He liked to be alone, but didn't like quiet.

James Tyrell had been an only child. He'd married once, found it didn't suit him and told her to leave. He didn't like negotiating living arrangements. He was definitive, could make decisions, it's what made him a good businessman, a good CEO.

He noticed the trees would be changing colour soon, moving into fall and hibernation. It meant he would be bringing out his 1980 Harley Davidson Sturgis soon. He stowed it in the garage, beside the SUV, so that he was afforded the opportunity to see it daily, to be reminded.

He kept it well maintained, even though he used it rarely, taking it out for his vigil the week after Thanksgiving and just before Halloween. It wasn't the best time of year to ride, some years it could be snowing, but he'd go anyway. He'd head up to Kleinburg, over to Aurora and New Market getting to Port Perry and Lake Scugog, then back to the city. He'd gone out the first time more than thirty years ago when the area was still patchwork farmland. In the ensuing time it had been dissected by traffic lights and transformed into suburbs and strip malls.

He'd gone there the first time because the trees had been starting to change colours, and he thought it was as good a place as any to scatter his parents' ashes. He was less inclined to undertake the ritual now with the stop and go nature of the traffic, the application of mandatory helmet laws and speed impediments. He also figured the trees that he'd dusted with his bucket as he'd raced along the empty highways were now part of the particle board that made up the new subdivisions that had sprung up in the area, and they weren't much to look at. It had been freeing, and now felt confining. He took his eyes off the trees in his yard and looked at the stack of letters on his desk. Hand-written correspondence to his home was a rarity, maybe a check-in from an aunt or a wayward inquiry. But it had been awhile, until the envelopes began arriving in succession. He'd thrown the first few out, not taking in their significance. But after a few days, when the letters kept coming, he'd become intrigued, curious, even frightened in the beginning to receive a letter hand addressed in his name. The letters came in white envelopes and concealed a single page of pink paper bearing a word, a sentence or a fragment bridging the previous letter with the latest. It took a number of weeks to cotton on to the intention, to realize what it was about, why it had been directed toward him. But by then, he found he'd looked forward to them, to reading them when he came home from work with the music filling the corridors. The latest one remained on top of the pile. It lay with the others he'd received, one every day for many months.

He was both impressed and annoyed.

He hadn't said a word to his colleagues. He liked to imagine that it was for him alone, that the woman was writing to him in a kind of illicit affair, or as prison correspondence between inmates.

He fingered the envelope and recognized the story was finished and that he would receive no more letters. He read them through, from start to finish, filling in the first few with a guess, from his incomplete set. He held up the last page to the window with the final line, light filtering through the paper. It had nothing else to share. He put the letters back together, arranged in a bundle and put them up on the side of his desk, beside the picture of the dog he had when he was six, before his dad found out he was allergic, and had him sold and out of the house before

James got home from school. He wanted to keep the letters awhile before discarding, but the light had given him an idea. His position and the status of the company were not going to be manipulated by a dead girl and her sister. He glanced at his fireplace and realized that as he had received one a day, he could begin by burning one a day.

. . .

It was late and Warren and Meena walked alongside each other, but neither spoke. Meena had intended to study. Warren was due for the late shift. Neither had anticipated the fundraiser would have held them captive to this hour. There was disquiet between them and the streets they walked reflected it. Activity on Bloor Street never ceased, but once they left the lights of the commercial district, it got dark and quiet.

They passed the light posts that had started the story and initiated their friendship with a wary glance. The posts were naked, Warren and Meena were left to imagine the tan line, indicating where the story had been. Warren pictured the pages, linking up the neighbourhood, connected on an invisible string. He wondered what his neighbours would think, if they would feel the absence and be curious about what happened to the author, wonder how the story ended.

Warren went to touch the last pole, but drew his hand back not wanting to bring it to Meena's attention. It had been an escape, it funnelled his daydreams, allowed him to imagine a world outside of his own, and he relished knowing someone had taken the time, made the effort and directed the story toward him.

He also knew that any return to his own here and now meant unsettling inquiries he would rather avoid. Sitting with Celina and Meena he had felt as if his insides had been ripped open. He still felt the pain, the sores still vibrated on his skin the way a new cut would throb from the extra flow of blood to the wound. He didn't want to draw attention to it, to be subsumed again in the injury.

They arrived at the porch, Meena's door to the right, Warren's apartment, up the stairs and to the left. It felt odd to Warren after their evening to just leave her at the door and say good night.

Meena kept her hands on the bannister. She turned to Warren, and looked at him, drawing in his eyes towards her. "Why didn't you tell me about what happened in Nova Scotia?"

The entire walk back from the house she had replayed the conversation. She found it hard to look at him, to see him as the man she had been getting to know. It shook her, that she'd misread him; she felt she was a decent judge of character, able to spot and dismiss the venal, conceited, the hyper self-absorbed, the criminal.

"I didn't know it was your business to know."

Meena's instinct was to turn and head into her house, leave it behind, leave Warren behind, and leave the whole thing to rot on the street. Instead, she willed her hand to the wood. He had been hurt, and was hurting she recognized that, she could give him a little.

"Come on Warren. Going to law school has at least taught me that a touch of vandalism and a little bit of juvenile homicide is kind of serious."

"Is this about you, Meena?" Warren was fried. "Is this about your law career?"

"It's about you not trusting me."

"What, so I could become another file for you, another test case? Fuck that Meena."

"Is there more you're not telling me?"

Warren felt his face get hot. He'd opened his darkest closet and showed her its most twisted skeletons. What more did she want from him?

"Who the fuck do you think you're talking to?"

"Warren, I like you, don't you get that?" She said it again. "I like you Warren," and took his face in her hands.

She kissed him with the light brush of her lips upon his, exploring the terrain in the way one might do upon first touching a baby's skin. Noting no resistance, she enhanced her efforts. Warren had been kissed on occasion where it was pleasant and nice. And at other times he'd been kissed out of his head to a place hot and pulsing. This was one of those times.

Warren stopped thinking about the past. She took his hand and led him up his stairs and kissed him deeply at the top of his steps. He fumbled for his key and Vamp let out a screech when he opened the door. He didn't know if he was supposed to invite her in, but she walked in ahead and gathered him in. He gently kicked the door shut behind him. The caresses became mutual, leading to fondling and pressing. It was what he wanted, but he hadn't seen it coming, he hadn't been sure if it would. She unbuckled his pants and removed his shirt. Warren stood in his boxers in front of her unsure how it had happened. He hadn't been able to lead the way, but he accepted the invitation.

He unbuttoned her shirt to reveal a black lacy bra. She had small brown breasts which he cupped, moving the fabric aside with his thumb to reveal a darkened erect nipple. Some fumbling clicks and awkward elbows released the catch allowing Warren access to brush, touch, and lick each in succession.

Meena had manoeuvred his boxers off and was exploring, gliding her thin soft fingers up and around. More clothing was removed till they stood before each other, naked. They explored one another with fingers, and lips, revealing through touch and learning through breath. The coupling was frenetic when they tumbled to the floor. Frenetic and loud.

• • •

It stood out because it was the only adornment in his apartment. There were no wall hangings, paintings or pictures. But in the bathroom, hanging from the mirror was a little wooden yellow duck, the kind that might embellish a Christmas tree or be affixed to the zipper of a toddler.

The yellow duck had red cheeks, a red beak, a blue bow-tie and a smiley face. Meena took it off the hanger and brought it to the kitchen where Warren was cooking up some eggs as a late night snack.

"What's this?" she asked.

"That's Wally."

"Hi Wally." Meena turned the duck to introduce herself. "What are you doing here?" she asked.

Warren turned the burner to low, took Wally from her hands and rubbed the duck's head between his fingers, polishing his cheeks and then handed him back to Meena.

"Wally's a friend," Warren said. "Wally found me when I first came to Toronto. I got off the bus, had twenty-eight dollars in my hand, didn't know anyone and didn't have a place to stay."

Warren had stepped off the bus with a sense of liberation. No one knew him, he was a blank slate, he could be anyone and do anything. He wondered if that was how people felt after a baptism.

"Wally was on the sidewalk, waiting at the lights. I waited for the lights to change three times before it was clear no one was going to help him. So I picked him up and went looking for a home and a job. And he's lived with me ever since."

CHAPTER 6
Kimi *(death)*

"There is no death—only a change of worlds."
—Chief Seattle

The boardroom was full when James made his entrance. The twelve directors of Magma sat around the table—members of the Brownley family, the original owners of Magma; a few other industry players; a lawyer and an accountant. In a pale nod to diversity there was one Asian woman amongst the eleven white men.

Most of the meeting consisted of business on policy, financial transactions, and acquisitions; standard board fodder that James managed with acuity. The last agenda item was miscellaneous board business and Scott Liddle, one of the younger board members asked for the floor. James nodded coolly. He didn't care for Scott, who was young, ambitious, and on the board because he worked with a telecommunications firm that resided in the same building, allowing the companies to engage in a relationship of corporate reciprocity, whereby they shared board members and stock tips. He was about to zone out, when the import of what Scott was saying cut through.

"The letters started coming to my home," Scott said, his voice cracking under the strain. He described the envelopes, the individual pink pages, the story that started and just wouldn't stop coming. James felt a twinge of sadness—he'd hoarded the story, he realized. Guarded it like a treasure, the little girl whose destiny he'd determined. But now, this public airing diluted the fantasy, and she became just another name in a long list of global tragedies that would occur and reoccur throughout the course of time. Sad perhaps, but inevitable. He let her memory drift away, like ashes into the wind.

"I got them too," the woman spoke up, and James accepted the lion was loose from the cage.

His obligation was to the welfare of his shareholders, not some ignorant girl in a faraway place.

"Looks like we all did." Scott surveyed the room, registering the nodding faces. "They know where I live," Scott said. "I have a wife and two kids, you know. I find this all very disturbing." Scott looked at the members of the Brownley family in turn. "I thought we had dealt with this?" His voice was high and tense. The room was silent, the faces of the other board members ciphers.

James cleared his throat. "Okay, listen," he said. "It seems that someone is trying to hurt the reputation this company has built for the past thirty years. That is neither acceptable nor legitimate. The letters are the rants of a disturbed person."

"James, I'm not stupid." Scott's voice quavered and he worked to control it. "What I'm asking is, is there any substance to these claims; are we vulnerable and open to any investor fallout? I'm concerned about our shareholders."

"Scott, I understand your concern," James adopted a fluid and conciliatory tone. "We dealt with this situation years ago. There was an incident in this community and the autopsies were performed—which we paid for I might add—and the toxicology reports were inconclusive, even so far as indicating an accumulation of cyanide due to the ingesting of yams and sweet potatoes; this, in fact, being a resultant factor in those villagers becoming ill. We brought in nutritionists and now these people know what to eat and how to cook in order to be healthy and not get sick. Investor confidence should not be affected in any way." James looked around and noted with satisfaction the nodding faces of the board members.

"Fine, but what's right and wrong is a reflection of public perception," Scott said. His glance flitted from face to face, looking for any kind of agreement or encouragement. "We all have a fiduciary duty here. What are we going to do to mitigate this so as to avoid any damage to our stock price?"

"We have the situation under control," James said. He pushed his shoulders back and narrowed his eyes at Scott. "We are taking the appropriate measures," he said with finality.

Scott barged on. "What does that mean?"

"It means we will not see any adjustments in our value alignments and you will not receive any more letters." James gave a tight smile. "I can assure you the matter is in hand."

James stood, smiled confidently at the other board members, except for Scott Liddle for whom he reserved a moment's pitying glance. He strode toward the entrance, pausing only briefly to whisper to the stenographer, a small woman hidden away in the corner. "Strike that last conversation from the record," he said, his voice low but commanding.

"Yes sir, Mr. Tyrell," she said.

And James strode back to his corner office.

• • •

Warren was late for the meeting. He hurried along Ossington Avenue wishing Meena was with him. Or maybe wishing he was headed somewhere else. Anywhere else. He'd assumed Meena would come, but she'd had some other thing on the go. Some aunty's birthday or the like. When she broke the news, his mind just froze.

"You have to go," she told him. "We have to see this thing through, wherever it takes us."

"But—what will I do at the meeting? What even happens at a meeting like this?"

"They'll probably sit around and talk, think about strategies or plan what they are going to do," she said. "You'll have to go and find out. Take notes. I want you to tell me all about it. Who's there, what they say, what they want us to do."

"Do?" he said. "But I am not going to do anything."

But Meena seemed not to hear him. "Oh, I wish I could be there," she said. He wasn't sure he felt the same way.

Still, he'd gone to the meeting. And now here he was in front of a semi-detached brick house on Delaware Avenue, about to ring the bell.

"I must be crazy," he muttered. But he reached out a finger and pressed the doorbell. And somehow kept himself from running away.

The door swung open a sliver and a head peeked around.

"Eduardo, right?" Warren said. His voice shook as he spoke and he didn't know why. "Warren," he said, pointing to himself.

"I remember," Eduardo replied. He swung the door all the way open and held his arms out. "Come on in, we've been waiting for you."

Eduardo led the way to a living room furnished with Ikea sofas and chairs and a wide-screen television tucked in the corner. He recognized Chantel and Bill, and Celina of course. But the room was full and Warren was conscious of his lateness, and his aloneness amid so many strangers. He wondered again what the hell he was doing.

"Welcome, Warren," Celina said, and he was comforted to see her smile at him as he found a spot to sit in the corner. There was an old-timer on a stool whose active years had since passed, a Jesus-looking fellow with long hair and beard cross-legged on the floor while a young fresh-faced woman sat behind him on the sofa and played with his hair. He guessed they might be students. In the back of the room, at the entrance to the hall leading to the kitchen was a tall, thin, bald guy with a goatee and a Spanish face.

Warren wasn't sure what he expected, whether he thought it would be a group of balaclava-wearing anarchists plotting the downfall of capitalism, or a conniving coven of communists with little beards and maoist berets. He had feasted on too many action thrillers as a teen, and was disappointed by the reality.

Warren tried to squeeze himself closer to the wall. He wondered when it would be polite to extract himself and slip away.

"So who's going to the shareholder meeting?" Bill directed the question to Celina.

"Who should go?" Celina redirected back to the group.

"They already know the four of us." Chantel indicated herself, Bill and Eduardo who stood like sentries on opposite ends of the room, and the thin guy standing by the door whose name Warren had already forgotten.

Warren tried to grasp what they were talking about, trying to keep his features neutral in order not to appear confused.

"That leaves Pierre, Mel, Ryan, you, and Warren I guess," Eduardo said. Warren figured they included him as a way to be polite, which he felt was nice, but unnecessary.

"And I can't go unfortunately," Celina responded

"Why not?" Warren found himself blurting the thought aloud.

"It's not safe," Bill replied.

Warren managed to keep his mouth shut and the skepticism off his face. He imagined they were trying to live out a James Bond fantasy. He had dreamt up his own share of heroic vignettes, as a kid he waited for the chance to save Amanda MacDonald's cat from a runaway bus, only to have her fall in his arms and strip off her clothes in a grateful embrace. Problem was there was no cat, no runaway bus, and Amanda thought he was strange.

He resolved to remain quiet, observe the proceedings, to see what lay behind the lamp post story, then move on. He regretted bringing attention to himself as he recognized it would make it harder to slip away.

Everyone in the room seemed to have an excuse not to participate, nary a hero among the do-gooders.

"Warren's new, they wouldn't recognize him." Chantel offered and all the eyes turned in his direction. He tried to look away to find a spot on the wall to redirect their attention elsewhere. He wasn't sure how he was going to extricate himself.

"It's a shareholders' meeting. We're going to put a proxy motion to the floor," Chantel explained.

He looked back at her in confusion. "But I'm not a shareholder." He was being swept forward on a weird tsunami, unprepared and unable to get off the forward-crashing wave.

"You don't have to be a shareholder. We've got a proxy vote from Gino's union." Chantel gestured with her thumb towards the tall thin guy. Everyone was watching Warren waiting for him to agree.

"Ah, no, I've never done anything like this before. I wouldn't know what to do..."

"It's okay, I do," the young woman said. "I'll help you out." She looked like she was twelve. Great, Warren thought, they are asking me to make a public spectacle of myself and take a member of the grade seven class with me.

"There's really nothing to it," Chantel said. "You present a motion to the floor for the Magma Mine to close operations in San Jacinto del Quiche and to compensate the victims of the cyanide poisonings and the community members who were displaced."

Warren stifled a laugh. "Oh, I'm sure that will go over well," he said, "Why should they care?"

"Because there are little bitty grandmothers, and teachers' unions and pension funds and a whole assortment of other people who are investors in Magma who know nothing about the company's real activities. And if they do, maybe they'll stop investing with them," Celina replied.

"I don't think so. Thanks though." His family had bred him with manners.

"No need to be afraid," Celina said. She gave him a warm smile. "You'll be fine."

But Warren knew that wasn't true. He'd never voted in any elections, let alone some kind of proxy vote. It didn't seem real that they were considering him for this undertaking. Warren was in over his head. He realized he should not have come alone. He realized further there was no point in speaking up—the room had erupted in chatter and his voice would be lost amid their excitement. At least, he thought, Meena would be impressed. That was something, at least.

Their voices rose in a kind of pep-talk before war. Warren picked out subjects from shareholders meetings to anti-apartheid rallies. Pierre, the older guy, was schooling them on corporate responsibility struggles that had achieved getting more women onto corporate boards , and creating ethical and environmental investment funds.

Warren slowly backed out of the room, and down the hall. He didn't make eye contact with anyone as he went, and no one tried to stop him. At the front door, he bolted. He felt like running all the way home, like a school kid, not because of something bad that had happened with his classmates, but because they had invited him to join their ring around the rosie, and after their hush, hush, he was the one who was going to fall down.

. . .

"So are you going to do it?" Meena asked. They were lying in bed, a place they'd been spending a lot of their time lately. Meena was multitasking—propped up on pillows, surrounded by law books. Warren lay beside her, stroking Vamp's head and thinking.

"I can't think of why I would," he said. "You said it yourself at the fundraiser—it's not our fight."

"But aren't you a little bit curious," Meena said, her brown eyes shining at the possibilities for romance and adventure. "Aren't you just a little bit curious to see where the story goes from here?" The lamp posts in their neighbourhood had seemed terribly naked since the fundraiser.

"Nope," Warren said flatly. He pushed Vamp off his lap and swung his legs out of bed. "Time to get up," he said. And he was in the bathroom running water for a shower before Meena could even form an objection.

He told Curtis about it that night, as they worked beneath a crescent moon. "It was crazy," Warren said, "the way they just assumed I would do this thing no one else was stepping up to do. I barely know these people!"

"So what are you going to do?" Curtis asked. He looked at his friend but the night was dark and he could barely make out Warren's features.

"Nothing," Warren said. "I'm not going to do anything."

But later still when he closed his eyes to sleep, he saw the face that was always waiting for him. Lalita looked at him with sorrow and disappointment, and he turned away in his dreams, but each time he did, she reappeared. And so he tossed and turned and dreamed about how hard it is to do nothing, after all.

. . .

"Thanks for meeting with me," Celina said. "There are some things we need to go over before the shareholders' meeting, so that you're prepared."

"About that," Warren said. "I'm not sure—"

"Don't worry," Celina said. She put a hand on Warren's arm. "That's why it's good that you could meet me, so that we can make sure you're sure."

Warren wondered if that meant there was still an out for him. He'd let her explain what she had to and then at the end of it all, he'd say, you know, I don't think it's the right opportunity for me. Maybe he'd even write a cheque for her fund, and then he'd be on his way. The cafe was busy, and he'd lost Celina's voice among the background babble for a moment. He shook himself out of his own thoughts and honed in.

"I started working in the sewing sweatshops on Weston Road when I first arrived," Celina was saying, "then with time and contacts I got a job planning events at the Centre for Spanish Speaking People. And then I went on to do translations, for universities, institutes, businesses, and government."

"That's a great asset," Warren said, picking up the thread, "being able to speak and translate into another language. We've got Gaelic way back in my family tree line, and they taught French in school, but I can't say I did a good job of retaining any of it." Warren remembered learning all the swear words in French so they could use them when the played the Acadian teams in basketball.

"My first language is Achi," Celina said. "It was something they didn't want us to learn. We only spoke it at home, or in our village. But in school, you would be punished if you didn't speak in Spanish." Curtis had told him the same thing had happened to his parents at the residential school, where they'd had the Cree beaten out of them.

"And now you use it to make a living," Warren noted, wondering how that made her feel.

"That's how I got involved again," she said. "Here I was doing all this translating for the government and businesses that were working in my country, and in other countries. Somehow I was facilitating this, it was like I had come to Canada and forgotten what had happened to me and my family. But you don't forget that stuff. I couldn't forget my family..." Celina's eyes began to well.

Warren squirmed in his chair. He was terrible at tears.

"Sorry." Celina wiped her eyes. She took a deep breath, then smiled and continued. "I only translate for universities now. Academics, requests for research, that sort of thing. It is more palatable to me and helps me send money back to my family."

Warren thought about his own family, and how blown apart it had been by the mine. He thought about Celina's family, the faces that were already familiar to him from his dreams, the faces he saw reflected in Celina's own. His dreams of Lalita—since the fundraiser she had come to him every night when he closed his eyes. They played together, they laughed in his dreams. She was like a sister he never had. Then she would turn and run, and he would chase after her, running as though they could glide above the world. Lalita would shout to him and then disappear over the bank of shale that bordered his town. He knew what was about to happen, and he called to her to come back, that it was dangerous. And then the sky turned red, and then black. Lalita had come into his story, and he could do nothing.

The dream became a nightmare, drowning him. He'd never learned to swim, despite growing up in proximity to the water, learning to fly fish, taking out a dory with his grandfather to catch eels or sea bass.

He didn't tell Celina about the dreams, that Lalita was crying out for him to respond. He knew in the cold light of day, in a crowded cafe on Bloor Street West that it was either swim with Celina and deliver the proxy or drown in his nightmares.

• • •

He hesitated on the steps to the house, but once inside, it reminded Warren of the Forty-fives card game parties his parents would host in their living room when he saw people arranged around card-tables. In this case there were stacks of letters and envelopes piled around their feet. Back home, there was always a hazy atmosphere where folks would be smoking, drinking, and sounding off. It made Warren feel at ease as he arrived to join the work party to stuff envelopes with fundraising letters.

"Here, come join us," Melanie said. She gave him a smile of complicity, anticipating their act of rebelliousness at the shareholders' meeting, perhaps. She was sitting with Chantel and Pierre, and she gestured to an empty seat at their table. She gave him a stack of letters and envelopes and he focused on folding the paper. He appreciated having something to do with his hands. He was still nervous about the group and his place in it. He was glad they were doing something and not just sitting there talking.

"So, does this work?" he asked, looking around at the stacks of folded envelopes and stuffed letters.

"Sure, we get lots of support this way," Melanie said. "We send some by email too, but there are plenty of folks who still appreciate a hand signed letter."

"No Meena today?" Chantel asked.

"She has exams and applications and things. Timing's been bad." Warren wished it weren't so. Meena was more at ease in social settings, could communicate much better than he could. But Meena's studies were at an apex and she found it hard even to find time to be with him. And Meena herself would rather have been there, she said. She hated to miss the action. But she pushed Warren to go to the meetings, to drink in all the details and bring them back to her so she could experience it vicariously. Warren figured in exchange for the side benefits, he was happy to share what he learned.

Being careful not to create a crooked crease and send a skewed message to donors, Warren asked Chantel where she met Eduardo.

She had been affixing stamps to the letters and placing them in a box for delivery. "Actually, we met in Guatemala. I was doing my masters research on post-conflict studies of feminism, and he distracted me long enough to make a difference."

"That's some kind of distraction."

"He's some kind of guy," Pierre piped in with a chuckle. "Anyone who is willing to leave the tropics for our winter wonderland is either crazy or notices a mark of quality and goes after it." He gave Chantel a poke and a smile.

Warren wondered about that decision. When he went to start his life anew he hadn't hesitated. Halifax, the nearest city, was too small and too close. He was intimidated by Montreal because he didn't speak French, and he wasn't sure if he could rise to the challenge of the fashionistas who lived there. He'd chosen Toronto because it was the largest city in the country, and he could sneak in like a country mouse.

"I'm not very good at making tortillas," she confessed. "And he was up for the adventure." Chantel looked at Eduardo as she spoke. He was in the middle of an animated discussion in Spanish with Celina at the other table.

"He's had trouble with English, it took him time to get adjusted and find a job. I don't know if we'll ever be comfortable with the decision, there will be a loss for someone either way. We thought there were more opportunities here, but that doesn't always translate well for everyone. There are more opportunities for me, but I'm not so sure there are more for him."

Toronto had provided Warren with plenty of opportunities, but he also understood what can happen when you land somewhere new. When he'd first arrived, he'd boarded the subway at Yonge Street and traversed the yellow horseshoe line slipping down to Union Station and then refracting back up again to Spadina Avenue. He hadn't realized that if he had taken the green transit line straight across he'd only have had to go to three stations instead of twelve. Being somewhere new could be hard, he couldn't imagine doing it and not knowing the language.

"How about you Mel?" Warren asked. "How did you get interested in Guatemala, and get involved with this?"

"Celina gave a public talk on campus and I followed up with her afterwards and we had coffee. Ryan and I are studying international development."

"For me it was the coffee brigade to Nicaragua during the Sandinista period in the eighties, when Ronnie Reagan enforced an economic embargo on the country in an attempt to stifle the spread of communism," Pierre said with a flourish as he waved his hands over the card table as if he were an evil sorcerer. "I went from picking beans and defending the communities from attacks by the Contra to backpacking through the region. That's where I fell in love with Guatemala, and maybe a few of the women who lived there too," he grinned.

Warren smiled to think of Pierre as a playboy given he was pushing eighty.

"Wanna beer?" Gino offered him a bottle. Back home, everyone drank booze at the card parties. There were some nights where he would be awoken by shouts and bouts of scuffling and he'd sneak to his window and peer around the curtains to see who had been thrown out. Though turfed one night, they would always appear again the next week, as expulsion for lousy behaviour didn't equate to lifetime banishments. Everyone would appear cordial again the following week and any slights were soon forgotten in the shuffling of a new hand.

He couldn't imagine anyone being expelled from these gatherings, but he was glad Gino joined their table, so he didn't have to drink alone. They tipped their bottles together.

"Cheers."

"And what's your story for being here?" Warren asked Gino.

"My union," he said. "I'm a geography teacher, into landscapes and topography. And I'd taught my kids about Guatemala—which is a great study with its highlands and lowlands, volcanoes, deserts, rainforests, coastlines. It's got it all," he said swigging down his beer. "An opportunity for an educators' exchange arrived and I jumped at the chance. I was there during a teachers' protest around wages, as they hadn't been paid in three months."

"Why didn't they quit teaching?" Warren asked. It seemed ridiculous anyone would continue working if they weren't getting paid.

"They quit their job, they lose their job. And in Guatemala, there aren't a whole lot of jobs." Gino put down his beer. "I saw them shoot three teachers that day in Guatemala, because they wanted to teach, but didn't want to be hungry."

Warren looked at the others in the room, taking them in and affixing them with the thread of their stories. People had joined in Celina's cause to find meaning and express purpose. They were all connected to the story, in different, yet similar ways. Everyone was linked to either Guatemala or to each other. Celina's struggle seemed to give their engagement a focus. They could weave themselves into the fabric of her circumstance and deepen their own connections to her, the country and to one another. While her struggle for justice for her sister was personal, it had become so for each of them.

At the last meeting, Warren had run away from this group, and now he found himself a part of the solidarity crew as he watched people in the room laughing, chatting, folding and stuffing, joining into this community to bring justice to Celina's family. It was similar to a card party, made up of friends and relations, but it was a party with purpose. Warren was beginning to see his own thread woven amongst them.

CHAPTER 7

Manik' *(hand)*

*"I think we dream so we don't have to be apart so long.
If we're in each others dreams, we can be together all
the time."*
—Calvin and Hobbes

Meena fantasized herself as a warrior, flying up on the back of a lion with her six arms spread out carrying spears, swords, shields and daggers. As a child she had imagined herself as Durga, the female Hindu goddess who had been sought by Vishnu to kill a demon, who had threatened the living, but who couldn't be killed by a man. Meena, as Durga, would often slay the villains and vanquish the enemies.

And now, as she stood before a row of elevators she wished she could summon her deity protector. She'd been told to go to the north tower and take the elevator to the fifty-ninth floor. The mirrored images reflected her, taunting her, displaying her mortal qualities with no lion, no weapons, only two arms, and the demons residing above.

She waited for the doors to open, and people elbowed past her. As the door closed, a few looked back as she remained facing the entrance. If she left now, there would be no harm, no foul. If she went up, she was putting her career and more in jeopardy. It had seemed like a good idea at the time. In fact, she had pushed for it. This was a way she could contribute—she could get inside Magma International, and find out what she could. Warren had been dead set against it—but then, Warren was against any involvement on her part or his own. But Warren, she thought, regaining some of her old Durga fire if only for a moment, Warren didn't get to say what she could and couldn't do. If people's lives were at stake and she could help, she couldn't turn away. Still, it was one thing to feel sure among friends, with Celina encouraging her. And it was another thing altogether as she remained at the elevator and contemplated escape and fairy tales, where the struggle against good and evil was always clear. She wondered if Durga ever had any doubts.

"Yeah, I know, it's pretty scary the first time. This is your first time, no?" A woman with short red hair and long legs sidled up beside her, awaiting the next elevator to zoom up the corporate ladder. Meena smiled weakly.

"I couldn't sleep the night before first coming to work. I threw up as soon as I got to the office. Shaking like a leaf I was." The woman's *t*s were *d*s and *w*s were *v*s, leaving Meena to surmise her origins were eastern and European. "My name's Petra."

Meena was struck out of indecision and led into the elevator. "Uh, hi, my name is Meena."

"Nice to meet you Meena. I almost didn't make it in today. The streetcars were all backed up. I had to hoof it three blocks." Petra was still talking to Meena while she replaced her running shoes with high heels that better matched her lime green blouse and black skirt. "Do I look flustered?" she questioned as she patted out the perspiration and put on her best face.

Meena thought the woman looked stunning and vibrant with her hair, flushed cheeks and bobbly earrings. She felt conservative and dowdy by contrast. She'd worn her most benign looking business outfit with straight black pants, mauve blouse and black jacket, a nice costume, but with no sense of play.

Petra saw Meena glance at herself in the surrounding mirrors of the elevator. "You look fine. What are you here for?"

"Interview, for an articling position."

There were no lawyers in her family, it was replete with managers and engineers, and now with the new economy in India, there was a smattering of IT specialists. She had one uncle who had joined an ashram, much to the chagrin of the family. He'd been fleeing from some bad debts and was considered crazy and was excised from the family genealogical references. Lawyers, though not at the height of the career charts, were acceptable.

"Well, good luck. And, oh, by the way, if you get the job, my little trick is to talk to strangers the whole ride up. It keeps the mind occupied. Cheers." Petra winked and waved as she headed down the hall.

Magma's logo was emblazoned on the wall. Beneath it sat a receptionist who was just as impressively turned out as Petra had been. Meena took a deep breath. "Hi, I'm here for an interview."

"You can take a seat on the couch and we'll call you when they are ready." The woman was young, efficient, and pleasant. Meena glanced around at the large Inuit carvings and paintings by First Nations artists on the wall. She thought one looked like a Morisseau original. Glossy brochures were lined up on the mahogany table in front of the black leather couch. She picked one up to occupy her hands. She already knew the contents.

She'd researched Magma, its holdings, investments, board of governors, and staff associates. There were no surprises in the glossy outline held in her hands. She considered a bolt for the door.

"Ms Awinyolan?" Meena glanced up as the receptionist pronounced her name. "Mr. Dawson will see you now. His assistant will be here to show you the way."

At that moment, Petra, the woman from the elevator, came back down the hall. "Meena Awinyolan I presume?" Petra smiled. "Follow me please."

Meena was startled, but Petra looked at her with warmth. "You'll be fine." She opened the door to a boardroom and beckoned to Meena to enter.

Floor to ceiling windows provided a panoramic view of Lake Ontario, the Toronto islands dotting the water below. A large conference table punctuated with leather chairs took up most of the room. A man was seated at the head of the table, engrossed in papers spread out before him.

Meena shrugged off her surprise at seeing her elevator companion in the board room, and went forward to introduce herself, propelling past the point of no return. "Greetings Mr. Dawson, my name is Meena Awinyolan. Thank-you for taking the time to meet with me today."

Dawson got up and shook her hand. Meena noticed his appraisal of her figure. He motioned her toward one of the chairs across from him.

She was glad for the high school drama classes, they had taught her to breathe through adversity. She sat down.

Dawson was in his late fifties, bald with short strips of grey hair on either side of his head. He wore a slim, expensive, tailored grey suit and burgundy silk tie. His features were sharp, and he was not unattractive.

"You've met Ms. Chemenkov I presume?" He glanced at Petra, his eyes trailing over her earrings and blouse. "So Meena, may I call you Meena?" His tone was smooth, but held a touch of ice.

Meena responded in the formal, "certainly Mr. Dawson," aware of the position articling students took in the pecking order.

He didn't begin with any niceties, diving right into her reasons for wanting to work with Magma, to work in the area of corporate law.

"I'm intrigued by all aspects of the law, as I mentioned in my application," Meena replied with practiced calm. "I'm interested in the places where environmental regulations and corporate interests are accommodated, cognizant of marrying the best ecological practices to solid financial imperatives." Meena and Celina had rehearsed this beforehand. It was crucial that it construe Meena's convictions, but be tempered with a business ethos.

"And why choose us, Meena? You've the pick of Tory Tory or Anderson Deloite." Dawson rhymed off the leading Bay Street Law firms.

When the list of articling positions came out to the students, Meena had seen Magma listed under corporate opportunities. She had been considering Parkdale Community Legal Services or interning with the International Human Rights program at the University of Toronto, and brought up Magma as a lark, not seriously considering it as an option. But Warren had mentioned it to Celina, and Celina had immediately seen the potential.

Though Meena wished she could say she'd been cajoled into it, she had relished the thought, imagining herself a modern-day crusader. It would be only for a few months, and she could perhaps garner information from the inside that they had been unable to attain on the outside. She rationalized that the skills she would learn would serve her well when she was on the other side of the courtroom, prosecuting individuals and corporations for their misdeeds.

"Magma is not a lawyers' den, but a geological corporation with a supporting cast of lawyers who, I might add, are subservient to the dictates of the lustre of mineral acquisition. We play at being lawyers as we navigate the firm through avoiding malfeasance, defamation, labour strife and the like." Dawson's voice was colder still and he looked at Meena.

"Working within an existing corporate framework will allow me to be involved in a variety of cases related to trial, litigation and negotiation. I enjoy the diversity and in particular," she paused, looking Dawson in the eyes, "corporate law is not without its benefits." She arched her brow and smiled. "Is it Mr. Dawson?" The words slithered into the room, she'd adopted a character, taking on the distasteful traits of fellow students.

"Indeed," he responded with equanimity. "Shall we proceed to your qualifications and see what you know about Magma?" Dawson looked from Meena down to the pile of his papers. Meena had passed the first test.

An hour later, Petra was leading her away from the interview boardroom. Meena was glad she'd kept her suit jacket on as she was soaking underneath.

"You did well." Petra touched her arm with feeling.

"Thanks."

"I'll see you soon." Petra smiled at her and nodded.

"I hope so, I may need an elevator-mate," Meena replied, relieved. If given her druthers, she would have sprinted down the hallway and discarded her clothes at the bottom and jumped into a fountain to wipe off her own stench.

The truth was, she'd begun imagining herself in the offices overlooking the city. She'd eyed the other women working there, and rated her own prospects. She felt she could hold her own, and when they complimented her on her marks and performance, she rose taller in the chair.

• • •

Meena had a gold watch that had been her grandfather's. He'd earned it working for decades with the Indian Tea Company. She never knew the man, but had inherited the watch.

It was the kind you could attach to a coat, with a long chain and click mechanism that opened the face. It hung from a bookshelf over her bed like a tetherball around a pole in a school court yard.

She felt guilty about having it hang there when she thought about the mine and where the gold came from. Most of the gold mined in the world went to India, for bangles, studs, necklaces. It was the bling that accentuated the saris.

She'd imagined pan handlers on a river bed in the Yukon washing the pebbles away to find the glimmering nugget. The Magma website showcased a different scenario depicting a wash basin appropriate only for the gods and the size of their stakes were ranges of mountains rather than riverbeds.

But what would it mean to sell it, or melt it down to its elements and return it to the earth? The metal held a memory for her, it kept time to a connection to her past. She wondered if the metal had held memories for her grandfather and if he'd experienced the same thrill when he opened the click that she did. She left it hanging by her bed, because it was a memory, but now, it also served as a reminder.

• • •

Each day she had come into Magma she had been hopeful she would find something incriminating or a clue that would help Celina. She was no Mata Hari. And the truth was, she was learning a lot about the law. Dawson was a skilled lawyer and had a competent team working with him, and the complexity of the issues they were dealing with was impressive. In the course of a day she had researched subsoil hydrology legislation, edited a briefing note related to a salary contract and written a number of responses to threatened legal actions around property disputes, a kind of lawyer to lawyer tit for tat, amounting to the firing of warning flares. It was a lawyer's bread and butter, the kind of thing lawyers do preceding negotiations, to mark the territory.

Dawson had given Meena responsibilities, and she had worked with diligence to prove her worth and gain access to more information and files.

That access could come none too soon. There was a case in Guatemala where human rights researchers found a warehouse full of files from the police, a secret stash of reports that detailed the names of the disappeared, the surveillance they had been under, the torture they had suffered, and the information that had been obtained from them—as in the Nuremberg trial of Nazi Germany, where the confidence of the perpetrators was such that they kept detailed records of their crimes and atrocities. Celina had suggested the archives in Magma as a place to search, suggesting maybe the company was cocky too.

Meena asked Petra about the old concession archives, as if she were asking who was supposed to wash the coffee cups in the staff room.

"Some are here and some are downstairs and others are scattered in satellite offices in the countries where we had the concessions. Why?"

She and Petra were working late on a Saturday evening. It was in her nature, Meena immersed herself into whatever passion was the endeavour of the day. Warren had suggested she had a perfectionist streak, and that she liked neither to either fail nor appear uninformed. The first time she made a soufflé, her father dropped a toolbox on the counter to better search for a screwdriver to fix a faulty light switch. The souffle collapsed and he ate the demolished scraps she tried to compost as penance, while Meena set about making another one that was fluffy and golden.

"Dawson mentioned something about a new concession and I think I might be confusing it with something else, so I wanted to verify it with the other ones to make sure I'm not, you know, confusing the two." Damn, Meena thought, she was not a very good liar. When she was sixteen, the use of a derailed streetcar as explanation for her breaking her curfew was weakened at the sight of her father waiting up for her in the living room.

Meena knew Petra was examining her so she kept her head in the papers she was sorting through, displaying as little interest as she could muster.

Petra told her she could find the information in the annual reports in the library, reports that Meena had already gone over in detail. She hadn't found mention of any scandals, or poisonings, it all displayed rosy pictures of benevolent corporate practices resulting in phenomenal returns for shareholders, the sort of thing that annual reports were supposed to say.

"Right, of course, but there were some details that weren't in the reports."

"What concession are you talking about?"

She considered an outright lie, but pictured her dad's disappointed face when she told him about the transit delay. "He was mentioning one in Guatemala."

"What about it?"

Petra and Meena had been spending a lot of time together at work, but Meena wasn't sure yet who she could trust. Still, she was going to have to trust somebody sooner or later if she was going to get what she wanted, what Celina wanted.

Meena knew she was better when she steered near to the truth, but obfuscated with omission and diversion. After the incident with her father, she learned to separate out the strands of honesty, proportioning their use to specific circumstances, and intermingling other strands into the mix.

"Why so many questions? I'm just trying to do some background checking." She looked up from the stacks of papers she'd been rifling through. She tried to look annoyed, as if she'd been bothered with an impertinent response.

Petra eyed the documents she had in hand. "The Guatemala work is very sensitive you know."

"I know, that's why Dawson asked me to look at it." Meena was in deep. She stood up, and left the files on the desk for Petra to examine. It was nothing of import, they were background deposition sheets for a right-of-way access for fuel trucks she was supposed to have filed a week ago. They indicated nothing, and that's why she left them there.

Petra flicked through the pages as if she were scratching the back of a dog's ear. "I don't think so."

"Don't think what?"

"Meena, I may be just another pretty face, but I do have a bullshit detector you know. Dawson is not going to ask you to look at a sensitive file mere weeks after you start articling here. It's just not done, that's not how Magma works. That's why you were hired, your background check was clean. But they want to trust you before they'd let you into anything as delicate as that." Petra stopped flicking and held her index finger on the stack of files, pointing downwards, holding the papers in place.

Meena sat at her desk, and rolled a second chair up beside it. She patted the seat, as if settling in for an Oprah chat. Petra raised an eyebrow. "I heard some things about this company that I didn't know about," Meena said. "Now I want to know. One, to cover my ass and two, to see if this is the right fit for me." She tried to disarm Petra with a smile.

Petra didn't speak right away, but she sat down and circled her long red fingernail on the side of the chair, twirling it around like she was wrapping up a coil. Meena took a yoga breath, the one that calmed the body and slowed the heart.

"It's a fine ass to cover," Petra replied with a glance. Petra rolled her chair till it blocked the exit out of the cubicle. Meena tried to imagine it wasn't on purpose. She was out of her depth, she knew. There was something about Petra that seemed to want to toy with her. Meena took another heart breath and dug deep. She wouldn't rise to Petra's bait. Instead she looked back at the right-of way file, a dismissive monarch.

Petra paused a moment, gazed at Meena under heavy lids, then sighed loudly and rolled her chair away again. "The archives require a security code," she said, sounding bored. "Neither of us has access on that level."

Meena considered this. She knew, weeks into her work at Magma that the only place she was even halfway sure of finding anything that would point to the complicity of the company—let alone tell her where the bodies of the villagers had been dumped—was in the archives. She considered her options. So far, she'd yet to break a law. But surely if she was found out, it could be construed as corporate espionage. It was risky, a fine line between crime and conviction. Still, she knew the others were relying on her—on her access, her smarts, and her ability to find something that would be useful.

And Petra, she knew, wasn't being straight with her.

She'd seen Petra respond to requests from Dawson as if she wanted nothing more than to photocopy stacks of five-hundred-page documents, or accept the error for reports that weren't prepared on time for board meetings, reports it wasn't her responsibility to acquire. She'd also seen Petra "lose" documents into a shredder, ones that were out of her jurisdiction. She'd heard Petra bait Dawson with a morsel of false information about a case they ended up losing. Meena knew Petra wasn't who she seemed to be—to those not paying attention, she was a dedicated and diligent employee. To Meena, with more at stake, it was more complicated.

Meena weighed her options. The archives were likely huge and it would take her years to search them by herself. Meena knew that at a trial, you had to give some things up in order to get other things you wanted—if you couldn't convict a person for murder without a smoking gun, maybe you could get them on manslaughter. "Get me the access codes Petra, or I'll let Dawson know why we're paying the damages suit to that family in Baker's Lake."

Petra raised an eyebrow in surprise, but smiled at Meena as she stood up and walked past her out of the cubicle. "Alright then, anything you need."

· · ·

"What do you mean you are not working for a legal aid clinic?" Meena's mother said, astonished. She pushed away the crossword puzzle she'd been working on. "I thought that's what you wanted?"

Meena slumped on the couch, flipping television channels, too tired to read.

"I know," Meena said, "but things change, people change."

"This doesn't have to do with that boy next door does it?"

"I thought you liked Warren."

"Not if he makes you change into someone you are not."

She hadn't wanted to tell her parents. She knew they would not be impressed, nor believe her porous explanations about working in a system to change a system. She knew it went against type, betrayed her idealism, her own efforts at making change, and her practiced righteousness. They, more than anyone, would know from which well of insincerity it flowed.

"Listen Amma, it's okay. Working at Magma is my choice. Besides it gives me a lot of opportunities—a chance to practice and learn about a wide range of legal issues." At this, Meena's father looked up from the *Manchester Guardian*, he'd had his head buried in stats and scores for cricket.

"Well, I must get ready," her mother said briskly. She stood, and put the crossword puzzle on the coffee table. "I'm off to see your cousin Pavindar. Do you want to come along?"

"No thanks, I've work I should be doing."

Raita bustled upstairs, and Meena would have felt as if her mother had brushed aside the decisions she was making in her life. But this was a well-worn conflict strategy. Not avoidance—delay. Anytime Raita was taken off guard, she changed the subject or left the room until she had time to decide on a response.

Vatu spoke as soon as he heard his wife reach the top of the stairs and close the bathroom door.

"She was baiting you. She doesn't believe you."

Meena was startled. Her father was a quiet man. He rarely meddled. "What do you mean?"

"You have changed since you started seeing this Warren fellow."

"I thought we were talking about my articling position?"

"We are."

"They're not related."

"Is that so?"

Meena squirmed. She loved her father, he had encouraged her to think for herself, expand her horizons and views of the world. He'd taken her places when she was a girl, explained the world to her through the discoveries. At the zoo they had watched the polar bears swim behind the glass with their massive paws digging at the water to propel them forward. It's where she learned penguins lived on the southern tip and polar bears occupied the north, belying what had been depicted by Disney. Vatu loved to go to the Kleinburg gallery to appreciate the vast space of his adopted country, and Meena responded by setting up her own preteen art collective that showcased pencil drawings and crayon blends in their living room.

He had helped her to learn about the world as a kid, but when she was no longer impressed by water slides and rarefied descriptions of

Egyptian mummies, he had faded away. Those days of in depth sharing had long ceased, at some point the minutiae gave way to synthesis, then to summary and there had come a time when there were whole chapters she hadn't shared with her father.

She didn't know if they still knew how to talk with one another.

"You don't like Warren?"

"I never said I didn't like Warren. I don't like him influencing you to do things that aren't like you. Or that haven't been, up till now." He left the implication hanging in the air.

"He isn't, he hasn't." Meena felt like she was reverting to her childhood.

"If you and he insist on being together, you should make it official."

Oh, I see, she thought. Here it comes, the marriage truck steaming towards her, the focus on her work was the prelude to the real discussion. "Marriage is a bit presumptuous at this point I would think."

Her parents would have noticed her early morning absences when she hastened up to Warren's apartment to cuddle herself up under his quilts when he returned home from work. Up till then, they chose not to talk about it, if it wasn't verbalized then it required no recognition or remedy.

"What's going on with Warren, this job of yours? What is happening?" Vatu put down his paper and looked at her with concern. It was how he had looked at her when she had buzz-cut her hair in a fit of solidarity at the death of Kurt Cobain. In India it was a sign of religious sacrifice or widowhood, not a fashion trend you wore for attention, though perhaps in retrospect that was why she had done it. Meena had known about the tradition, her grandmother had shorn her hair upon the death of her grandfather. Her father hadn't reproached her, but spoken to her with great sadness, which made it worse.

She was beginning to see his reluctance to interfere as him not knowing how to recapture the string-less bonds between parent and child.

She didn't want to make him sad. So Meena told him. She told him everything, as she had when she was a kid, and gone into great detail about getting on the bus, what she had for lunch, the interesting bug they had looked at under a microscope and how Zia had worn purple barrettes with orange pants.

"Do you love him?"

"I don't know, maybe..."

"And this job, at Magma. Do you think you will be okay?"

"I hope so." She replied and Vatu nodded, looked at her with a small smile and then picked up the paper again and resumed his reading.

. . .

Warren had never been to anything like a shareholders' meeting. Procedures and etiquette were not his strong suit, and so he was nervous for days beforehand. He knew he'd be out of his element, a hillbilly crashing a debutantes' ball. He had nothing to wear, for one thing. His wardrobe was appropriate for someone who moved gravestones for a living and spent his spare time reading in coffee shops. Curtis had a nice suit though, one he'd worn to a niece's wedding. It was blue, conservative, with a paisley silk tie. Warren's wearing it doubled its public appearances. Curtis was a bit taller, so they had to make a few adjustments so that it sat right. Warren accessorized with shoes from Honest Ed's.

The Toronto Convention Centre hall was packed. Warren waited nervously in the lobby for Melanie. He barely recognized her when she arrived. She wore a tailored maroon suit, the conservative equal to his own, and had exchanged her hippy flower earrings for faux rubies. Her hair was sleek, pulled back.

"You look nice," Warren said.

"You look nervous," Melanie replied. "Don't be." She squeezed his hand.

The hall was stocked with distinguished, middle-aged people and seniors of all shapes and sizes, awash in suits and a scattering of skirts. It occurred to Warren that these people spent more money on their clothes than his community kept in their credit union. And they likely bought their diamonds off the proceeds from the shares in the local mine. The thought irritated him.

He and Mel were made to pass through security and verified they were shareholders or held the proxies that allowed them to attend such an august affair. It felt more like going through an airport than attending a business meeting, but they passed the screening and were cleared for entrance.

The gathering had begun. Mel and Warren partook of the free coffee, with a choice of regular, latté or cappuccino. Warren also took a small plate of smoked salmon over a multigrain cream cheese bagel, a couple of kiwi rounds and a slice of gruyere cheese. It was a force of habit to fill his plate, part of the legacy of church suppers and community funerals.

They found a spot to sit amongst the crowd. People were seated on stackable chairs, the kind that were upholstered with burgundy backs and matching cushions. There was a large screen buttressed by a huge banner proclaiming Magma International, and a number of people were on stage and had begun to address the crowd as Warren glanced through the glossy folder of materials he'd received when they'd arrived.

The speaker was outlining the successes of the company, droning on about 'low-risk operation with superior stock performance.' There was a series of pictures beamed on screen with images of gold rings and necklaces, shining machinery, and happy investors.

The speaker continued "…our advantage and competitive edge is realized through our low-cost production and large and expanding reserve base." Pictures of the mine splashed on screen. Warren had seen similar photos from Celina where the clear devastation of the open pit was on display. But the company had altered and distorted the images adding greenery, trees and even what looked like a fountain in the corner. If Warren hadn't seen the original pictures of a mountain with its top blown off, leaving a gaping pit with rock piles spewed across the land where villages once stood, he'd have thought it was pictures of a luxury resort they were looking at.

The speaker continued "…and we've consolidated operations, working with the local population to allow for sustainable communities, economic improvement and overall well-being for the Guatemalan people."

Pictures of little kids appeared on the screen: an impish boy missing a front tooth and a young girl holding his hand. They were basking in the munificence of Magma, which had its logo affixed to the bottom, ensuring no one would mistake who had brought such great fortune to these children.

Warren dropped the bagel back onto his plate. His mouth was set in a grimace. He wondered if the investors that had owned the mine in his hometown had once sat here and airbrushed his community in the same way.

The speaker droned on about extraction-to-cost ratios, balance sheets, and showed graphs illustrating stock performance for the last quarter. Warren's hands had begun to shake balancing the food and the stockholder meeting material. He put his coffee on the floor and felt pressure building in his chest.

He looked around at the group of investors. Didn't they know? Didn't they care? And if they didn't know, shouldn't they find out? Wasn't that part of their moral obligation?

"It's coming up," Mel whispered to Warren as she checked the agenda. A new speaker had taken up the mic on stage. He'd been presented and people had clapped, but Warren had missed who he was.

"As many of you know," the speaker began, "in an attempt to secure democratic privileges at this meeting, and so as not to be bogged down by gratuitous motions, we've gathered together the proposals and motions we have before us and will vote on them based on the order of presentation. If you look in your folders you'll find the appropriate…"

Warren wasn't thinking about motions or investor confidence. He was experiencing a dissonance—he knew first-hand what happened on the ground, behind the gloss. He knew they didn't show the pictures of the dust that spewed out over the town after blasting days, where everyone would be out washing their cars, and spraying down their houses. He didn't need to do the math to know that what the workers in the mine made and what the investors received. The picture of his mine didn't include the smiling faces of children, he saw the face of his grandfather.

The speaker intoned "…you'll find the ballots…"

"Shit," Mel exclaimed.

"What?"

"They're not going to let us put forward our motion."

"How do you know?"

"They've limited it—only letting majority holders put motions forward. You have to go to the mic and do it anyway."

Warren hesitated.

"Do it now Warren, or we won't have a chance."

When he was a kid, Warren hadn't dreamed of other ways to protest his disdain. People where he was from didn't sit in trees for months on end or blockade roads, or write letters to shareholders. Warren looked at the smiling kids on the screen and walked to the nearest mic.

"Excuse me, Mr. Speaker." He cleared his throat, and felt his voice wavering as he addressed the crowd. He'd never spoken in public before, let alone in front of hundreds of business people. The man on stage, withholding a frown, turned his attention to Warren.

Warren continued. "I have a motion from the floor."

"Yes, well, as I said," the man's voice was sharp. "You can bring the motion to one of the assistants on stage and we'll make an amendment after an appropriate review."

Warren broke in, gritted with a determination that came from a deep pit of memory, oblivious to the fretful sleeps that had preceded the meeting and urged him to flee. As he started to present the motion, he didn't need to look down to read the text in his hands.

"...and we demand that..." someone on the stage tried to interrupt, as if that could stop the surge coming out of him "the families of the victims of the San Jacinto cyanide poisoning, the town it dislocated..." Warren pictured the victims in this town, like victims in his own town, like his own grandfather whom a similar company had left to die.

Warren was forced to yell "so that they will not be forgotten..." They'd turned off his sound and guards were trying to wrestle him away. He didn't hear the other people shouting or responses from the floor when he starting reciting the names of the victims, "Lalita Arayo, Maria Hernandez Ical, William Alexander Peace, Dillon Edward Peace..." he recited the names, shouting at the top of his lungs, names he brought to the hall so they wouldn't be faceless, anonymous bodies. He felt like he was standing at the head of the silenced multitudes from mining towns everywhere. He was speaking into the mouth of the devil.

They tried to muzzle him, and he shouted out wordless rage. It took five of the guards to haul him out of the convention room, and then throw him down outside the doors of a service entrance. A couple of the guards gave him a few kicks to his ribs, forcing him into a ball. Mel interrupted the beating and the guards pushed past her and marched back into the building.

"You okay?" she crouched down.

"Let's get the fuck out of here." He groaned and rolled over and pulled himself up, his throat raw, his ribs sore. He felt bad that he'd ripped the elbow on Curtis's suit jacket, and scuffed the shoes from Honest Ed's. He wouldn't be able to take them back now. Mel helped him up, and they made their way to the streetcars on Front Street.

Inside the hall, the speaker on stage turned to an assistant. "Find out who they are."

"Yes Mr. Tyrell."

• • •

"You did the best you could." Mel remarked as they rolled along the tracks. Warren's face was set. He'd heard that before, and it was cold comfort. He stared out the window and watched the buildings pass them by as they travelled along Front Street. He wished he could press himself into the glass, but the images flooded forward.

Warren and other kids would spend Sunday gathering the empties and filling up shopping carts. There was no recycling program so they took the bottles to the quarry to smash on the rocks or set-up for target practice with BB guns and slingshots. Someone had seen a Molotov cocktail on the news and using reference books, and veiled questions to chemistry teachers, they deduced that Palmolive dish soap mixed with gasoline gave the best flash.

They blew them up at night, for effect.

His father had died, and Warren was trying to sort it out in his head. He was scared for his brother. He had seen the ads for Mothers Against Drunk Driving and squirmed from the television.

Their few interactions involved roughhousing where Dillon would wrestle him into all sorts of contortions till he squealed in pain. He didn't mind, it meant they were communicating through arm holds and leg pins. When his brother was beating him into submission, he knew his brother was aware he existed.

It was a Friday evening and Dillon was finished his shift. He came into the house, it was late and the smell of the pub announced his arrival. He didn't stagger, or stumble or even mumble his words, no one in his family did when they'd been drinking. It's why they were acceptable in the community, they all still performed while intoxicated, were gregarious, spinning yarns, lighting up parties, creating laughter. They weren't argumentative or violent in public, so everyone loved them, and admired how they could hold their liquor.

Warren cornered Dillon and gathered his resolve.

"Dillon, you've gotta stop drinking and driving." His brother hit him with a sidearm smash across the face. Blood escaped down his lip and the conversation was over.

His mom came in and grabbed a dishtowel and tried to help clean him up, fussing over the cuts and ignoring the wounds. That worked when he was six, and had a scraped knee, but as the drink soaked deeper into the roots of their family the wounds would fester.

Six weeks later, his brother wrapped the car around the McCluskey family, and when they came home from the memorial service his mom dug out a bottle of vodka from the cupboard and turned to him as she poured a drink. "You did the best you could, son."

It was a few months after that he perfected his own cocktail, of the Molotov variety.

. . .

"What do you think?" Warren asked Curtis as they drove the long haul to Beechwood cemetery. It had taken him a few days to broach. Curtis never asked him why he had a bruise on his cheek and he moved so stiffly getting in and out of the truck. Warren was grateful for the space, but eager to talk about it now.

"Dreams, death, gold, native folks, and ancestors, it's messy shit. You white folks have fucked around with Indians for far too long and in far too many places," Curtis replied.

"I guess."

"Shit yeah, man. Columbus and his merry band of torturers were the first wave. We've been fucked over for the past several hundred years since the European arrival, with the rape by the Spaniards in the south followed by the pillaging by the Brits up our way. So, some company kills some Guatemalan Indians, no news there. The news would come, although we'd never be allowed to hear about it, if the company bastards were put in jail. 'Fraid we don't have a whole lot of examples of that. Most of them grow old, die, and get buried here." Curtis scanned the passing graves.

They passed the shadows of markers, dark reflections lined in rows acting as the battalion guards of the night. A sliver of light from the new moon afforded them a glimpse into the evening as they glided towards the stone marked for removal.

Curtis backed the truck up to the site and Warren hitched up the gears and clamped them on to the rock, then lifted the gravestone into the air, where it hung suspended for a moment above the ground where the bones were left, unmarked. Warren shifted the the levers drawing the stone towards the bed of the truck. He lowered it down slowly while Curtis guided the descent. Warren's eyes were trained on the distance, paying no heed to his actions or the stone they were removing. He hadn't even bothered to look at the name on the inscription.

"What the hell do I do with it?" Warren asked.

Curtis was focused on the task at hand and patted the stone lying on the bed of the truck and raised an eyebrow, "I kind of thought you would have figured out your job by now," he said.

Warren glanced inside and shook his head, "No, I mean with Celina."

"What do you want to do?"

Warren shrugged. "I don't know what I can do," he said as he secured the crane and closed the hitch.

As they drove off, Warren watched out the side mirror as their red taillights trailed away from the patch of land that now lay bare.

They left the gravestone in the storage unit at the cemetery and Curtis drove Warren home. A late night jazz station played softly in the cab while each was absorbed in their thoughts. Warren wasn't confident in his abilities. It seemed all his efforts at redress backfired or had disastrous consequences, it was hard not to feel impotent.

"What's that?" Curtis said as he drove up Warren's street and stopped near his house.

"What?" Warren said.

"You starting to take your work home now?" Curtis pointed to the house, in front of the staghorn sumac. There was a grave, not unlike the one they had just left behind, with a stone standing upright, indented into the lawn as though his front yard had been made into a cemetery plot.

Warren jumped out of the cab and Curtis kept the headlights lit on the spot.

Warren only went as close to the gravestone as it took to read the writing on it. He turned to Curtis his face contorted and his eyes bulging. He hadn't noticed the name on the last stone they removed, but this one he recognized.

"What is it?" Curtis said getting out of the truck.

"The gravestone." Warren backed away from the lawn and his house.

"What about it?"

"It's mine."

CHAPTER 8

Lamat *(venus)*

*"...after a person dies the spirit is somewhere on the earth
or in the sky, we do not know exactly where, but we are
sure that the spirit still lives..."*
— Chased-By-Bears Santee-Yanktonai Sioux

Warren was in shock. He lifted, moved, removed, and touched gravestones every day. And each was unique, like snowflakes. He knew who was memorialized in each stone, he greeted them when his hand met marble. Sometimes he didn't need to look at the epitaph to see the name engraved there.

"Angle the truck," Warren said. "I want them to see."

Curtis nodded and obliged. He cut the engine and looked at Warren. "You okay?"

Warren was ashen, but he nodded.

"Okay then," Curtis said. He opened the truck door and swung out on the pavement. "You coming?"

Warren took a deep breath and nodded again. He hopped out of the truck.

His heavy knock on the front door brought Chantel, wrapped in a terrycloth robe and yawning. "Hey boys, this is an early visit." Warren nodded grimly. "This is Curtis," he said, gesturing with his head. "He's cool. Where's Celina?"

"I'm here," Celina said, coming in to the front hallway. She was bleary-eyed, but awake. She nodded at Chantel, who scooted off to the kitchen.

"What the hell is this?" Warren strode to the front room and moved the curtain aside. He thrust his finger toward the truck and its cargo.

She put her hand to her mouth and backed away from the window. "I'm sorry, Warren," she said.

"Sorry? They put up a gravestone with my name on it. They know where I live, what I do." Warren stood in front of the fireplace. "They want me dead Celina."

Chantel returned, on light feet. She slid a plate onto the coffee table. "I've got some muffins," she said quietly, "and tea and coffee will be ready shortly." She sat next to Curtis on the sofa.

Warren paced the living room, unable to remain still.

"This isn't some high school gag. I didn't buy into this shit when you asked me to go to that shareholder meeting. They bust on my ribs, then put a fucking grave up in my name." Warren was shaking. "I've been beaten up and that's one thing, but them telling me they want me dead, that's a whole other level of commitment."

"Warren, I'm sorry," Celina said, her gaze never wavering from his. "We should have warned you."

"Warned me! Warned me they wanted me dead? What the hell is this you're getting me into?"

He'd agreed to help her, in a way to assuage the dreams that came to him when he slept, dreams that cajoled him into actions. He'd become involved because Celina had presented an option that suggested there were ways to do things that seemed right, ways to respond to the callings he heard. And her cause seemed reasonable, legitimate. These were not the kinds of repercussions he was expecting. Beatings he could take, he'd had worse meted out toward him and survived to tell the tale. But finding his own grave—no. That was too much.

"You knew from the first night they were dangerous people. You knew what they were capable of doing," Celina said.

"Yeah, but that was in Guatemala. This is Canada for fuck's sake. We've got laws in this country."

And he knew as he said it, it wouldn't matter. They couldn't go to the police, he couldn't go to the police. He knew that no seasoned officer would give him the time of day when they came across his record. He was a misfit with a grudge and he'd soured his legitimate opportunities for protest. It seemed he was doomed to repetition, his fate had him swing at windmills only to have the blades cut him off at his feet.

Warren looked at the two women in turn, then outside to the stark reminder in the truck, and then at Curtis. They were waiting, watching him. He unclenched his fists and slumped down on a brown-cushioned chair. "I don't know." He grimaced. "I don't know." And then he whipped back to standing as if on a spring. "What the hell is that? A fucking grave? That's sick."

"That's what they do," Chantel said. "That's how they play the game."

"But it's not a game," Warren said.

"No, it's not. It's deadly, I'm afraid."

He hadn't considered what it would mean becoming involved in this group. It had felt the world was offering him a taste of something, tantalizing him, and he'd consumed the story like a crack vial. But he'd never considered death a possible outcome of his involvement.

"You're not the first to receive a threat," Chantel said. "I got phone calls at all hours of the day and night. Celina had a package of ashes delivered to the house with condolence cards. And Eduardo, they put up posters around the neighbourhood accusing him of being a convicted sexual predator." Chantel shook her head in disgust.

"Jesus!" Curtis said.

"Yeah, Eduardo had to move and Celina's been followed, I use an unlisted phone now, it goes on."

Warren felt his courage ebb, being faced with his own tombstone brought the stakes sharply into focus, and he wasn't sure he had the fortitude to participate.

"Do we go to the media?" he offered. "Maybe if people knew..."

"No proof," Celina broke in. "Circumstantial evidence. They'd never take us seriously, and if they did by some miracle, we'd be sued for defamation and slander faster than we could issue a press release."

"But what if we found out who ordered the stone?" Warren wouldn't let the idea go.

"Do you know?"

"No."

"Did anyone see them leave the stone at your place?"

Warren shook his head, it was late at night, people had seen gravestones in the back of the truck at his place before, it would not have appeared unusual.

"Yeah, they cover their tracks," Chantel said.

And get away with it thought Warren. It was becoming all too familiar a scenario.

. . .

They kept the stone in the truck, though neither wanted to be near it. But they needed a place to store it, as they had other deliveries and removals. Curtis had suggested dumping it in the Humber River or throwing it off the Scarborough Bluffs into the lake. In the end, they left it in the garden's administrative facilities, in the back storage area that housed lawn care tools, a menagerie of broken pottery pots and overflowing bins of discarded plastic flower stems.

"Hurry up," Warren urged Curtis.

They moved boxes of defunct funeral service programs and dusted an area off in the back corner where they frog-hopped the rock to settle against the wall. Warren wore gloves to act as a barrier between skin and stone. He pushed past Curtis, wanting get out of the shed and away from the stone as fast as he could. He took one last look at it where it stood. It was a dark granite rock, flecked with grey, with veins of yellow and green. Despite himself, he was drawn to touch the rock with his bare hands, to see if it had something to tell him. Warren took off his gloves and set them on a shelf, he moved gingerly as if he were expecting a shock and dragged his finger along the lines that spread across its surface. He pressed his palm against it and waited to see if he could conjure up his image. The stone was cold.

"Are you trying seduce it or polish it?" Curtis said.

Warren retracted his hand. "What do you mean?"

"You touch these things like you're making love to them. What's up with that?"

"Nothing." Warren gave it a glance and shrugged it off, moving to grab his gloves again from the shelf.

"You gonna tell me or what? Do you have a love for geology or are you looking for fossils in the monuments of dead people?"

"Something like that," Warren whispered, shoving the gloves in his back pocket.

"Something like what?"

Warren looked at Curtis. Celina and Meena had pulled long held secrets out of him, and now this. "I see images," Warren waited to see Curtis smirk, but his features remained neutral. Warren hesitated and then continued, "of people, the people whose names are on the stone."

"Hmmm."

Warren hadn't told anybody, taunts against his grandmother's seeing eye kept him silent. The supernatural and superstition were loaded topics back home, best avoided, and only broached in myths or stories.

"I can see that."

"You can see them? " Warren hadn't considered he might not be the only one.

"No dude, all I see is a pretty piece of rock. But if you're telling me you're seeing spirits, who the hell am I to tell you you're not?" Curtis straightened a stack of flower pots they had knocked over in their haste.

Maybe he wasn't crazy.

"There's all sorts of stuff that happens in this world we don't know or understand. Hell, Shirley's niece, Beatrice, was so sick, the doctors had her on the way out, couldn't determine what was wrong, what to diagnose her with, so the whole family trudged up north for a ceremony, did their prayers to the spirits, and the ancestors, went into the sweat lodge, tied the tobacco, the whole bit. The little girl walked out of there five days later, symptom free. So yeah if you tell me you're seeing spirits, do I believe you, sure."

Warren suddenly felt a stiffness he held in his body begin to soften.

"Now let's get the hell out of here," Curtis said.

Warren pulled the door to the storage compartment closed behind him, and checked to make sure it was latched. He put his palm against the metal, testing. If there was something there, he wanted it locked behind the door, unable to get out.

He felt nothing, no spirits, no visions or images. His hand felt cold. Warren remained at the door a moment longer to see if anything stayed, or lingered, or protested its confinement. All was quiet, he removed his hand and shook out his arms.

Curtis was already in the driver's seat. "You okay?" he called through the truck's open window. "Yeah," Warren said. "I'll be right there. He went to the nearby washroom and held his hands under hot and then cold water, washing and rinsing them thoroughly. He looked at himself in the mirror and tried a smile on for size, then looked away quickly.

In the truck he was quiet. He wanted to tell Meena about the gravestone, but he knew she'd be gone to work by the time he got home, and lately, she wasn't making it back before he had to leave for work in the evening. He missed her. She was totally caught up in her work at Magma, and all his spare time was going to Celina and her group. He remembered the feeling of wanting to just be left alone, and shook his head. He'd give anything now to be surrounded. He thought about texting Meena or calling her, but how could he possibly tell her about a gravestone on the lawn with his name on it? That seemed like the kind of thing you'd want to do in person. He wondered if she would have noticed the divot in the yard, at least.

• • •

Meena and Petra were entombed below the surface. The archives, accessed by a special code, were in one of the storeys below ground.

The rooms were protected with special elevators you had to know about to locate, and the codes for the rooms were recorded, restricting access. Petra used a different code each time, having appropriated the access information from the central database. She knew the video key and every night after she and Meena left the archive room, she would delete the taped portion of their presence.

"One can't be too careful," she'd said.

"How did you get the codes?" Meena asked feeling like an espionage amateur learning at the feet of Lara Croft.

"Extracurricular diversions require extra particular cautions."

"What's that supposed to mean?"

"I enjoy having sex in unusual places," Petra said, and looked at Meena, who tried not to appear shocked. "But I'm not as keen on video evidence. Not that I'm unhappy with my performance," she pointed out. "But videos have a tendency to make it to the Internet. My proclivities, I'm happy to say, I like to keep as private performances."

Meena felt plain next to Petra with her tight white shirt and short red skirt. Petra was the kind of woman who made an effort in her appearance, while Meena was sparing and erratic in applying eyeliner. She'd been a David Suzuki acolyte in her teens, and after being brought up on *The Nature of Things*, she bought all her clothes at thrift shops. Petra was Paris Hilton to her Laura Ingalls.

She pictured Petra splayed out on the countertop on top of the pile of folders, and blushed. It was the kind of distraction that could keep her mind from going numb as they continued the research. She wondered if that was why Petra had shared it.

"You're blushing," Petra said.

"It's hot down here," Meena said, and blushed some more.

"Try to focus," Petra cooed.

Meena rolled her eyes.

They'd tried to be meticulous, beginning with the earliest files detailing the explorations, leading up to the first year of operation of the mine. The corporate documents displayed none of the flavours of the story as Celina had described it. While there were references to community consultations they were centred on obtaining of permits or outlining access routes. Some documents referring to land titles suggested there may have been bribery and illicit dealings. But Meena was certain there was enough obfuscation to preclude the concrete evidence required for prosecution. Petra found security documents outlining payments to the military for guarding the property of the mine. They photocopied these for future reference, but found nothing nefarious or conclusive in them, other than to wonder why a private company's assets would be guarded by a nation's military.

Meena was going through an endless pile of receipts, her vision at times blurred by repetition. She stared at the sections in Spanish, and failed to make sense of them. She was tired. She looked up from her work, and stretched her neck, rolling her head one way and then the other. "Let's take a break," she said. "How did you end up in Canada?"

"Typical Russian story. Face persecution, look for an opportunity and then find the holy land."

"What was your opportunity?"

"I was a dancer."

"Really!" Meena was impressed, but not surprised. As she had followed Petra down the hall, Meena had noticed her carriage, the way she held herself, back straight, muscular calves, broad shoulders, and strong arms. Meena had tried to emulate her grace on her walk home after work.

"Ballet? Modern dance?"

"Exotic."

"Exotic? Oh my god, are you serious?"

Meena felt her cheeks burning. "I grew up in Toronto," she said, "but it might as well have been a convent next to you."

"Oh, we had nuns too, boys love the virgin and the whore," Petra said breezily.

Meena looked at Petra with sympathy.

"Don't worry darling. I was a stage dancer. The lap dancers had it worse. A means to an end. It allowed me to come to Canada."

Investigation into Dancers Revealing

Lacey Dipietro

TORONTO – Recent revelations from an investigation at a local strip club on Yonge Street found performers from Eastern Europe who obtained their immigration status by scoring points as "exotic dancers." According to immigration officials there is a labour shortage

"Still," Meena said, "my greatest misdemeanours involved petty thefts of lipstick my parents wouldn't let me buy. I felt so guilty I volunteered at a seniors' home bringing them meals and holding their hands to make amends. I can't imagine—"

"Do not pity me for my choices," Petra said. "The decisions were mine. I made them freely and consciously. You have not been forced to make the same decisions. That is good for you. Yet, you are naïve and I must say I enjoy corrupting you." She winked at Meena.

"So how do you move from dancer to legal department?" Meena asked. "That must have required an interesting bit of footwork."

Petra laughed. "I saved the money I made dancing, while my...colleagues...added to the junk tracks that snaked up their arms."

Meena pictured young women with diaphanous sleeves, and dollars stuck into strings, wrapped around poles, flying high above the desperate outstretched hands of patrons.

"A means to an end. Dancing allowed me to study and I knew I needed to know the law. But I have no interest in lawyers." She smiled at Meena. "Present company excluded of course. The law allows me to know rights and knowing rights helps me to fight those who don't know or respect them."

"Then why work here? Why not work at a legal clinic or women's shelter or something?"

"For the benefits of course." She replied with a grin, then shifted her eyes to the walls of boxes they were searching and the smile slid off her face. "Listen honey, working in the bars made it clear what junk circulates around this world and the johns who finance it. Working here, the junk and johns come in a different form. In either case, no one should be buying it." Petra grabbed hold of a box, opened the cardboard lid and pulled out a stack of manila folders.

Meena thought about the vagaries of circumstances and opportunities, choices and obligations. She considered where she would be if her family had remained in India. The female cousins on her dad's side were married, many with children. Some had cooks and gardeners, few of the women worked. Their lives seemed to involve mostly shopping and incessant gossip. She wondered how she would have found purpose and meaning in their midst.

Meena watched Petra for awhile, appreciating her anew, beginning to see the depths behind the facade. She suspected that her cousins too, were enclosed in complexities she had never ventured to uncover.

"Are you going to stand there staring at me all night? This is your project, Meena," Petra said. "Better get in and get your hands dirty."

"Sorry," Meena mumbled. She shook her head to clear her thoughts, and bent again over a dusty box. They worked in silence for a time, the boxes accumulated, but there were still so many more to go. The hours seemed to fold into each other, with no windows to look out of, it was hard to know what time it was.

FACTURA OFICIAL

Fecha:
12 de feb, 1,996

Contenido:
Reportaje de los
autopsies toxicólogo
por MAGMA

International Monto:

Q4500 Firma:

"Here's something." Meena whispered at last, holding a receipt in her hand.

"What is it?"

Meena flipped it looking at it from back to front. It was a small piece of paper with rough edges and a smooth surface. "It's a toxicology report. Or at least it's a receipt for one." Because it was in Spanish, it had crept into her consciousness, staying her hand.

"Holy shit, it refers to an autopsy." Meena scrutinized it with care, lest she rip the one piece of evidence they had. Petra hurried over to her side and looked at the paper over her shoulder.

"Although my Spanish is pretty weak, I believe it says it's the receipt for an autopsy they must have done on one of the victims."

"How do you know?"

"It's dated two days after the poisoning of the river."

"That's a smoking gun."

"Almost, it establishes a link, proof that an autopsy was performed, or at least paid for, but we can't prove who it was performed on unless we can find the report."

"Or the bodies."

"Right, or the bodies."

"Don't lose that."

"Don't worry. Let's see if we can find that report."

· · ·

"Do you want me to wait till you get upstairs?" Curtis asked.

Warren was still rattled, though two days had passed without incident. Every time he approached his house, he expected to see a gravestone. And every time he didn't see one, he felt a moment's relief, replaced by what was becoming constant worry that something worse was just around the corner. But he didn't want to let on just how haunted he was. "I'll be fine," he said.

Warren watched as the truck took off down the street.

He circled around the indent on the lawn—he was going to have to fill it in, and soon; it wasn't helping his state of mind—and brushed past the sumac. The tips of the leaves on the top of bush shone in the night. Warren looked at the bush and then at his apartment and back again. He stopped in his tracks, his heart pounding, his stomach tight. Light poured through the windows of his apartment. He never left the lights on. Warren looked back out onto the lawn and then up to his window. They were goading him.

He considered his options. He could wait on the porch till the street awoke, or he could arm himself and face whatever awaited him upstairs. They were making him scared, and he didn't want to be scared, he didn't want to live his life constrained by threats.

He took a deep breath and crept up the balcony and snuck past Meena's darkened living room window. There was a shovel that had been retired for the winter tucked in the corner. He grabbed it, took another breath and snuck up the stairs. He paused in front of his door, his heart hammering, he willed his hands to stop shaking. He lifted the shovel over his head with one hand and placed his hand on the doorknob with the other. The shovel had a wide blade which would make it awkward to swing over his head, but it was all he had.

"Ahhhhhhh..." Warren yelled, lurching into the room shovel swinging wildly.

"Aghhhhh," screamed Meena as she sat upright on the sofa. and pulled a blanket protectively towards her chest. "What the fuck!"

His eyes darted around the room. He slowly put the shovel down. "Sorry," he said, "I ah, I didn't know you would be here." He closed and locked the door, and peeked out the window, just to make sure.

"I repeat, what the fuck?" Meena said, taking in the shovel, the door, and Warren himself.

"You scared the shit out of me," Warren said.

"I scared the shit out of you?" Meena said. "You have a shovel. I have a blanket."

He looked out the window once more, then closed the curtains. "Ah, yeah, we probably need to talk." Warren leaned the shovel in the corner by the door. Meena stayed crunched up, with the blanket to her chin adrenaline coursing through her.

"We definitely need to talk," she said. She'd been excited by what she had found in the archives, and as they'd been slipping by each other too often, she didn't want to miss the chance to tell him in person. "I was thinking of surprising you naked in the bedroom, but I'm glad I didn't do that." She shivered beneath the blanket, dressed only in one of his t-shirts and boxers.

"How did you get in?" Warren asked. He darted to the door to make sure it was locked.

"The key you leave at the top of the steps under the rock," Meena said, impatiently. "It was either there or in the mailbox. Everyone has a spot, it's just a matter of finding it." She stood and grabbed a thin piece of paper from the coffee table. "And speaking of finding things, look what I've got!"

"What's this?" he took hold of the paper.

"The beginning of their downfall," Meena replied with glee. "Now your turn, what's with the shovel and the samurai entry?"

"Not important," Warren said. He stared at the autopsy receipt, trying to make sense of it. "I'm going to make us some coffee," he said, making for the kitchen with the receipt in his hand. "And I'm going to put a shot of Baileys in it. And maybe some rum. And you're going to tell me all about this."

Meena sat on the kitchen counter while Warren ground beans and poured water into the coffee maker. She described her efforts in the archives, uncovering the receipt and the accompanying toxicology report. Warren listened in silence, the fright of the last few days mingling headily with excitement over Meena's discoveries till he felt quite worn out. He gulped his coffee, the booze in it smoothing out his nerves despite the early hour.

"And if we have the toxicology report it means there was an autopsy. It's our smoking gun. It proves they killed Lalita, or at least they felt guilty about it and had possession at one point of the bodies," Meena said.

Warren ran his hands through his hair. "This is amazing," he said.

"Okay, now you," Meena said. "What's with the shovel."

Warren sloshed more coffee into his cup, topped it up with a generous shot of rum. "The shovel," he said. "Yes. It also has to do with this, all of this..." he grimaced, took a gulp of his coffee and told her about the gravestone written on his behalf.

Meena ran to the window and peered down at the lawn. Dawn had broken and she could see the marks left on the grass. "This is getting serious," she said and turned back to Warren. She felt instantly cold and grabbed the blanket that had protected her when he'd burst into the room. She huddled down beside him, she wanted to be near. "What are we going to do about it?" she asked.

"I don't know," he said. He drained his coffee, put his arm around her and held her close.

• • •

Celina and Warren remained long after the lunch crowd had departed from the Café El Asador on Bloor Street. They were finishing up the last of the pupusas, and Kola Champagne cream sodas. "I feel...*entre fronteras*," Celina said.

"What does that mean?" Warren asked wiping the salsa from the corner of his mouth.

"Between borders. I feel like I live between borders. It's like when you've lived in one culture and come to a new one, it's hard to find your place, hard to belong. You compare everything to back home, in your old country. The weather is warmer, the people are friendlier, the food is different."

"Sure, I consider that when thinking about my move from Nova Scotia to Toronto," Warren replied.

They had met several times that week as their trip to Guatemala approached. At first they met to go over details, to give Warren some idea what to expect when they got there. As they got closer to the departure date, they talked less and less about the logistics of their trip, and more about themselves. It felt good to Warren, a budding friendship.

"No, it's different than that I think. You are a Canadian. You understand the cultural cues, the subtleties, what someone means when they say something. People in Canada are polite, but you never know if they are telling you the truth."

"Ouch." Warren liked the polite indifference of his fellow compatriots, that "How are you doing?" took the place of hello, with no real intention to find out how in fact the person was doing.

"It's more than that though. There are things about being in Canada that I love. There's a freedom of movement, of possibility. There is some degree of respect that you get, on the surface, and that tolerates difference, protests against discrimination." Warren was familiar with impacts upon those who stood up and got a bashing to remind them of their place.

"I'm not immune to the looks and acts of fear, the racism. Here, what's on the surface, and what's underneath are not always the same. But, here, at least, there are laws that are supposed to protect, something we don't even have in my country. And the level of machismo is not as prevalent, there are the appearances of equality. Here things are more subtle, not as extreme."

In Cape Breton, there was a hierarchy of discrimination. Mine managers did what they liked. The job your father did indicated what jobs that would be available to you. "You're a Smith kid? Okay, you're alright. A MacKinney? Your dad's a bum, sit over there in the corner." Warren's dad was a union leader, which was another type of marker, and because of that, he landed in trouble at school. They expected him to misbehave.

"The whole problem," Celina said, "the crux of the thing, is that I'm not Canadian—I never will be because of my accent and the tone of my skin. But I'm not Guatemalan anymore either. It's like I live in a vortex; damaged goods from having left Guatemala, and not Canadian because I come from Guatemala. Someone who doesn't fit in anywhere—*entre fronteras.*"

Warren wondered how he'd be viewed if he went back to Nova Scotia. Toronto was an evil viper's den to some back home. No one ever seemed to want to live here, though plenty of people did, looking for jobs, school or opportunities that couldn't be found back home. But there was a certain amount of suspicion placed on those who left for Toronto. If you went out west, that was fine, understandable even. But the wrath of envy was reserved for the largest city in the country.

"Are you going to stay after we get things sorted out in Guatemala?"

"I don't know. I'm just as scared about thinking of going back home as I am about thinking of leaving it again," Celina replied.

"Sounds about right."

CHAPTER 9
Muluc *(rain)*

"Paharh ki haddi tootegi, desh ki dharti doobegi." (If the backbone of the hills breaks, the plains below will be submerged).

—Slogan of the Chipko movement

Huge billboards lined the highways, and as they got closer, the Magma logo was prominent alongside pictures of lush forests, clean drinking water, and smiling faces.

The mining site was a huge scar ripped through the earth. Lush greenery bordered the rocky gashes of dirt roads which crisscrossed the browned exposed terrain where trucks extracted the innards of the land. The Jeep jostled along the road that ran beside the mine.

As they approached the gates, they exchanged nervous glances and then with gravity assumed their personas as the driver stopped in front of the large imposing metal gate. Armed guards flanked either side of the entrance and other guards looked down upon them from sighting towers. Celina, in her role as translator and assistant, spoke with a guard, explaining their interest in visiting the mine, describing Warren as an inspector with the Securities Investment Review Committee concerned about the assets of investors. Given fraudulent claims following the Bre-X salting of core samples in Indonesia in the late nineties, the SIRC, as it was known, performed independent verification of company claims through site visits. The scheme was to have Warren impersonate the reviewer to gain access to the mining site and its records.

Warren looked down the metal fencing, noting the guard towers that appeared every two hundred metres.

"The driver is going to stay here, we're to be met by the site manager."

"Did you get a sense they knew we were coming?"

"No, I think we're good. The rest is going to be up to you."

Great, thought Warren. Confidence in his abilities was marginal suddenly with the mine in their sights.

The security guard was joined by more of his mates, one of whom motioned them out of the car. Warren, in his haste, almost forgot his briefcase and reminded himself to look as if he belonged there, as if the frisking were a mere formality and he had every right to be investigating.

The guards were thorough, noting his clothing, inspecting his shoes and rifling through his briefcase, looking for hidden compartments.

A Jeep drove up scattering dust in the air and a tall, big-bellied, ruddy complexioned white man in beige dress pants and a sky-blue, open-collar shirt emerged from the passenger side. He came straight to Warren, extending his hand in greeting.

"Welcome to Magma. My name is Charlie Smits. I'm the site manager here."

"Hi there Charlie. My name is Reg Boland and this is my translator Maria Valentes." Warren butchered the pronunciation of Celina's alias. The man gave her a cursory nod of appreciation.

"I wish we'd been notified of your arrival. We'd have picked you up from the airport."

Warren assumed a magisterial demeanour. "That's fine, I prefer to make my own way; see things for myself."

"Sure, sure," Charlie waved it away. "Come on, we'll get you past Checkpoint Charlie and up to the offices." Warren feigned a smile as he and Celina climbed into the vehicle.

Charlie turned around from the front of the seat. "Since we didn't know you were coming, would you mind if we asked to see some identification?" The man spoke with an amiable tone, but Warren detected a hardness. He was glad they'd planned in advance for this.

"Sure, I have my SIRC and Toronto Stock Exchange identification and a driver's licence. Is there anything else you will need?" Warren hoped the documents—a mix of authentic and doctored materials—would pass the scrutiny of a manager not schooled in duplicitous conspirators.

"We've got to be pretty careful as you can imagine." Charlie took the papers from Warren's hand.

"The internal security procedures are an integral component of securing the assets of the company, I'm glad to see your adherence to high standards," said Warren doing his best to sound officious.

This time, Charlie responded with a forced smile. "Of course."

Warren resisted peering at Celina. This was where their scheme crossed the line to criminal intent. Fraud, impersonation, falsifying documents, and a plethora of other laws Warren chose not to think about. He maintained his veneer, hoping it came across as nonchalant.

Charlie looked up. "Yup, seems all good Mr. Reginald William Boland of 36 Elm Street Toronto. Isn't that right?" Warren wasn't sure if Charlie was having him on, or the inspection of the documents had uncovered their ploy and the jig was up.

But Charlie wasn't finished yet. "You don't mind if we place a call through to Toronto do you?"

"Please, go right ahead …" and shoot me now he thought. That was it. They hadn't even gotten through the door.

CHAPTER 10

Oc *(dog)*

"*Every betrayal contains a perfect moment, a coin
stamped heads or tails with salvation on the other side.*
—Barbara Kingsolver

Melanie's mother lived in Etobicoke, and Melanie lived there with her while she was in school. The house was neat and tidy, a nice house in a good neighbourhood, tucked away on a quiet street. Warren found it surreal, sitting in a Martha Stewart living room while Mel's mom served tea and biscuits on fine china while they talked about gold mines and vindication for dead children.

"Hey Mom, we're fine with the biscuits; we'll help ourselves."

"Sure, of course. If you need any more tea I'll be in the kitchen." The older woman was solicitous and Warren wondered if she had any idea what her daughter was engaged in.

He took a homemade cranberry scone and tasted the tart on his tongue. The air felt different in the room, people's faces seemed more serious. There was a tingling. Just before an incident in Juvie, where the gangs would target a rival or snitch, the air would shudder. Even if Warren was raking the grass, oblivious, his skin would alert him to the changed mood, the electric hum of anticipation. No one spoke about it, but everyone could taste it, and prepare.

The events of the previous week at the shareholders' gathering and the gravestone drive-by on his lawn had cast a pall that was palpable. So they stood straighter, were more attentive, and their eyes were cautious.

Their action at the shareholders' meeting hadn't resulted in much beyond Warren's still sore ribs. The leaflets the others had handed to shareholders outside while Warren and Melanie were inside didn't seem to have made a difference.

"I think we were a little optimistic about the goodwill of seniors," Chantel noted.

"We did get a bit of press for our press conference," Ryan said.

"But nothing mainstream," Celina pointed out. "And nothing about Warren being beaten up by Magma's goons."

They continued deconstructing their progress, follow-up calls from the media and contact with the teachers' pension fund manager about the nature of their investments. They talked about phone calls and lobbying, and assigning tasks as if they were engaged in a campaign for a high school election. Warren wasn't sure he was suited to be in the command hub moving chess pieces around a board, he was antsy and felt contained. He didn't feel like talking about press releases.

"And we need to make sure everyone's safe," Bill said. Warren was glad someone spoke about the elephant in the room. Wasn't everyone else a little worried about what was happening?

"So far they've only issued threats," Chantel said. "They haven't acted on any of them."

"Not here they haven't," Celina noted and Warren glimpsed a little girl running, black hair flashing as he ran after and tried to catch up.

Bill exchanged a look with Celina and began to speak, outlining the precautions people in the room needed to begin to take "...give no information over the phone, we'll move our meetings around. You probably should keep an eye on your surroundings..."

Warren put the scone back onto his plate and watched as Gino shut the door to the kitchen. It was no longer a lark, following someone's story on a lamp post. Warren moved to the edge of his seat.

Warren could feel electricity building in the room. He wasn't the only one struggling with the talk and no action. Ryan sat on the floor, cross-legged, drumming his fingertips on his knees and looking increasingly agitated. Finally he spoke up. "Maybe rather than be in retreat, we should increase the pressure," he suggested.

"How?" Chantel asked, directed first at Ryan, who shrugged and then at the others.

"I have an idea," Pierre, the old-timer, said with a gleam in his eye.

Warren's stomach lurched. He imagined Magma as a snake, coiled in anticipation. He wasn't sure increasing the pressure was such a good idea, and even less so if members in this group were in line to be bitten.

. . .

The billboard was twenty-four feet wide and twelve feet high, in colour, bright, compelling, and unavoidable. It had a huge picture of Lalita Arayo's face on it with the date of her birth and her death, and in large print on the bottom right-hand side, it said, "Ask Magma." It faced the entrance to the Magma office tower from a car lot across the street and no doubt every employee, in fact, anyone who walked up and down Bay Street, could see it.

Scott Liddle was frantic. Lalita seemed to be looking directly in his office window. Tyrell had told him it was under control, but surely this proved it was anything but. He emerged from the elevator percolating with rage and fear. He went straight to Tyrell's office, but Sonya, the personal assistant, said James was in a meeting. Liddle was in no mood to be stopped. He barged into the boardroom and looked around wildly. James was at the head of the table, flanked by Magma's lead lawyer, Dawson, and two young women.

"And just what the hell are we going to do about that?" He threw his hand out in the direction of the billboard below.

Tyrell was unruffled. "Good morning Scott. You know Mr. Dawson. This is Petra. And our new articling student, Meena isn't it?" James looked over at her for confirmation.

Scott grimaced and continued. "This is not good James, we've got to—

James cut in, not allowing Scott to finish. "We're handling it. It's already in the process of being dealt with as we speak."

"Most of our employees will have seen it."

"Yes, Scott. We're just dictating a memo to Petra for all the staff, notifying them of the exciting new program we have developed."

'What program?"

"The Lalita Arayo Memorial Fund to train young Guatemalan women in primary health care and nutrition."

"When did we do that?"

James smiled. "Just now. It was Meena's idea. A good one at that."

Meena shifted at the mention.

Scott did not appear appeased. "But who did this, I mean—"

"It's taken care of Scott." James stood. "We're just waiting on the final details." James brought his hand to Scott's back and led him to the door. "And we'll have all the documents on your desk by noon to keep you up to date and informed." He gave Scott a little push into the hallway, then eased the door closed and turned to those remaining in the room.

"Uh, Mr. Tyrell, that wasn't my idea—" Meena began.

James turned in her direction, smiling, "Oh, not to worry my dear. You were here in the room, part of the flow and exchange of ideas. It was just as much your idea as it was mine."

Meena knew better than to protest any further.

James continued, "I think we've done what we can for the moment. Thanks to you all." And he led the legal team out of the boardroom and headed back to his office.

. . .

"Come over to my place. I'll cook you dinner," Petra said, as she and Meena passed the security desk in the lobby.

"Umm, I don't know," Meena said.

Petra persisted, "C'mon. Whatever you were going to do tonight, this will be better. I love to cook, you can relax. We'll have some wine, a nice pasta, and watch a movie. What do you think?"

Warren was working and wouldn't be home till dawn. Their schedules were still not in sync, as he would get home in the morning, she would be heading off to work. And with the late nights in the archives, he would often be gone by the time she returned to her house. It was becoming a strain, not being able to communicate and see him when she wanted. She was worried about him, about what was happening. She was looking forward to the weekend when she thought she would sneak into his apartment again and greet him in bed, properly this time. Then they would have the whole day together.

The problem was it was only Thursday.

An evening with Petra beat sitting at home waiting for the weekend.

"Sure Petra, that would be nice."

"Get your stuff," Petra said. "I'll meet you at the elevator. We'll grab a cab. I live at Yonge and Eglinton."

Meena watched her walk away and felt a momentary twinge of fear. She was increasingly isolated from everyone—Warren, her parents. And that business this morning with the billboard. She pulled out her phone and texted Warren. *Going to Petra's for dinner. Will send the address later just in case.* She was probably being ridiculous, she knew. But she couldn't help it. *Love you,* she added. She tucked the phone back in her pocket and went to grab her purse.

• • •

"There's a plant."

"Pardon me?"

Celina and Warren were in Robin's Donuts near Christie Pitts. Celina had sent him an text to meet her as soon as he could. Since there wasn't much to do that night, Curtis told him to shove off, he could handle things alone. Warren had found her sitting in a booth that took in a view of both the park and the entrance. Other than a couple of teenage skaters and their girlfriends, and a drunk in the corner, they were alone in the restaurant.

"Magma has planted someone into our group," Celina explained as he sat down.

"How do you know?"

"They knew about the our motion to the shareholders' meeting. They knew about the billboard, they got your name to send you the warning. They've cut us off at every turn."

Warren thought about the people in the group, he'd liked them, he'd even begun to think of them as friends. "It could have been prudent management. Magma has more money and resources than we do to pre-empt our efforts."

"We had to check up on people. On everyone."

Warren fumbled with the napkin holder, suddenly nervous. "It wasn't me."

Warren knew he was blameless, but he began to sweat anyhow. He could barely look at Celina.

"It's okay," she said at last. "We know it's not you." She leaned in closer. "We're going to set a trap."

"I should tell Meena," Warren said. "She could keep her ears open, see if she hears anything. If there's a mole—" He thought about Meena cloistered up in that office tower. "Oh, shit, Meena could be in trouble." Warren threw down the napkin he'd been wringing in his hands and jumped up from the booth.

Celina grabbed his hand, kept him at the table. "When she agreed to work there, I didn't tell anyone about her. I wasn't sure if people would accept it. I didn't want it to become a big debate. Only you and I know about that."

Warren looked at Celina and wondered if he should have trusted her.

"She's at Petra's place right now, a colleague from her work."

"Is she a tall woman, with red hair?"

"I don't know, I've never met her."

"This could be a problem." Celina's face had gone grave.

Warren didn't wait for further explanation. He raced out the door and ran towards Bloor Street to find a cab.

• • •

They'd had a lovely evening. Petra had made a nice dinner, they'd had some wine. Petra had shared Russian stories she'd learned as a kid.

"It's nice to see you relax," Petra said. "You're so buttoned up at work."

Meena slurped the last of her wine. "There's a lot of pressure," she said. "My parents are upset with me right now, I hardly see Warren. It's been really hard." She smiled at Petra. "But this is nice."

"Do you like swimming?" Petra asked.

"Uh, sure. Yeah, I guess."

"Great, then let's go swimming. There is a nice hot tub in the building, that's good for relaxing too. I'll lend you a suit."

"Okay," Meena said, rising slowly.

In the hot tub, Meena finally started to feel loose. "This was a great idea, Petra, thanks," she said. "I don't think I realized how stressed I've been. Now all I need is a good massage," she mused, almost to herself.

"I am an excellent masseuse," Petra said. "Come over here." She stood, rivulets of water running off her, and held a hand out to Meena.

"Oh, no, Petra," Meena protested, modesty overtaking her. "No, no. No need. I have a great massage therapist, and anyhow, you're probably just as tired as I am."

But Petra took Meena's hand and pulled her to standing. "Nonsense," she said. "I used to do this for the girls after their shifts at the club. Let me look after you."

Meena felt her reluctance ebb. Between the wine and the pasta and the hot tub, she was finding it increasingly difficult to take a stand on anything. She let Petra lead her back to the apartment.

Petra showed her to a daybed in the living room. "Just take off your bikini top," Petra said. "I'll be right back." Meena lazily slipped out of the bathing suit as directed and lay belly down on the daybed.

Petra had not oversold her ability. Meena relaxed into the massage, feeling the strain ebb away as Petra rubbed her back and used her knuckles to knead along her spine. She had just about fallen asleep when the doorbell rang.

"How inconvenient," Petra said. She wiped her oily hand on a towel and adjusted her satin robe. "Don't move a muscle," she said to Meena. "I'll be right back." She sauntered to the front door.

But Meena's modesty got the better of her once more, and she sat up on the daybed, pulling up the towel that was draped around her waist.

She saw Petra peer through the peephole and then open the door.

"I'm looking for Meena?" The voice was familiar. Meena's heart leaped.

She pulled the towel around her and tucked in the end as she made her way to the front door. "Warren, what are you doing here?"

Warren had been a frantic taxi passenger from the Annex up to Eglinton. He'd urged his driver on, cursed the traffic and the endless string of red lights, and finally stuffed a wad of cash into the cabbie's hand and leaped out of the cab almost before it stopped curbside in front of Petra's building. Frustrated by the wait for the elevator, he'd bounded up the stairs to find Petra's front door. He stood in the doorway now, panting and relieved to hear Meena's voice. He had been so nervous thinking about what might be happening to her that it took him a moment to take in the scene, Meena covering her breasts with a towel and this woman, Petra, who stood remarkably close to her, with her robe slit open so he could see the length of her leg and know she was naked underneath.

"Excuse me," Petra said. She turned to Meena, ran her fingers along Meena's bare shoulder, then kissed her on the cheek and disappeared into the apartment.

Meena smiled broadly at Warren and reached for his arm. "Warren, what are you doing here, shouldn't you be at work?"

"I was, but Celina called me." Warren could see into the apartment. The daybed still rumpled, the outline of a woman's body still visible in its sheets. He looked at Meena and the towel that clung to her body. He felt like a tool.

"I guess you're doing fine."

"What are you doing here?"

"It's not important." Warren turned and closed the door behind him.

Meena stood for a moment as the towel unravelled and nearly dropped to the floor. "Surely he didn't think that—" She ran to the bathroom and scrambled into her clothes, didn't bother with her shoes, and ran out the door, and looked for him down the hall. It was empty. She ran to the elevator and urged it to the fifth floor. She squeezed in as the doors opened and jammed at the ground floor buttons. "Come on, come on…" she implored as the elevator began its descent, thinking only of trying to catch him before he left the building.

The doors sprung open and she leapt out, ran into the lobby and out onto the street. It was empty. The lamplights shone on the rows of apartment blocks and she saw nothing and no one. Not a soul. "Shit." She stood on the sidewalk. "How could he think that?" She felt equal parts shame at the scene in the apartment and anger at his assumption.

Only when her feet became cold on the hard pavement did she move back into the apartment building. The elevator was waiting for her. She pushed the button for the fifth floor and ascended to Petra's apartment to retrieve her shoes.

Warren was in the stairwell with his hands to his face and his elbows to his knees for a long time.

CHAPTER 11

Chuen *(frog/monkey)*

"All actual life is encounter."
—Martin Buber, I and Thou, 1923

Charlie returned to the air-conditioned office where Warren and Celina had been left to wait. They had a panoramic view of the mine in action, stretching out to the scraped and blunted horizons. "Impressive isn't it?"

"Yeah, sure is," Warren replied, waiting for the sound of his voice to echo above that of his heartbeat. He thought they were sunk, and Midnight Express-style jailhouse scenes played vividly in his imagination.

"Looks like we were scheduled for a visit from you folks after all, according to the team back in Toronto," Charlie said. He handed back to him their identification and faux Securities Commission letter.

Warren tried to keep a look of confidence on his face, but he couldn't resist a sidelong glace at Celina. She was doing a much better job than he was at keeping cool. Still, Warren wondered, was Charlie playing it straight? Or was Charlie bluffing, had he been bluffing all along, was he just waiting for them to further incriminate themselves? Warren pushed down his rising panic, and tried to arrange his features in a way that suggested boredom with this bureaucratic inconvenience.

"How about you give us a tour?"

Charlie looked at Celina. "You can leave her behind," he said speaking to Warren. "It's more comfortable here and it's kind of dirty and dusty out there."

Warren looked at Celina and felt a need to be protective. One look at her face, however, told him she was damned if she was going to be denied a chance of touring the mine site. This had once been her home. As painful as it was, it was still her ancestors' land. Or what was left of it anyway. "That's okay. Maria should come along in case I want to speak with any of the workers. If that's okay with you, Maria?"

"Of course Mr. Boland!" Celina replied, laying on a thicker Spanish accent than Warren was accustomed to hearing. Warren admired the way she was holding up, and wondered how he would respond if they were walking on the land that once lay beneath his home.

"Suit yourself Miss. Don't say I didn't warn ya." Charlie stole the opportunity to eye her figure.

They left the cool offices and were greeted by the hot, dusty, choking air. He noted that the mine was still weeks from being operational, explaining they'd had a few technical and supply difficulties. He directed them back to the Jeep and they all popped in and the driver headed off on a road leading away from the office. Charlie took them around, like a tour guide at a heritage site. They found themselves in a desolate world of blue sky, brown dirt and grey stones.

Warren wondered if there was a geological colour map that offered hints to prospectors where minerals may be found based on the colours of the stones on the ground. The rocks here were light in colour with hints of yellows and reds amidst the drab of grey.

Charlie had continued highlighting aspects of the site, citing load content percentages, and mechanical sophistication that took an ounce of gold from a tonne of rock. Warren imagined gods injecting substances into the veins of stones with gigantic syringes, and humans crushing rocks like they were cactuses in the desert desperate for the elixir.

They were still touring the areas of the mine that had been worked and then left idle since the nineties. "Why did you stop mining here?" Warren asked. He and Celina had discussed it at length, the role he'd need to play. This delicate balance of gaining information without revealing any himself.

"Whole assortment of factors. Price of gold was declining, there was a war going on here, so lots of security challenges and costs—had to hire the army at one point, and it was a challenge to get the locals to work."

Warren was surprised how forthcoming Charlie seemed to be. But then, he was speaking about things that occurred many years ago.

Charlie seemed to like to talk, so he led him to do so. "Why was it hard to get workers? I'd imagine they'd be lining up to get a job."

"Sure, yeah, that's what we thought. But they sent some witchdoctors or something around telling all the Indians the mountain was sacred and if it was desecrated all sorts of fire and brimstone would come their way."

"And did it?"

"Hocus pocus bullshit really. There were a few accidents, but they were the sort of thing you'd expect at any mining site. They sure milked that tit though." Charlie leered at Celina's breasts. "Kept the local Mayo people away." He pronounced Maya, indigenous Guatemalans, like he was ordering condiments on a cheeseburger.

Charlie went on, oblivious to offence. "So, we had to truck them in from the coast, or other towns and the city. Meant we had to feed and house them too. It all became quite a scene."

"You were here then?"

Charlie was not going to miss an opportunity to boast. "Been working this shithole for a fuck of a long time. What can I say, beer and putas are both cheap. Watered-down versions of both compared to back home, but you can't beat the price, just the bitch." He laughed.

Warren thought of what Celina had gone through, what her whole community had gone through, and how they were being depicted by this man. He still held a briefcase in his hand, on his lap, part of the role he was playing. It reminded him why they were there.

"Listen, Charlie. This is a professional investigation, what you do on your own time is your business, but let's try to maintain a little decorum and a hint of respect." He brought his eyes away from his lap and glared at Charlie, so his intent was clear, and Charlie could see his anger.

"Hey, I'm shitting you guys. C'mon, no disrespect intended."

Warren felt Celina's tension at his side, and he knew they couldn't blow their cover, what they were after was bigger than the the mine manager's offence. "Anyone else still working here from that time?"

Charlie was happy to change the subject. "Sure, yeah. Lopez, one of the crane operators. What do you want with him?"

"As part of our examination of the market and environmental conditions, since this mine was mothballed for some time, we need to determine if there is sufficient operational value to continue, and sometimes it's wise to get that perspective from the workers themselves. Besides, it helps to quell complaints that could emerge from the labour sector back home," Warren said with a smirk. "If the workers here say it's good, not much the unions back home can say is there?"

"Guess you're right there," Charlie replied and instructed the driver to head off in search of Lopez. They drove on in silence, through the compound, over lanes and lanes of compacted dust and crushed rock. It felt like a moonscape, and Warren tried not to think of the composition of the dust.

He imagined what the land must have looked like above the rocks, the community he first envisaged when he read Celina's story, before he knew her, before he knew all about the mine, Lalita, and all the damage that had been wrought. He thought of the abundance of greenery, what he had seen in other parts of the country, where villages existed, children played, where plants grew on brown earth. He thought about the rocks that fed the soil from the tectonic shifts of subsurface plates, releasing minerals to be taken up by plants, that died and composted or petrified and ossified, beginning the cycle again. Except here all around him was just dust and rock, the cycle interrupted.

They came to a shack perched on the edge of a large crevasse overlooking a gaping pit. "Lopez is probably taking a sip of the guaro. His shift was over about an hour ago," Charlie explained.

"Why don't you stay in the Jeep, it shouldn't take us more than a minute," Warren said.

"Whatever you say." Charlie seemed happy to comply and blasted the air conditioning a little higher. Warren and Celina made their way to the clapboard shack.

Celina knocked on a door of withered wood. There was a small scrub of dead vines lying out front—a vain attempt at gardening atop the hardpan.

They was no sound so she knocked again. Warren heard a muffled response from inside the shack, so Celina opened the creaking door to a pale, stinking room. Sprawled on the bed in the corner was an older man with Maya features that had been distorted by years of drink.

The old man struggled to sit up.

Warren and Celina approached the bed.

"Señor Lopez," Celina began to introduce themselves.

The man's words came out slurred. "Mi hija."

"What'd he say?" Warren wanted to understand him.

"He's drunk; he called me his daughter. He's mistaken us for someone else. I don't think this is going to do us any good Warren, let's go."

The man grabbed at Celina's wrist and held her. His words didn't sound Spanish, but Warren brushed it off as a symptom of the years of abuse. "Alright, that's enough," Warren said, brushing the man's hand away. "You can let her go. We're leaving now."

"Wait, let him finish." The man's grip tightened on Celina's arm.

Warren felt uncomfortable in the room, and with Charlie waiting for them outside, out of sight. Celina stroked the man's face, looked into his eyes, spoke a few words and then turned to Warren.

"Ready then?" Warren reached for the door, anxious to get back into the light.

"Wait, Warren."

"What?"

Celina looked at him with fear, sadness, and longing. "He knows me, Warren."

"What?"

"He called me Itzel, my name, my Maya name. He knows who I am and why I'm here."

"Oh shit."

The old man finished talking and Celina turned to Warren with tears on her cheeks.

"Let's go," she whispered.

Warren took in the sorrow held in her body and demurred from asking questions.

They left the wretched shack and climbed back into the Jeep.

"Pissed to the gills, was he?" Charlie said. Celina stared stonily out the window. "Best crane operator we've got, but the son of a bitch is working himself into pickle juice." Charlie turned to them in the backseat and noted their silence. Warren arranged his features in disapproval, hoping Charlie would read it as disgust with the man's inebriation.

"Terrible little shack you've got him in," Warren said.

"Hey listen, the old goat could live at the staff quarters, but always seemed to want to live here at the lip of hell, as I call it. Even tried to gussy up the place with some pansies, the old bastard. Planting pansies eh, what a—"

Warren interrupted. "Charlie, just take us to the office building. We need to check the records."

"Sure, you bet. *Hasta la oficina.*" Charlie enunciated each syllable, oblivious to the cadences of the language.

CHAPTER 12

Eb *(skull/tooth)*

"Those who profess to favour freedom, and yet deprecate agitation, are men who want crops without ploughing up the ground. They want rain without thunder and lightning. They want the ocean without the awful roar of its waters. This struggle may be a moral one; or it may be a physical one; or it may be both moral and physical; but it must be a struggle! Power concedes nothing without a demand. It never did, and it never will."

—Frederick Douglass, 1818-1895

Meena had come to Petra's cubicle and because of the cavernous offices she had to keep her voice to a whisper, despite her fury. "What are you playing at?"

"I don't know what you mean." Petra remained impassive behind the desk.

"Come on Petra, what's going on? The other night—"

"Yes?"

"Warren was trying to tell me I was in danger."

"The boyfriend?"

"Yes," Meena replied in exasperation. She felt a hot blush, contrite and furious in equal measure as she remembered the scene. Warren hadn't called yet to apologize and she wasn't going to call him to explain why it wasn't okay for him to doubt her loyalty like that. She hadn't done anything wrong, but she needed to take her anger out on someone.

"This morning I got a message telling me to be careful."

"Because of me?" Petra raised her eyebrows in disbelief.

"Maybe."

It all seemed to be coming to a head, her parents questioning her choices, Petra's coy manoeuvres, Warren's absence. It felt like the whole house of cards she'd built was starting to collapse.

Petra remained calm, turned away from the computer console and crossed her hands on her lap. "Why don't you sit down and tell me what's going on; then we'll see what kind of wicked danger you are in, shall we?"

"Why have you been helping me? The late nights, the archives, all of it?"

"I like you."

"You were doing all that, for what? To get a date?" she whispered as she glanced around to make sure the other cubicle dwellers were not paying them undue attention.

Petra reacted as if she'd been stung, twisting her features to protect her face.

"I'm attracted to you." Petra made no effort to drop her voice, affecting the same tone she would if they'd been discussing appellate court. "In fact, I have been since the day I met you on the elevator. But," Petra angled her head to the side and arched her brow, "if you think it was a fuck I wanted, I would perhaps have chosen a less complicated target. Procuring sex, for me, has never been an issue."

Meena bristled at her candour, she was conscious of being overheard. "What do you want from me?"

"A chance."

"What do you mean?'

"For god's sake Meena. I like you," Petra replied. "You're intelligent and sexy, with a hint of mystery. I'm no different than you in that I'm looking for intimacy, tenderness, companionship. If there was a chance at a relationship with you, Meena, I wanted it. That hasn't changed." Petra looked at her, guarded, yet hopeful.

"So then Petra, I need to know, did you know about the billboard?"

"You mean the Lalita whatever one?"

"Yes."

"No."

"Do you know why I'm here?"

"Because you want to talk about what happened at my apartment?"

Meena fairly stamped her foot. "No Petra, why I'm here at Magma?"

"Of course, it's clear, we spent time in the archives looking for ways to undermine the company. I'm not a stupid woman, you are associated with that group of people."

"Have you told anyone?"

Petra raised her eyebrows, surprised. "Of course not."

Meena was desperate. "This is important Petra, I need to trust you."

The phone rang. Petra looked like she was going to ignore it, but picked it up after glancing at the caller ID screen. "Yes, Petra here...yes she is...I'll tell her."

Petra looked up at Meena. "Mr. Tyrell wants you in his office." Meena felt a rush of cold and saw on Petra's face a flash of fear.

* * *

Despite her apprehension, she was impressed by the opulence of Tyrell's corner office. It was the largest with the firm. The office tower windows cocooned them from the high winds she could see roughing up the water on the lake. She tried to sweep Rapunzel and Sleeping Beauty images from her mind, princesses caught up in towers and prisons. She preferred an active damsel, like Rani, Queen of Jhansi, who was a revered freedom fighter against British rule in India. Then she remembered the Queen died fighting the cause, so that didn't help either, she was on her own.

"Welcome Ms. Awinyolan. Please sit down." He pronounced her name with surety and invited her to take a seat on the couch located at the far corner of the office, away from the door and the phone. He was behind his desk and moved over to join her in the faux homey atmosphere created by the jade-coloured couches, upright gold-toned antique lamps and a glass coffee table.

"What can I do for you Mr. Tyrell?"

"James, please. And it's Meena, is it not?"

"That's correct James," she tried on. "How can I be of assistance?" If Tyrell wanted to get something out of her, he was going to have to work for it just like in an interrogation lab they'd practiced in class.

"That remains to be seen. First, I have a question for you."

"Answers I'm good at. I was a straight A law student." She hoped it sounded boastful, in the way one has to sell oneself in an interview, highlighting positive attributes. She knew her articling position, her assistance to Celina, and potentially something more was on the line.

"Yes, I heard that about you." He paused and sat on the edge of a chair, taking her in. He looked feral, ready to pounce.

"And the question?" she asked.

"Do you know a Mr. Warren Peace?"

She was startled and she hoped her face depicted confusion rather than deceit. "I think my neighbour's last name is Peace. His first name is Warren, I'm sure. A tall, white, dark haired, good-looking guy?" Don't say too much she told herself. The trap hadn't yet clenched its teeth. What the hell did he want? Where was this going?

"Maybe so. But, do you know him?"

"Sure, as much as anyone knows their neighbours in Toronto. I say hi to him when I see him on the porch—but do I know what he has for breakfast in the morning? I have no idea," she said, thinking about toast with marmalade, grapefruit, poached eggs, and coffee. "Why?" She was terrified, but tried to appear confused.

"Does he know you work at Magma?"

If Petra had given her away, she would be caught in a lie. "No, I don't think so. I don't know why he should. I never talk about it. He knows I am a law student because he asked me about it once. That's it as far as I know."

"He's part of the Lalita Arayo group, you know."

She tried to sound innocent. "You mean the Magma Foundation-nutrition program thing?"

"No." She sensed his anger. "The original billboard design team."

"Really, how do you know that?" Oh shit, maybe she shouldn't have asked that.

"Part of the research we do here—to cover the bases so to speak. Quite a coincidence huh? To live next door to him. It's a big city. Three million or so, no? And one of our newest employees happens to live next door to one of the major organizers trying to destroy this company."

"I don't know what to say." She didn't. She hoped other people had watched her come into the office. She resisted looking for an escape.

James waited, not saying a word, letting the pressure mount.

Meena reviewed her options. If she bolted, she was done. They'd grab her. Would they kill her? She shuddered at the thought. Maybe they didn't know; it was her only shot, that somehow they suspected, but also considered it might be a coincidence. She decided to call his bluff.

"So, do I get fired for having a nefarious neighbour? Is that why you brought me here?"

James demurred, "No, of course not. We just thought we might try to take advantage of the situation."

"And how do you expect to do that?" Meena sat back in her chair, trying to appear relaxed.

He smiled. "I think it would be worthwhile for you to make friends with Mr. Peace. Get to know him and his cohorts a bit and perhaps neglect to mention your association with Magma in your interactions."

Meena hesitated, not sure how to respond. James wasn't finished. "You'll be compensated for the extra work of course. A corporate perq shall we say?"

Meena figured they were stringing her either way. "Oh, and Meena... your father's parents live in Mumbai do they not?"

"Yes," Meena sat up, her body rigid. Where was he going with this?

"I don't think as a good and respectable Indian family they would want a video of their half-naked granddaughter getting a massage from a buxom Russian woman careening around the Internet, do you?" he said as he toyed with a DVD case that lay on the table.

So Petra had played her.

She wanted to get out of there, get away from him, and all of them. Tyrell didn't mention the archives. He eyed her, she could tell he was waiting for her reaction. If he had known about her searching, he would have her quartered, expelled from the building, up on charges, with the video held in his back pocket. But he didn't so much as hint at it.

She needed to know what Petra was up to.

"I understand, Mr. Tyrell," Meena said. Until she knew what was at stake, and how things were situated on the playing field, she was going to stay in the game.

"One more thing Meena. This is a verbal contract between you and me. This meeting didn't happen and you will keep everything in that beautiful head of yours, nothing to be written down. And of course, you will report only to me."

"Yes sir."

"Thanks for having this chat Meena. We appreciate having you here at Magma with us."

Meena shook all the way to the women's washroom, and threw up in the toilet.

. . .

The café-bar off Brunswick Street, behind the Tarragon Theatre, was small, dark, and intimate. Meena waited for her eyes to adjust to the dim lights, scanned the room, then spotted Celina, and greeted her with a hug and a kiss on each cheek, sliding into the booth, on the opposite bench. She took a quick glance around to make sure they would be alone when they talked. She didn't know how double agents did it, she felt nervous all the time.

Celina was direct. "What do you have to tell me?"

Meena hadn't told anyone what had happened at Magma yet. She had to disentangle how it related to what took place at Petra's with Warren, and later with Tyrell. She felt ashamed and duplicitous.

"Well, as I told you before, I wanted to do some investigation. There are some leverage points, but not a lot." She'd thrown herself into some legal research, to see if she could find a legal remedy or loophole they could use against Tyrell.

The bartender took their order. Meena noted Celina was drinking tea, however, she needed something with a bigger kick. "I'll have a scotch, on the rocks."

She barged on, not wanting to leave any space in their conversation.

"Here's the deal." She pulled out her notes and looked around the room again to make sure no one was paying them undue attention. "The ILO —" she glanced at Celina for recognition and clarified the acronym. "The International Labour Organization has some standards to which Guatemala is signatory. ILO Convention 169 states there must be community consultations with the local indigenous community prior to any developments and they have to be in accordance with said developments. It's called free, prior, and informed consent."

Celina shook her head. "Won't work. They 'consulted.'" She made quotation gestures with her fingers. "They held community meetings where they came in and told us what they were going to do, not asking for our consent. In the renewed phase, they've held additional consultations to justify the mine's expansion. The one source they do cite for support is the mayor who drives around in a new SUV with tinted windows in a community with dirt floors and no running water. The community held a referendum, denouncing the mine, with over ninety-eight percent voting against its operation and expansion, and yet they still proclaim the community's support for their project."

Meena was not surprised. She knew the Convention indicated a need for consultation, but stopped short of defining the parameters, so the loophole allows companies to slip through with staged or manufactured talks where people come to a meeting and sign their names and the companies call it a consultation. She also knew the popular referendums organized by communities held no standing in law, even if they demonstrated widespread opposition. It frustrated her that companies were able to circumvent the intention of due process and responsibility.

The bartender dropped off her drink, but Meena was no longer paying attention to the room around them. She was immersed in sharing the intricacies of the law, as though, through dissecting international covenants on civil and political rights she could find a solution and get the stink of Tyrell's eyes off her body.

"They kicked us off the land, and said we never owned the land in the first place. So where does that take us?" Celina said.

"These things are complicated, but what I'm trying to say is, there is some recourse in the international systems that we have." She needed there to be an answer, if she spent more time researching, building a case, studying precedents and implementation mechanisms, maybe she would find something that could be useful to them.

"And how many of these covenants, as you call them, have worked, saved lives, made a difference? None of these international covenants or conventions did anything to stop the genocide in my country, nor anywhere else as far as I've seen."

"The Lubicon," Meena said, determined there was something. "They're a First Nations band in Alberta, their Chief, a guy named Bernard Ominayak, went before the InterAmerican Commission on Human Rights and won. Canada was found to be in violation of Article 27 which said that Canada's support for oil and gas exploitation threatened the Lubicon's way of life and culture."

It was a case, a bright light. It meant there was a breach in the armour of impunity. It was a lance she could use on Tyrell, to take the smirk off his face, to make him worried. And maybe they could bring Warren to witness the spectacle, to prove her allegiance. She looked up from her notes into Celina's weary eyes. She looked tired. Meena was another in a long list of enthusiastic advocates of the cause, with a solution to the problem that had been entrenched in inaction for more than a decade. Celina had been waging a campaign far longer than Meena had been licking wounds. In her enthusiasm for research Meena had procured some interesting findings and documents, but she got lost in them, maybe even was hiding in them.

"You know, these things are all great, but they're all after the fact," Celina said. "These companies go in, kill, rape, exploit, and then look at us—years later we're still trying to get them to stop what they are doing." She rubbed her eyes.

"Are there any other options; are there no laws in Canada about the activities of Canadian companies overseas?"

Meena had to admit defeat. She looked up to the dark ceiling, where the pipes and tiles were spray-painted black. "I'm ashamed to say it, but no. They can pillage at will."

"Even if they get Canadian dollars?"

"I'm afraid so. If they say they are operating within the laws of the country of operation, there is nothing we can do about it."

"Even if the laws in that country are corrupt?"

"Yup."

"*Madre!*"

"Yeah." Meena put her hands up to her face and rubbed her brow. "I spoke with a government official, as a Magma rep of course, and she gloated that companies have to monitor themselves and public opinion will police their activities."

"You have an expression in English about wolves guarding the chickens, I think you've demonstrated a good application."

They sat for a moment in silence, Meena running over the information in her head, trying to find an option, some solution. This was what law was supposed to be about, why wasn't it working? They needed something to work.

Celina spoke up, "What if we find the bodies and did a postmortem—would we be able to prove that they were criminally responsible and bring about a criminal and civil suit? Maybe that could lead to a moratorium on the mine."

Meena had focused on the international instruments and had ignored possible criminal charges. She smiled at Celina, renewed. "That could work."

"Did you find anything at Magma to help us prove the case?"

"No." This was the tricky part. She and Petra had searched the archives for weeks on end, going through some of the boxes twice. They'd found no more records other than the autopsy receipt. But, without any other evidence, or the bodies, it might as well have been a receipt for the dissection of a pet rat.

They both contemplated their drinks, Celina swirling her teacup, seeming to look to the leaves at the bottom for a solution.

Meena sipped at the scotch, and took an ice cube and began swirling it around her mouth, unsure of where to go, what to say.

"Who's Petra?" Celina asked.

The ice shivered throughout her body. She'd not told anyone about her. She spit the ice back into her drink. "Petra is my colleague at work."

"What else do you know about her?"

What did she know about Petra? She would have been able to say that she knew Petra liked to shop, and had stunning and impeccable taste, she'd even procured some upgrades to Meena's wardrobe, adding some colour and panache to her style, she liked it, it made her feel sexy. And now she could add she was being blackmailed by her, or at least Petra had given Tyrell a compromising video so he could blackmail her and get her to do his bidding. But she didn't. She wasn't able to divulge this part, not yet, she didn't know how, what she would say.

"She's good at her job, she's from Russia, lives alone," she told Celina, "and she was a dancer, an exotic dancer."

"Is that what she told you?" Celina looked sceptical.

Meena's stomach lurched. She recalled the relationship they had developed. The hours in the archives room, lunches in the office, how she had been strung along.

"Celina, she helped me in innumerable ways. We wouldn't have the autopsy receipt if it wasn't for her."

"Jesus, Meena, you didn't tell her about us did you, what you're doing there?"

"Not in so many words…" She recalled how Petra had befriended her, how she procured their access into the archives. Petra never disclosed how she managed to get the pass codes for security, or how she knew how to erase the surveillance tapes.

"Oh my god. I was the mole, wasn't I?" Meena said, making the connection. "Shit, I ruined everything…"

Celina's face was ashen. "You couldn't have known Petra is Tyrell's mistress," she muttered.

Meena's jaw dropped open and she sank into her seat as if all the muscles in her body had slipped away from the bones. "God, I had no idea. I am so stupid."

Meena felt doubly betrayed, having been lied to, violated, blackmailed, and had maybe even lost any chance at reconciliation with Warren. She began to cry.

She was the bright girl, the one who excelled, succeeding in sports, in school, was one of the highest academic achievers in university. Her success had bred cockiness in her abilities, she'd felt invincible, that she could do whatever she wanted and achieve great success. Meena gulped for breath as the tears flowed down her chin.

Celina closed her eyes and leaned back in her seat.

"We've been tracking Tyrell and some of the others," Celina said, her voice low and measured. "Watching them to see if we could learn anything of value. At the beginning, when you started to work there, Tyrell went to Petra's apartment late one night, and left the next morning. We don't think they were preparing a prospectus."

"Fuck, I'm so stupid," Meena mumbled. Anger began to seep into the place of pity. "Celina, there's one more thing you need to know."

"Yes."

"Tyrell knows about Warren. And they know we are neighbours, but he didn't seem to know about my connection to all of you."

"Uh oh."

"He's asked me to make friends with Warren and to begin to spy on you guys."

"Really? Wow. *Qué interesante.* Either he doesn't know, or he wants to turn the spy on the spy."

"So what the hell do I do?"

Celina considered things for a moment, calculating and forecasting different scenarios and outcomes, possible repercussions. "It seems to me, you might as well spy on us, then we can control the information they receive."

"And with Petra?"

Celina paused, and pursed her lips. She had been thinking about that too. "That's your call Meena. But I would say that it might be good for you to keep some kind of relationship with her. It may prove useful down the road."

Great, thought Meena, Celina wants me to keep a relationship going with Petra, who's sleeping with Tyrell, but whose information I can pass on to Celina. And Tyrell wants me to keep a relationship with Warren so I can pass on information about Celina. And Warren hates me for thinking I'm sleeping with Petra, and I'm pissed at Petra for using me and sleeping with Tyrell. And in the midst of all of this, what I'm supposed to do, is try to be a lawyer. What a rat's nest this is turning out to be, thought Meena.

CHAPTER 13

B'en *(cornstalk/reed)*

*"Mostly it is loss which teaches us about the worth of
things."*
—Arthur Schopenhauer, Parerga Und Paralipomena:
Kleine Philosophische Schriften, Volume 1

"Find anything?"
"Nada, you?"
"Nothing so far."

Celina had recovered from the shock of seeing Lopez and was
focused on looking through the records at the office mine in San Jacinto
with Warren. Celina took care of the documents and receipts in Spanish
and Warren went through the English correspondence. They'd been at it
for hours since Charlie had left them with the books and files.

Warren felt feverish. "Celina, he's not going to like us spending all this
time going through these records." Warren spoke in a whisper, worried
about being overheard. He'd felt like he'd already pushed his luck when
he'd asked for a private room to review the archival documents.

They weren't sure what they were looking for, and time was closing in
on them and they hadn't found anything. They'd come to Guatemala and
played an elaborate con game on the company to get past the front gate.
They'd hoped to build on the autopsy receipt Meena had found in Canada,
but so far they had nothing. Warren was beginning to feel desperate.

"Got ya!" Charlie burst in on them.

Warren froze.

"Ha, just kidding ya. What the hell's taking you so long? Christ you'd
think you were looking for gold or something." Charlie chuckled to

himself. "Listen, we're closing up shop here. We got some rustic accommodations to put you up in. We're closing in ten minutes."

Warren tried to hold his voice steady. "That's okay, we'll just keep looking through some stuff."

"No can do buddy boy. Against company policy having folks in here when staff are gone. You guys pack up, and we'll set you up in Hotel Magma; then tomorrow you can bore your skulls with this shit first thing in the a-m." He pronounced both syllables.

Warren looked to Celina who twitched a shrug. They didn't have a choice; they had nothing to show for their efforts, more time might afford them the break they were seeking. "Sure, that's fine," he responded.

"I'll leave you two to clean up, and then we'll hustle you out of here and take you over to the plaza." Charlie shut the door on Warren and Celina.

"What do we do now?"

"As he says I guess." Celina replied.

"How do you feel about spending the night at the mine?" Warren wasn't comfortable about the prospect himself.

"This was once my home."

"Yeah, hard to see that now though."

"Warren, generations of my family lived on these lands and are buried in these hills. It may be good to spend the night with them. They'll protect us."

God, I hope you're right, he thought.

They left the building and Charlie took them to a part of the mine they had yet to visit. They passed another of the large terraced mounds of rock and debris that reached from earth to sky, then turned a bend and went through a gate, entering a paradise, transformed from moonscape to lush California suburb. They entered a large compound with concrete walls that obstructed their view of the surrounding mine. They drove along cobblestone roads buttressed by low, white duplexes with red tile roofs and multi-coloured flowers hanging from pots outside the windows of the immaculate structures.

Charlie noted their surprise. "Yeah, our own little piece of Eden. Staff quarters. Old man Juan might like to live like shit, but the ex-pat staff are used to a little higher standards. Just down there, there's a pool even." Charlie pointed to a shade of turquoise shimmering in the late sun down a side road. "No skinny dipping though, unless I'm around," he chuckled.

They both remained silent as the Jeep pulled up to a small house. "This will be your spot Reg, and I'll drop Maria off at the Latin Quarter."

"She doesn't stay here?"

"Well, local staff are a ways down the road. They don't like their privacy same as we do, so we have a little apartment complex for them."

Warren turned to Charlie, anxious that he and Celina not be separated. He leaned over to Charlie as they walked out of the car. "She can stay here with me tonight, huh?" he winked.

Charlie slapped Warren on the back."I knew that respect shit was a put-on. You like a little Indian pussy yourself. Ha ha, not to worry." He called to Celina. "Come on darling, looks like you got yourself a hotel upgrade."

Celina pushed the driver aside as she went to get her bag out of the Jeep. Then she stood in front of Charlie, in his space, inches from his body. She looked at him hard. "I will stay here tonight because we have some work to go over and this will make it easier. Reg is a gentleman and will sleep on the couch. I will find great comfort to sleep on the foreigners' bed. Goodnight Mr. Charlie." She stomped off, not before muttering "*maldito cabron*" as she passed him, loud enough for him to hear, but not enough to comment on.

Charlie turned to Warren. "Got yourself a feisty one. I'll pick you up for supper at six-thirty unless you want a little more time, eh cowboy?" He nudged Warren.

"That's fine. See you then."

Charlie hopped back into the Jeep and Warren went into the guesthouse. The room was beautiful. There were bright tiled ceramic floors, wicker chairs and couches in a sitting room flanked by tropical plants basking in the sunshine from the bright windows. There was a kitchenette at the back of the room and off to the side were a bedroom and washroom. Pictures of beaches and palm trees were hung on the white-washed walls. The room felt breezy and fresh.

"Fucking bastard," Celina exclaimed, throwing her bag on a couch.

"Hey, don't let him get to you. He's a creep is all." Warren went over to soothe her.

"I don't mean him. I meant you!" She shook off his hands and gave him a look that was all daggers.

"Me!?"

"You fucking bastard. You played right into his macho shit. Now he thinks I'm no more than your little whore."

"But I didn't think it was a good idea to be separated."

"Me neither, but didn't it occur to you that it's fucking demeaning and degrading to play into his stereotypes? I wanted to throttle him, but now I feel like I want to kill you."

"Celina, I'm sorry."

"Sorry's not good enough Warren. Maybe you don't understand. This bastard and his friends have been exterminating, killing my people, my own sister. They think indigenous women are here to serve their sexual needs; they can fuck us, beat us and then bury us. We are not human, we are not equal to them. Jesus, Warren, you played right into that, without even thinking about it. Is that what you think of me too? Fuck me and have a good time?"

"No, come on Celina." He hadn't thought about what he'd been doing. He didn't think they should be separated, but hadn't known how to justify it to Charlie. And besides, she was attractive, he was attracted to her, but not the way she was twisting it. He wasn't like Charlie; he just didn't think.

"Warren, you don't get what this is all about do you?"

Warren knew he couldn't and shouldn't respond to the missiles she was firing at him.

"We are not here to be raped, or bullied, or degraded, or beaten, or killed for your or their profits and pleasures. Fuck them Warren and fuck you too if that's what you think."

Celina went into the bedroom and slammed the door.

Warren slumped down on the chair.

CHAPTER 14

'Ix *(jaguar/magician)*

My life is a perfect graveyard of buried hopes.
—Lucy Maud Montgomery, Anne of Green Gables

Warren stood outside the church and contemplated just how much had changed since his last visit there, for the fundraiser. Last time he'd stood on this spot, he'd been a casual observer, a curious onlooker. Now he was fully engaged in—in whatever it was they were doing. Instead of going to the event room this time though, he headed to the basement and made his way through the catacomb of supply rooms and eclectic offices. The Marxist-Leninist Society had a red-sickle poster adorning its entrance with a stack of *Granma* papers pushed to the side; the Vegan Association of Toronto stated its name on the plain, brown door. Warren also passed something called the Ayurvedic Healing Group, which would have baffled him were it not for the poster with a pair of hands and chakra symbols around it.

The church was housing the real movers and shakers of the Toronto dissident community, Warren mused. He wondered if that's why they were meeting in the basement. He found the right room at last, and pulled open the door. Celina was already there, as were some of the others. As was, he was startled to see, Meena. She'd never been to one of their meetings. He'd had no thought of encountering her there—and in fact had been fairly carefully arranging his life to ensure he wouldn't even run into her on his own verandah. He felt sick.

"Warren, I…" Meena began. He interrupted her and mumbled an excuse, making an escape to the dingy, dank bathroom at the end of the hall. He considered fleeing. He didn't want to see her. He felt a rawness that ached in his belly. He waited in the washroom, keeping his ears alert to the sounds of the stairs.

He listened to the clatter of shoes on the steps, each one representing a new arrival. Warren fought with flight or fight, the push and pull of connection and release. He cursed everything and everyone as he toiled the tissue paper between his fingers into little balls of indecision. He muttered to himself about how much more stupid it would look if he didn't return as he tossed each one into the toilet.

The roll finished, Warren flushed down the paper and went back to the room to join the circle, hoping the crowd would provide a buffer. They'd kept a space open for him, assuming his participation, allowing the circle to close. Warren tried not to imagine it as a serpent with prey, squeezing tighter and tighter. He did not look at Meena. Or anyone else, for that matter.

There were discussions, updates, the grist mill that fed the meetings, people taking turns to talk about their engagement and activities. Warren half-listened, plotting an escape that would result in the least collateral damage. He wished he'd discovered dormant super hero powers that he could take the opportunity to activate, like Invisible Man or the Flash.

He almost missed Celina's announcement.

"This may seem hard to believe, but Scott Liddle wants to work with us."

They all knew who was on the board at Magma. Melanie had done research, put together a Wanted Poster with all the board members' names, pictures, and affiliations.

There were raucous outbursts, and faces etched with shock, worry, and anxiety. Some of the group were opposed, others liked the idea of having someone from the board close at hand, even if they couldn't be trusted, there might be a way they could find out information. Some thought it was a trap.

In the chaos, the cacophony, Warren chanced a glance at Meena, covered by the dissension of the ranks. She stared back intently, as if trying to speak directly into his mind.

He looked away, scared of what she might learn, that she could penetrate with a glance. He didn't trust his thoughts.

Ryan was exuberant and righteous, he pushed hard to have Scott join them. Pierre, the octogenarian from Quebec who'd been active during the Padlock Law days of the Duplessis government, was opposed. Warren stayed silent. He knew Celina was floating the idea, and that it would go against the principled stands of other members of the group, with little chance of success. It didn't have to be true, it just had to be considered. He'd little interest now in the intrigue that had once consumed him.

There was no consensus, but the seeds had been sown. One way or another the false information would spiral back to Magma, either through Meena, or through another if Meena wasn't the leak. Either way it would germinate in the company, causing the struggle Celina and Chantel sought.

Warren couldn't concentrate on the plot, he longed to talk with Meena. He was paralyzed by a fear of failure, by the fear that his own actions, and his own temper would not be in held in check, that he could not be trusted and would create another rupture, an irreconcilable one. Fleeing was his other strategy. Postponement meant he could pretend for another day. The meeting was coming to an end, so he grabbed his coat and rushed for the door, ascending the steps and emerging to a flush of cool. He exhaled the fetid air from the basement that had constricted his lungs, breathing as if it could wipe away stains of embarrassment, vulnerability and longing.

A voice followed him up the stairs.

"Wait Warren, one more thing." Celina had followed him out.

He turned to her, fixing her in his field of vision so as to block penetrating eyes.

"I think you and Meena need to talk."

"I don't think that's any of your business," he responded, heading out the oak doors and down the ramp that allowed seniors and the mobility challenged access to the church, and he ran for home.

• • •

He remembered waking to her stares. Meena would watch his eyes as he searched her face in the morning.

"Where does the grey come from?"

"The trauma of abrupt awakenings."

"I'm talking about your origins—not your hair."

"Thirty comes quickly you know. One moment it's diapers, the next it's Depends and before you know it you're drooling spittle on the arm of the wheelchair in an old-age home."

Meena ignored him. "You have black hair, grey eyes, you're what, five-eleven?"

"I am when I'm forced to stand up." He rolled over onto his side, covering his body and bringing the blankets up over his shoulders, trying to savour the last vestiges of a now-forgotten dream.

"And?" Meena continued.

He remembered wanting to drift off again and hoping the long pauses would be a clear enough signal and Meena would become bored or distracted.

"You've figured out some of my Southern India roots. How about you? Who is this naked guy beside me with the nice butt?" she said, grabbing a piece and giving him a tap. "How far back do you trace to Eve? Which colonial post did your foremothers arrive from—or was your mother the first?"

"Great-grand, actually."

"How many?"

"A couple."

"From?"

Sleep was done. He pushed himself up and let the blankets fall from his body. "The Scots, the Celts, the Irish, and probably a little Roman and French thrown in during some European pillaging."

"A regular genetic smorgasbord eh?"

"Hence the grey. The sum of all colours and none."

Meena took his chin in her hands and peered closer. "The blue, green, and gold flecks?" She eyed him as though he were a painting or prized stallion and she was checking his teeth.

"Grade nine art project gone wrong."

She climbed out of bed, fixing a blue terrycloth robe around her. "So, you don't know your heritage or history?"

"Are you going to hide behind that robe, or can I have another flash?"

"You answer a little, I'll flash a little," she said, playing his game and opening her robe like an Academy Awards dress, with lots to view but all the good bits just out of sight.

Warren grinned. "I grew up in Nova Scotia. I'm a white guy, probably mostly Scottish. But nobody in my family knows for sure about the boat, nor from whence we sailed. Why?"

"Curious."

"You show me yours, and I'll show you mine," Warren offered.

Meena gave him a kiss and then took his face in her hands, "I don't want to be surprised some morning and find haggis on a breakfast plate."

It was something she needn't have worried about.

He didn't like going back into his apartment, with the memories trailing after him. He tried to sweep them out of his mind, but he thought he caught a whiff of her scent. She could have left it here, or it could have drifted up from her side of the wall. He found his key in his pocket and let himself into his apartment, alone. He had nowhere else to go.

• • •

"Did you always want to be a lawyer?" Celina asked Meena after they finished clearing up the cups of coffee following the meeting.

"Sure, I wanted to be lots of things I guess, a ballerina, a fireman, a hero. I wanted to be a baker for a long time too, till I discovered they got up early and worked so hard. Then I realized I just wanted to eat baked goods, so I thought about marrying the guy who makes brownies. But, he was seventy with hair coming out of his nostrils. So, that didn't work out either."

Celina laughed.

"How about you?" Meena asked.

"I don't know. The world was a smaller place where I grew up. It's not that I didn't know about those kinds of things, like being a dancer, or movie star, it's just that I didn't know anyone in my world who was like that. Those kinds of things were more make-believe than real. I did have a crush on a guy who rode a motorbike. As close as you'd get to a kind of James Dean." Meena imagined Celina driving around with a bad-boy biker and smiled at the thought.

"Yeah, well, lots of guys have bikes in Guatemala, but he liked to slick back his hair and he always wore white shirts and blue jeans. Which, if you knew Guatemala, was kind of silly, because in the dry season you would be caked with dust after travelling the dirt roads."

"So, what happened?" Meena asked.

"A girlhood fantasy. He was too old for me, but it helped pass the time of hours and hours of washing clothes in the river."

Meena liked Celina. She found her easy to talk to, not pretentious in any way. It was nice to have a friend she didn't have to compete with.

"Is Warren your James Dean?" Celina asked her.

Well, maybe she did feel a little competition.

. . .

In the kitchen, Warren hunted through the cupboard for a new packet of espresso. He pushed aside boxes of tea, and saw one Meena had left behind. Chai. He took it down and inhaled the scent.

Warren didn't realize there was an art to making tea. In fact he wasn't aware there was more than one method or variety. He'd been taught you put cold water into the kettle, add two tea bags into the pot—one bag just coloured the water—pour the boiled water into the teapot, steep it till dark, then pour it into a cup. Sugar was for infants and when you were of an age, you took it black.

Warren had watched his mom prepping and serving tea three to four times daily in his childhood. The only variety to the routine was which cracked mug you could choose. Warren liked getting the Lady Diana memorial cup with the gold detail on the rim. He could imagine himself a prince sipping tea before the lion hunt.

Often the tea would come dressed with white bread and molasses, and when his mom wasn't looking, his grandfather would sprinkle the bread with sugar.

Red Rose was served in the Peace home. He thought he could make his own once, and had cut down the rose bush his mother cultivated beside the front stoop. He mashed together the stems, leaves and petals and tried to sieve it through a colander into a bucket.

"Red Rose doesn't come from roses you moron," his brother told him, flicking his head with his finger. He helped Warren flush the mess down the toilet and trample the grass around the stemless bush with the end of a soap dish made to look like deer prints. His mother never knew.

Meena had served him Chai spiced with cinnamon and cardamom pods, steeped and flavoured with milk and honey. He had assumed she was cooking the first time the scents wafted through the apartment. He was surprised when she put the tea before him. He had seen it offered in restaurants, but since he'd left home, he'd stuck with coffee.

He took a sip. He wasn't expecting sweet, he was used to bitter.

Darjeeling, Earl Grey, Tiger Spice, Green Tea, Chai, Jasmine, he drank them all after that. Meena had opened up a world to him, and helped him discover tea could come from roses. Just not in his family.

He put the box back into the cupboard and closed the door. He resigned himself to the couch, staring at the bleak, white walls of his apartment. Meena had chastised him for the lack of embellishment, or colour, but he liked the clean look, it suited his aesthete ethos. He looked over at the digital clock on his stove; time seemed heavy, dripping and clinging from one second to the next, like over-ripened jam.

He tried reading and threw down the book, unable to concentrate, returning to stare at a nick on the wall. Then he got up and tried to fill the apartment with soft jazz, and when that didn't work he moved to hip-hop and reggae. He turned them all off in sequence as the noise bothered his ears.

But he was not depressed. With his family back home, people didn't get depressed. He figured it was because they were all so damn unhappy that if someone were to utter the dreaded word, they'd all file like lemmings to a cliff for the suicidal plunge: recognizing and naming the condition they all suffered from would be too much.

"He's got a touch of…" or "She's a little under the weather"—a perpetual state of loneliness and unhappiness. Maybe it was part of the genetic condition. Even in the midst of the city, he was still "not quite himself" these days.

He had been himself, once, even more than once. The city had been an intoxicant when he first breathed in its life and revelled in its pleasures: heady days of escape and rebirth.

It was like nothing people had scared him into believing. His own fears at the unknown were surpassed by the terror and dread of remaining where he'd been.

And then, after he learned he didn't have to live with cockroaches in the basement apartment near Dundas Street, and that the multi-hued strangers were not going to pounce upon him, and that the ubiquitous Toronto shootings didn't happen everywhere, every night in the city, he became less afraid.

In time, he realized he walked into the Korean grocery store to pick-up kimchee and drank beer at the Sri Lankan resto-bar as easily as he'd once eaten baked beans or fished for mackerel.

That was when he'd realized how far he'd come. Those memories he liked he draped onto his identity, those which pained him he discarded, to keep them from being recycled.

Over time, the haze of euphoria had lifted, but never dulled. He'd slipped into the contemplative as he went from moving van jobs, to warehouses and factories, and culminating in graveyards—where he'd felt most at home. He'd embraced cemeteries as emblematic of the spectrum of expressed emotions: places and scenes of sorrow, but also, joy, celebration, reverence, and memory.

These were communities he could engage with on his own terms, such as it was, surrounded by spirits and souls. It suited him.

Until it didn't.

He realized he was romanticizing his time in Toronto. Discovering Lalita Arayo, and all that ensued had changed him. He found he was excited, anticipated the day and became energized by existence. He was no longer content cocooned in a bubble, surrounded by a history that wasn't his own, that was static and provided a narrative that he consumed, but had no part in shaping or experiencing.

Lalita coincided with Meena. Meeting one had led to the other. He felt a wisp of her still, like she'd had just left through the door. She wafted through the kitchen, in the tea cupboard, the couch was indented with her form where they'd cuddled to an action movie or shared the reading of books, each exploring the other's world but partaking together in the space, the warmth and quiet.

Her spirit had infected him and now he was at a loss.

He stared at the clock and felt a painful helplessness as it ticked forward. His eyes went back to the wall and over to the door. There was no one there but Vamp, clawing to get out.

As if in a trance, Warren got up and grabbed his jacket, opened the door and followed the cat down the steps. He walked to Bathurst, looked south for the bus, seeing none, started north and kept walking.

It was a sunny but cold. He turned east on St. Clair and kept going, his breath leaving rhythmic streams in his wake. He went past Avenue Road, all the way to Yonge Street, crisscrossing the sidewalks so as to avoid stopping and waiting for lights.

The cemetery was quiet, with few mourners straggling on the horizon. He headed to the grave and stopped. He brushed the fallen leaves from the top of the headstone, and touched the words scratched onto the marble. Then he waited.

He sat in the empty space that had once held Lalita's stone, and pressed his back against the rock where Pablo's name had been scribbled. He sat as you would in a convalescent seniors' home, his presence providing a comfort as much for himself, as for anyone.

CHAPTER 15

Men *(bird/eagle)*

If you cannot work with love but only with distaste, it is
better that you should leave your work.
—Khalil Gibran

H e'd been forced to go to dinner alone with Charlie. No degree of cajoling, pleading or apologizing had convinced Celina to open the door to him.

Though he felt terrible, he didn't identify with the accusations she launched at him, and he felt she would see that in time. Meanwhile, he'd go to dinner with Charlie, elicit some more information and perhaps, upon his return, he'd have something to share with Celina, and all could be forgiven.

Dinner, a kind of beefsteak as Charlie had described it, was good, a touch of lime setting off the grilled meat and boiled rice mixed with beans and a slice of avocado on the side. They shared a few Gallo beers, but Warren had not jarred anything loose from Charlie. In fact, he felt like he needed a shower to clean the remnants of the guy from his pores.

Charlie had stuck to his stories, extolling his conquests. The man pined for a return to Canada but Warren concluded the real reason Charlie stayed in Guatemala was that his salary allowed him to be king. At home he was just another sorry loser; here at the mine, he lorded over the rock.

Warren was depressed and sickened when they finished dinner in the ex-patriot lounge complex near the swimming pool. He was beginning to understand how awful it was to have insinuated allegiance to this man and to degrade Celina by association. He wanted to get back to the guesthouse to grovel and repent. He felt any more time spent with this Neanderthal was going to bring up the dinner for a repeat.

Charlie, however, insisted on taking Warren for a ride up the mountain, so they could look down on the lights of the mine and see it in its unfettered beauty. Warren thought the sights at night would be the only time one could conjoin beauty with mining.

They headed for the guarded front gate, their silent driver navigating the night trails. Warren could see a ceremony of fireflies dancing in the distance.

"Fuck."

"What?"

"Goddamn voodoo shit they're doing."

As they drove closer, Warren spotted a large group of Guatemalans on the other side of the double layer of reinforced fence topped with curled barbed wire. Their faces shifted in and out of shadow with candles flickering in the wind.

"Who are they?" Warren asked.

"Goddamn nuisance. Don't worry, we'll get them moved out of here. I'll go call the colonel."

"What are they doing?"

"Praying. They show up every so often, make a fuss and then we bring in the army to set them straight and get them the hell out of the way."

"What are they praying for?"

"Not to my God, I'll tell you that right fucking now. For all I know, they're sacrificing little kids or virgins, like bloody Aztecs with their satanic rituals."

"But why here?" Warren persisted. There was a low humming emanating from their group interrupted by the shouts of the guards yelling at them to shove off.

"Some bullshit ancient religious site." Charlie glanced at Warren and in alarm at the disclosure, added, "Ah, don't worry, we haven't found one goddamn piece of clay, nor bones, temples, nothing. It's all a ploy for them to get their greedy hands on some of the gold here without having to work for it. Lazy bastards." He shrugged and turned away from the sight of the vigilant petitioners. "Well, we won't be seeing the lights tonight till we get this horde out of here." He grinned at Warren with a drunken smile. "Guess it's back to that pretty little bitch of yours back at the guesthouse. And once you're done with her, feel free to send her on—" Warren grabbed the neck of Charlie's shirt as he contorted himself in the backseat.

"Shut the fuck up Charlie. She's not your goddamn piece of ass, nor mine. She's a brilliant and committed woman. If I hear one more stupid sexist or racist thing come out of your ignorant mouth, I swear to your Christian god I'm going to punch it till it will open no more. And, I'm going to make sure you get a failing report from the Securities Investment Review Commission and your little ass will be fried for a good long time." Warren released Charlie, who looked shocked. "Is that clear?" he added, trying to regain control of himself.

"Clear as goddamn mud," Charlie said, rubbing his his neck and smoothing down his shirt where Warren had grabbed it.

They rode the rest of the way in silence, Warren still seething.

The lights from the windows of the guesthouse illuminated the night. Warren stepped out of the Jeep and closed the door without another word. The Jeep tore off, heading back to the lounge complex, and Warren went in to tell Celina how sorry he was.

Except, Celina was not alone.

CHAPTER 16
C'ib (owl/vulture)

A work of art is a confession.
—Albert Camus

Everything was distasteful, being at the meeting, what they were about to do, facing Meena. He'd arrived late, hoping it would be over, and everyone would have left. But the group was crowded into the living room, and they all fit in the way that small spaces expand and contract to accommodate different numbers of people. Photos of Gino's kids looked down on them the way his mother had the Virgin Mary stare at guests in the vestibule back home, even though everyone came in through their kitchen.

Warren didn't like suspecting people, he tried to keep his eyes averted, he didn't want to look at anyone. He snagged a banana chocolate chip muffin from the tray set on a table in the centre of the circle of Solidarity Association members. Chewing on something might help.

"Unfortunately, we have a mole." They hadn't hit the ugly part yet, the part he had been trying to avoid. Chantel wielded the axe. "Someone who has been talking to Magma about our group,"

Warren focused on the chocolate that stained his fingers. He'd been picking at the crumbs on his napkin, bringing little morsels to his mouth. It gave him an opportunity to hide behind his hands. He could sense the tension in others in the room. No one stepped forward, no one offered a mea culpa, so everyone focused on their drink, photos or the threads of the carpet. If there had been a Mother Mary present, Warren imagined a few of them would have directed their prayers in her direction.

"Someone alerted Magma to the billboard campaign, pre-empted the declarations at the stockholders' meeting, passed on all our names and information of the group members to the company." Chantel waited for someone to respond, to set themselves apart from the others.

Warren wished he were elsewhere. He'd been corralled into a school interrogation where a classmate had broken into their science teacher's office and used the Bunsen burners to torch their grade nine mid-term exam. All the appropriate suspects had been brought to her office for a confession, except none of them had done it, so they'd sat in silence, feeling guilty and responsible, and looking at one another, silently imploring someone to confess to end the scrutiny. Instead, they were all punished and the student council rep who was responsible hadn't had to stay after school for two weeks, like the rest of them.

"I was hoping someone might confess," Chantel said and people squirmed, hoping not to attract undue attention. He imagined they were searching their minds for improprieties, and wondering who was responsible for using the lead pipe in the library on Mrs. Plum or Colonel Mustard.

Gino looked to Mel and Ryan who in turn stared at Bill, Pierre portrayed a profound sadness towards Chantel and Eduardo. Warren watched Celina and waited for her to make her move. He avoided looking at Meena.

Celina's eyes scanned all their faces before turning to one of their younger crew.

"Why?" she asked Ryan.

"Ryan?" Mel looked at him in shock.

Warren kept his eyes on the young man, wondering if his body language would tell a tale, wondering if he would confess. Ryan sat on the floor, arms rigid in his lap, he looked up, cornered, his eyes searching for the door. Eduardo, who was standing propped up by the frame, shifted to block the exit.

"It wasn't me," he said.

"We have proof," Bill replied.

He tried innocence with indignation. "I don't know how you could have come to that conclusion."

Everyone remained silent.

Then he went in for righteous anger. "I've put hours and hours into this shit and you guys treat me like this?"

People shifted away from him. No one jumped to his defence.

Mel watched his performance with her hand covering her mouth, suppressing the sounds emanating from her body.

He tried pity and looked pathetic, finally breaking the facade with a shrug. "What's the big deal?" he said, as if he'd made a blunder in a Euchre tournament.

Melanie looked at him, incredulous. "Are you kidding me? What the hell were you thinking?"

"They'd get the information anyway," Ryan replied, as if he were shooing away a gnat.

"So you gave it to them?" Melanie yelled. "What did they give you? What did you get out of it?"

Ryan didn't say anything. He couldn't take in Melanie's eyes, so he looked away.

"You did it for money," she declared. "You goddamn coward, you did it for money."

Ryan tried to look at Pierre, as if he would come to his aid.

"Get out of here Ryan. Get the hell out of here," Melanie screamed.

Ryan stood up and grabbed his knapsack. Gino held Melanie's arm.

Eduardo moved away from the door he had been guarding.

"This is a bullshit lost cause anyway. What the hell do you think any of you are going to get out of this?" Ryan's gaze darted from face to face around the room.

Melanie made a leap for him, but Gino held her tightly. "You bastard," she shouted as Ryan shot from the room. Bill slowly closed the door as Melanie crouched down and burst into tears.

· · ·

"Scott Liddle?"

"Yes."

"You don't say…" Tyrell looked out onto the sweeping waters of Lake Ontario. Meena noted he didn't look surprised by the information.

"And pray tell, what is Mr. Liddle planning on doing?"

"I don't know. They weren't sure if they wanted him to join their group or not," Meena responded.

Tyrell snickered. "That is indeed rich, I'm not sure if we want him either."

Meena was uncomfortable both being there and divulging false information. She had begun a slide down a slope. It was one thing investigating evidence of Magma wrongdoing; it was another to falsely accuse someone of betrayal. She had witnessed what had happened to Ryan and here she was doing what he did, but for the other side.

Although Liddle was part of the corporation and responsible for any malfeasance, she realized as she shared the details with Tyrell that this could have far worse repercussions than she could imagine. And she recognized that she knew nothing about this guy: if he had a family, if he cared about the world, rode his bike to work, kissed small babies. He'd been chosen because he was the youngest and newest board member and not part of the family conglomerate. She became aware she was transforming into all the things she despised.

"Ah, but nothing was totally certain. In fact, they weren't even sure if it was Scott Liddle. I'm not sure we can—"

"That's fine Meena. Don't you worry about these things. We do have ways of testing loyalties you know." His eyes were penetrating.

She swallowed hard. "Between the devil and the deep blue sea," she muttered.

"Pardon me?" Tyrell had missed it.

"Nothing sir, is that all?" Meena needed to get out of his office, and out of Magma. She wasn't sure who she was, who she had become. She didn't like it, didn't like herself. It was different from when she was a teenager, and self-loathing was a stage of adolescence. She was an adult who had trapped herself into this quandary through her own decisions.

"Yes. Thanks for this. My assistant will have a little package of appreciation you can pick up on your way out."

Meena nodded, trying not to look hasty as she made her retreat.

"Oh, Meena?" Tyrell turned back towards her as if he'd forgotten something. "Would you like to join me for a late supper this evening?"

He smiled at her, all crocodile charm. "There's some more work we could go over," he added.

"No, thanks Mr. Tyrell. My mother has asked me to fill out the wedding invitations for my arranged marriage." When in need, pull out your mother and the cultural stereotypes.

"Congratulations. Maybe some other time…"

Oh my god, I truly am working with satan's spawn. I gotta get out of here, she thought as she sprinted to the elevator.

• • •

"On the discovery channel."

"What?" They had been waiting in the funeral director's office for the Abacha paperwork and Warren hadn't been paying attention to his colleague. He had been thinking about Odelia and wondered if spirits ever returned home and what her life would have been like if she'd stayed in Nigeria.

"The Asmat in Papua New Guinea. They create these giant poles, like the totem poles in BC. You've seen them?" Curtis asked.

> **ABACHA, ODELIA**
> *46 years old. Taken from earth to God's holy land. Odelia was born in Nigeria and came with her family to Canada five years ago. She is survived by her husband Paul, and her six children, Constance, Kenneth, Hortense, Paula, Samuel, and Portia. Funeral services will be held at the Mississ-*

Giant carved trees, stripped of the bark and made into depictions, ravens and eagles and representations of other animals and creatures. Warren had seen them but had missed what Curtis was referring to. "Yeah, so?"

"They're monuments, spirit poles. I was just wondering if it's what happens to you? Totems are monuments of clan lineages, and for the Asmat they believe the spirit lives in the wood."

Warren had seen the BC variety in a picture of Stanley Park, where the pole had an expanse of wings ready to soar off the land where it had been perched.

Curtis continued, "And then you've got these things coming out of the stone. So, I was just wondering if it was similar, and you get to decide where you go when you die? Like, hmm, I think that oak tree is quite nice or there is a shiny bit of onyx I could get stuck in for the next millennia. I doubt they'd do that in plastic though, don't you think? Can you imagine finding spirits spinning out from milk cartons or made in China whirly tops?"

Warren had a hard time picturing spirits in plastic.

"So, what's it like?"

"What?"

"I don't know anyone who sees ghosts, what's it like?"

"I don't know." Warren was hesitant to explain further.

Odelia could see through him. Warren wondered if she was looking back at her children, or forward, seeing all the antecedents, all the people who had come before, as well as those who would join her after. She was beautiful.

"Images. Faces."

"Like Odelia's? You see what she looks like, like the photo they'd put on her casket?" Curtis asked.

"Like that, yeah, but not static, these aren't pictures."

"It's real?"

"I don't know."

Warren knew Curtis would leave it for now, but he'd come at it again, from a different angle. He'd launch little volleys and collect the fallout that would settle to the ground. He'd put the pieces together, constructing an understanding, and then when all was clear for another approach, he'd fire another flare. Warren appreciated the pace.

Warren went to the library on College Street and searched for details surrounding the Asmat. Curtis had once told him why there were so many Cypress trees in cemeteries. The Greeks and Romans believed it was the first tree one would see upon entry into the underworld, and they used the wood in the construction of coffins as it deterred insects and all sorts of other kinds of evil. It was a tree that once cut, would not live again. Warren was curious whether other cultures were infected with spirits in the same way he was.

His Asmat discoveries led him to learn that the Spirit poles were erected in honour of fallen warriors, as reminders to avenge their deaths.

Warren hoped his spirits didn't share that expectation.

...

Warren was grateful it was only Bill, Eduardo, Chantel, and Celina scrunched in his room. He wiped a rogue dust spot along the window sill. He'd arranged Korean walnut cakes on a plate resting on the trunk which served as footstool and serving table.

He busied himself getting classes of water for everyone and once that was done there was nothing left but for the discussion to begin.

"We've got to go to Guatemala," Celina said. Warren had been waiting for this moment. The mine was in Guatemala, the bodies were in Guatemala. Celina was going to have to return home.

"I agree," Bill said. "We've tried everything else. We've done the shareholder thing, public pressure, PR, even searched their inner sanctum. We need to get to ground zero and see what we can find there."

"Yeah, fine," Chantel said, drumming her fingers on her water glass. "But she can't go alone."

Bill put his hands in the air. "I'm out; caught in a couple of protests and misdemeanours means I can't leave the country."

And Eduardo was shaking his head, he was a busy cabinetmaker, and couldn't take time away from deliveries and contracts. Chantel was in the middle of her dissertation.

Warren felt a pit enlarging in his stomach. He didn't like the way they were looking at him.

"Oh no," he said. "This is the shareholders' meeting all over again."

"Your family were miners, Warren," Celina said, her eyes deep pools of brown turned toward him. "You know the lingo, what to say, where to look. You're our best bet." She paused, reached a hand across the trunk toward him. "Please."

He knew things were desperate if they had settled on him as their choice as travelling partner. But he was no less desperate not to be the one to go. "I couldn't leave my job," he said. It had worked for Eduardo. Why not him?

"We'll cover it, make sure your friend Curtis has some help," Eduardo replied.

"I've never travelled overseas. I haven't even been out of Eastern Canada."

"They won't expect you to fly the plane the first time," Bill said with a chuckle.

He felt like he was at a dinner where you had to turn down offers of food twice before you were expected to accept.

"I don't speak Spanish."

In some ways he knew all along, since he'd made the discovery and met Lalita, he knew he was headed south.

"Do you have a passport?" Celina asked. There was a note of hope in her voice. She could tell his resistance was wearing thin.

"I've got a suspended driver's licence. You think that will cover it?" He hopped up. "Tea anyone?"

Celina had requested his help and he wanted to say no. He'd never wanted anything as badly as he wanted to say no to Celina and be done with it. But she'd appealed to him, she'd written a huge plea on a stack of papers that she'd taken the time to post outside his home.

He knew a part of him wanted to go, was desperate to leave. He could get away from his apartment, get away from Meena and the failed relationship fog that hung around him like a spectre.

"Think about it," Celina said. "That's all I'm asking right now." She nodded to the others and they rose as one. They gathered their coats and he ushered the four horsemen out the door.

Guatemala, he thought, as he went to his bedroom and closed the door, falling onto his futon. He felt thrilled and scared. He didn't set his alarm, feed Vamp, nor take his clothes off. He lay in bed with scenes of adventure, heroism and terror playing on simultaneous screens as he fell into a dream.

· · ·

Warren had taken to sprinting from the sidewalk up to his apartment. That way he avoided unpleasant encounters with Meena and her family. But he was so preoccupied with everything that had happened, that he forgot to hasten his pace, and he didn't notice Mr. Awinyolan waiting for him on the porch.

"Warren," Meena's father said. "So nice to see you. Please come in and take tea with me."

Warren, red-faced, fumbled for the right words, the ones that would get him out of this situation and safely into his apartment before Meena's name was mentioned by either of them.

"Uhh..." was all he managed. It was not going to be enough.

"Please Warren. I know it is polite to do this, both in my culture and yours. Join me for tea."

Warren was befuddled by the overture. It came from a man who had once invoked a cone of silence in his presence. But his indecision allowed Vatu to draw him into their house. He sat facing Meena's father at the cherrywood dining room table, awaiting what was to come.

"Raita," Vatu called out. "Raita, please come and make us tea. We have a guest."

From upstairs Warren heard Raita respond, "I cannot. I am sorry. You know how to make it. I will come down later."

Vatu shook his head at Warren. "I cannot guarantee it will be drinkable, but we will at least be able to say we had tea." He smiled at Warren and went off to the kitchen to boil the water.

Warren sat and looked around the room bewildered at the turn of events and relieved Meena wasn't present to complicate them further. He shared a glance with Ganesh, an elephant mask overlooking the table. The Hindu god of good fortune oversaw all the activities and transactions of the Awinyolan family.

Vatu returned with a plate of Indian delicacies. "I found these treats in the cupboard. Raita doesn't like me to eat too many, but we must have a snack with tea, no?" He winked at Warren.

Vatu went back to the kitchen and returned with a tray bearing a silver teapot and two intricately patterned white and scarlet teacups. He pushed the tray of goodies toward Warren. "Please try these rasgula, they are Indian milk balls, or the kalakand, which is like a cheesecake," he said. "I must be able to tell Raita I am sharing these."

Warren took one of each to occupy his hands and his mouth.

They sat in silence with Warren picking at the delicacies, and waiting for Vatu to sip on his tea before he brought his own to his lips. His mind raced, worried what Vatu was going to say. He rebuffed thoughts of a poisoning, then panicked thinking Meena was pregnant and Vatu was going to urge a marriage to ensure her respectability. It was not how he imagined having a child. He tried to slow his mind. While Vatu fiddled with the tea, Warren took a close look at the older man, and saw Meena had inherited his eyes and shared an odd contortion of the mouth which became visible when they smiled.

"Do you like cricket?" Vatu inquired.

"Can't say I follow it, or understand it much for that matter," he said.

"Big match this weekend at the BMO at Exhibition Place. Pakistan national team is playing Australia as part of the colonies tour."

Warren nodded his head. He was uncomfortable, and impatient. "Mr. Awinyolan, I know nothing about cricket, I barely pay attention to hockey and the Maple Leafs, but I know you didn't ask me here to teach me about cricket. I'm happy to have tea, but I want to know why you asked me in. If it's about your daughter, not to worry, she and I are finished."

"Meena is unhappy," Vatu responded without hesitation, the worry so close to his surface that any traditional cultural niceties were squelched.

"And?"

"And I want to help."

Warren was unhappy too. He wondered if Meena'd moved past him, a momentary blip that she might not remember years hence. He imagined becoming an anecdote, a warning not to date your neighbour.

"I'm sorry Vatu, but I can't help you."

"Maybe not, but I can help you."

It was a strange twist. Warren had imagined Vatu considered him to be the archetype of evil. Any rapprochement had to be suspect.

"What do you mean?"

"My daughter is working for some crazy mining company. That is not her. She told me why, and now I want to help you."

Warren tried to follow the logic. "And by helping me, that will help her?"

Vatu looked pleased. "Yes."

"But you don't want her to know?" It was clear, if Warren were no longer a threat to his daughter's integrity, then he could be used as a tool.

Vatu was smiling now. "Oh yes, you are a very astute fellow. I can see why she likes you."

Warren doused the compliment. "Meena and I are over."

"Yes, yes, that is as you say. But if we help you, this will make Meena happy."

"Okay, fine, so what do you want from me?"

"You tell me."

"Let me think about it." Warren felt safer maintaining his options, till he could determine the score. Best not to reject the offer outright, nor acquiesce to some kind of contract he was unable to pay.

"Fine, fine, yes this is fine." Vatu was beaming.

They spoke awhile longer, eventually turning back to cricket with Vatu beginning to explain the intricacies of the sport. Warren played along till there was a pause allowing an extraction. He thanked Vatu and hopped back up to his apartment.

Vatu closed the door and heaved a long sigh. Raita hurried down the stairs with a flourish of expectation flushing her face.

"Did he agree?"

"Yes dear, he did." Vatu looked worried.

• • •

Warren and Curtis were heading back to the cemetery office with Mary Angevine's tombstone in the back of the truck.

"You're really heading to Guatemala?" Curtis shook his head, glancing at Warren and then focusing back on the road.

"Yeah."

They were comfortable driving and working in silence sharing an anecdote or commentary as it related to current affairs, talk radio or the CBC. Curtis preferred music, except when the CBC ran the *Dead Dog Café*, best comedy in Canada he called it. Warren's tastes were aligned with the public broadcaster. Whoever drove got to call the radio shots.

"What about Meena?"

"I don't know, I haven't seen her."

"Does she know?"

"I don't know." Warren figured she must know by now. He hadn't told her.

"But she hasn't called you or anything?"

"No."

The quiet between the words meant topics could be changed, as if any statement could be definitive and stand on its own. Warren could watch the traffic, note the changes as they moved through neighbourhoods, passing the Sri Lankans who nestled next to the Portuguese. And as they moved through the cultural communities, the conversation could have passed, moved elsewhere, leaving traces behind in the neighbourhoods they passed through.

"You got a death wish boy?"

"Hey, if I do, you'll fix me up with a nice stone?"

"We already got one with your name on it. Won't take much to get it back."

"I'm kind of hoping not to have to use that one yet."

"Won't cost much, it's already been engraved."

"Yeah, but I'm hoping to change the date on it. I'm kind of thinking this year's not a good one to die."

"Suit yourself. I'll miss you though."

"I'm only going to Guatemala; I'll be back in no time."

"Sure, whatever you say. I'm telling you this much, you better not be coming back in a box."

"That's not my intention."

"That won't make me none too happy. Not that I'm adverse to one less white boy kicking around."

"Thanks."

They drove the rest of the way in silence.

$$\cdot\ \cdot\ \cdot$$

Warren went to the Awinyolans' house. He'd reviewed the options, thought of his mother and rejected the possibility. He petitioned Curtis who had to decline because they'd forked over a mint for their eldest to get braces. He rested on Vatu's tender of assistance. If it had been genuine, it would result in getting him what he needed. If it was a ruse, it would be revealed, so Warren determined it was worth the risk of rejection.

The money was for an opportunity to squeeze into Guatemala. Meena had seen a notice regarding an upcoming Securities Investment visit. They had a limited timeframe in which to get Warren and Celina to the mine to impersonate the inspectors before the review. It was risky, illegal and dangerous, and perhaps stupid. But their efforts to date had floundered, the company was impervious to dissent, legal avenues were impeded and remote, and stockholders clung to their dividends. It was bold and improbable, but it allowed Celina to return home in the presence of a foreigner with a Canadian identity who could rally supporters if things were to go awry.

But they didn't have the money they needed. They'd used their cash reserves on the billboard scheme and there wasn't time for another fundraiser. And Chantel pointed out that asking people to give them money to undertake illegal activities was not in their best interest.

And so Warren found himself stationed at the Awinyolan dining room table asking Vatu for money. Asking your former girlfriend's father for money was not high up on his list of appealing and amusing ways to while away his time, particularly prior to sacrificing himself on an adventure to places that had rattlesnakes and men with guns. Yet, here he was with Vatu who had approved providing money to the cause, when Meena walked in the door.

Warren felt trapped and ready to flee with Vatu's cheque like a self-realized huckster. Meena was caught by surprise.

Homecomings were tense now for her, with both the thrill and dread of running into Warren mediating her steps. Every day, when she closed her door, she found herself relieved to be facing the altar that sat in their entranceway protecting them from evil spirits, yet disappointed to be back inside her shell.

But discovering Warren in her dining room wasn't something she'd prepared for. Not even once. She was shocked into silence.

It was Vatu who broke the silence. "Meena, you two need to go somewhere, to talk," he suggested.

Meena reverted to the girl rapt to the request of her father and headed up to her bedroom. She passed Raita, who was watching with stunned, widened eyes out of the swinging kitchen door.

"Uh…" Warren hesitated.

"Up, follow her up," Vatu cajoled him to go after her.

Warren climbed the steps, his heart pounding and his thoughts offering no alternative course of action.

Her room was nothing of what he'd imagined. He'd pictured posters of Bollywood actors lining her walls, and soft things, like teddy bears and the stuffed creatures of her childhood displayed on her bed. But, in addition to shelves of books, her room was adorned with enlarged photographs—one of markets in India, and another with women draped in red and yellow saris washing clothes in a murky brown river. She had a tiny wooden desk cleared except for a small framed picture off to one side. He was astonished to see it was a series of black and white portraits from one of the instant photo booths they'd gone to early in their courtship at the Eaton's Centre. A purple blanket with white, embroidered elephants and yellow-and-red lotus flowers adorned her bed.

She sat down on the quilt and Warren took the chair out from underneath her desk. She looked him in the eyes, "I'm so sorry Warren," she began.

The pulsing rejection wounds, eviscerations from frustration, loneliness, and hurt weakened.

"Me too." He looked at his hands and saw her wanting to reach out to him. His fingers extended, but his hands remained in his lap, playing the dance of remorse and uncertainty.

"I shouldn't have run out and showered you with my stupid anger, and then Petra, I hope you understand that…"

Warren interrupted her. "I missed you," he said, cutting through his own misgivings and insecurities.

Meena's eyes filled with tears. "Oh my god, I missed you so much." She reached for him, and Warren moved over beside her on the bed, taking her hand. Meena grasped him in a hug and it felt like a piece of him that had been missing was being affixed back into place. They held each other, compressing together as if they could push away that which had festered between them, finding lips and tongues and bruising hard into the other, kissing deeply.

Their mouths and bodies were frantic. Warren wanted to hold her and feel her, all of her, all at once. He'd manoeuvred his hands under her shirt and felt the warmth of her skin and the firmness of her back.

"Hello in there." Vatu knocked at the door and Warren threw himself to the end of the bed, away from Meena. Vatu came in with a grin, and a tray carrying two cups of tea and a plate of sweets which he placed on the bed between them.

Meena jumped up. "Thanks Dad, but we're going to go for a walk, get some fresh air." She grabbed Warren's hand and led him past her father.

An hour earlier, Warren had been pacing his apartment to gear himself up to make a pitch to Vatu to get money to go to Guatemala. He wanted to get away so that he wasn't reminded of Meena every day he came and went from his apartment. It had been torturous to be so close, and yet apart. And now he let Meena lead him as they left her house, went down the steps, around the banister and up the stairs to his apartment.

Vamp gave an appreciative purr when they came in the door, she seemed to smile at Meena as though they had covertly communicated during her absence.

Meena kicked off her shoes and pushed Warren down onto the couch and climbed on top of him. "God, I missed you so much."

Warren held her off. "Wait."

Meena sat up, surprised. Seeing him in her living room had brought to the surface hope that had been submerged under layers of mistakes. Warren had responded in her bedroom. He had told her he missed her. She didn't understand his restraint.

"A lot happened Meena. We need to talk." Warren saw her face begin to cloud over and he rushed to clarify, so things wouldn't be misinterpreted. "I missed you, I did, I do. But your dad's right—we need to talk about what happened." He felt like a two-year-old who didn't have all his words yet.

Warren sat up and Meena moved over to the end of the couch and stared at him with her mouth set and her eyes tight.

"Listen Meena, I've missed you. And I wanted to be with you, to have you in my life. To touch your skin, to wake up beside you..." Warren moved towards her and placed his hands on her lap.

Meena softened her stare. She resisted pulling him towards her. It was hard not to be desperate when something that had been taken away had come back.

Allowing someone behind his veil, permitting them entry into his experiences had exacted a toll. He couldn't face losing it all over again. "What I'm saying is that yes, I want you. I miss you. Meena I don't want to lose this. I want to make it right." Warren didn't have any other words. He looked into her eyes and expressed all the things he couldn't form into words.

Meena took in his eyes and then she smiled.

"I love you too, Warren." And she crawled into his arms and they cocooned together on his couch with Vamp purring at their feet.

CHAPTER 17

Kaban *(earth)*

"Almost as soon as the sun touched them, the bones started telling their stories."
—Dr. Clyde Snow, renowned forensic anthropologist and member of the UN Human Rights Commission.

"They're in a well," Celina whispered, as he walked in the door to the guesthouse.

She looked towards the old man, who was seated in the wicker chair. Lopez had cleaned up. He was wearing a nice shirt, and had pressed his cotton pants and slicked down his hair. Warren would have thought he'd come courting if Celina hadn't looked so distraught. "Juan has been watching," she said, her voice wavering, "keeping an eye on the site all these years."

Shaking off his encounter with Charlie, Warren was slow to assimilate the scene. Celina spoke in a whisper. "My sister," she said, then put her head down and wept into her hands.

Warren saw pain seep out of her, and he took her in his arms, holding her up against collapse, but letting the sorrow flow. "I'm so sorry." Celina's sobs wracked her body and Warren held her.

The alcohol and Charlie wiped from his mind, Warren didn't notice the old man get up and walk out, to honour her mourning, to offer privacy to her anguish.

"Oh my god Warren, *lo dejaron en una posa.*" She spoke in English, Spanish, as well as Achi. Celina apologized to Lalita, over and over again. "*Lo siento hermana.* I am so sorry, *mi amor,* I am so sorry."

Warren took her to the couch and held her hand and rubbed her back, soothing her, the way his mother had when he was a boy and ill with fever.

He drew her hair from her face, running his fingers along the strands from her head, trailing down to her shoulders. When one strand was complete, he took another, as if combing out the sorrow, the way his mother had coaxed out the fear and sickness.

Warren held Celina till she nodded off, exhausted by sorrow, falling asleep to his rhythmic voice and touch.

He gathered her in his arms and had to shake his legs to resume their circulation when he went to stand. Celina coiled up toward him, holding her body small and close. Warren carried her to the bedroom and laid her on the bed.

She was awakened by the movement and held out her arm as he tried to steal out the door.

"Please don't leave me Warren," she whispered. He observed her as she lay there, vulnerable and exposed. He sat by her side and kissed her forehead, caressing her cheek as he would a newborn.

She let him remove her shirt and pants which he folded and placed on the dresser. He took a nightshirt she had stuffed in her bag and pulled it over her head and drew the woven blankets over her body. He removed his shoes, socks, and pants, and crawled in beside her.

She curled up into his arms and pressed her body to his heart as tears slid down her face onto the sheets below.

. . .

"What the hell…" Warren heard the door bang against the wall and shouts rousted him out of bed. Piercing light blinded Warren as three men burst into the bedroom.

"You lying little bastard, sleeping with your bitch after all?" Charlie loomed over them at the foot of the bed.

Warren scrambled to pull the blanket up over his shoulders and cover up Celina. "What the fuck are you doing in here? Get the fuck out of my bedroom!" His heart was racing.

"That would be my bedroom you little shit." Charlie motioned to his two thugs to begin to rummage through their bags.

"What's happening Warren …" Celina awoke, caught herself.

"I thought it was Reg, from the Securities Investment Review Committee?" Charlie grabbed things out of Celina's bag and threw them around the room. "Guess fucking not huh? Get them the fuck out of bed." Celina screamed as one man pulled her from the sheets.

"Hey!" Warren was wrenched off the bed and nearly slipped on the clothes he had left on the floor. The other thug kept a firm grip on his arm while Warren's eyes darted around the room, looking for escape.

"Listen Charlie, I don't know what you think you're doing, but I can guarantee you, you're out of a job, right here, right now."

"Stuff it! We did a double check with folks in Toronto. Seems you're not exactly who you say you are. Are you?"

• • •

"This is stupid Meena. It's not like I don't notice you're avoiding me. The least you can do is tell me what I did wrong." Petra waited outside the stall. She had followed Meena into the bathroom, locking the door after they'd entered.

"I'm trying to take a piss, in peace, if you don't mind," Meena's voice reverberated in the chamber. She flushed, fixed her skirt, and emerged from the stall. She pushed past Petra and made for the marble sink. "What do you want from me?" She kept her eyes on the water, letting the soap expand into clouds that covered her hands.

"Well, I thought a little friendship, but now I'm thinking I'll settle for civility—and a dose of honesty would be nice." Petra stood with her arms folded, her back to the stalls.

Meena grabbed a paper towel, rubbing the moisture from her hands, as if she could remove the stain of their association. She stuffed the paper into the wastebasket and turned on Petra. "You want honesty Petra? Why the hell didn't you tell me about Tyrell?"

Meena noticed the change, the muscles in her face drooping and Petra's hands dropping to her sides. Feeling self-satisfied, she turned to leave, but Petra grabbed her. "What about me and Tyrell?"

Meena pulled her arm back. "Don't play coy. I know about your affair with Tyrell and you stringing me along. What I can't figure out, is why you didn't tell him about me searching in the archives."

Petra stared at Meena for a moment, calculating. Petra closed her eyes and went over to the sink, leaning against it, bent down with her hands on her thighs. Meena crowded close and stood in front of her with her arms crossed, eyes blazing.

Petra looked up. "He used me."

"Sure, that's what he's good at," Meena said.

"He found out I was here illegally and he threatened to tell Immigration where I was."

"I thought you came here as a dancer."

"I had a Performance Visa. I didn't want to perform anymore and they were going to send me back."

"Who are they?"

"The ones who brought me here."

"You told me you came on your own."

"Meena, it amazes me how naïve you are some days. You'll make a good lawyer because everything presented to you is like out of the mouths of innocents."

"So enlighten me."

"They advertise, or go to the dancing academies. They waited for me outside the gates, after practice. I didn't go right away. I thought they were jerks." Petra's eyes were welling and Meena could see her hands were beginning to shake. Petra turned toward the sink, speaking as though she were talking to the mirror. "They persisted. Some of my friends wanted to go. They made it sound great. And it wasn't great in Russia. But I didn't know how bad it would be."

Meena was trying not to soften, she didn't want to be played by Petra again.

"It was bad. They took our passports. Told us we had to work it off. I was lucky, I was a dancer. Some of the other girls never made it out of the rooms they kept us in. I had to work in their clubs, in the bars. I had done ballet, and modern dance. My mother had seen Nureyev once, and told me how he used to float in the air, she called me her little hummingbird." Then she did start to cry. "They kept our documents, renewed our visas, kept adding to our debt, room, board, health care costs, entertainment tax. We couldn't pay them off, no matter how much we danced." Petra looked up at her and Meena could see anger and defiance in her eyes.

"They would threaten us, beat us. They told us they would attack our families. I didn't even know my mother had died." And she dropped her head and began weeping again into her hands.

"That doesn't explain the Tyrell connection."

Petra regained herself, wiping the tears from her eyes. She turned around, back towards Meena. Her face looked hard and determined. "I came to work here, it is hard for illegals to find work, but with some connections, I was able to come to Magma. I once studied to be a lawyer, but there was no work. And things in Russia for me, well let's just say dancing was better."

As she talked, Meena fought her instinct to soften, but she sympathized with Petra. She always had. She'd sensed vulnerability in Petra, had seen it in her eyes, felt it in her body. She hadn't been able to point to it, as Petra was a strong figure, held herself upright like a ballerina warrior. But the dancer in her held softness, fragility, like an egg that could hold up a stack of encyclopaedias when standing erect, but once turned on its side, would be crushed under the weight of applied pressure.

"Who were your connections? Tyrell?"

"He came to see me dancing. We talked, because I always talked with my clients, I never pretended to be somebody I wasn't. He found out what I used to do, so he talked to my captors, and then he bought my contract and gave me a job here."

It was incredible, a living nightmare. She both believed and disbelieved, not because she trusted Petra, but it was plausible, and it appealed to Meena's sense of injustice. And the one outstanding factor was that Petra hadn't betrayed her regarding their search for information on the old mine in Guatemala. If she had told Tyrell, Meena would be in jail by now or worse.

"Why didn't you leave?"

Because for Meena it would have been that simple.

"Protection, money." Petra told her she was going to work at Magma until she had enough money to go somewhere else where they didn't know her, so she could disappear, start again.

"So you're his paid mistress?"

"If that's how you want to look at it."

"What about the pictures, the video of the two of us together?"

Petra had betrayed her, she hadn't forgotten that .

"He saw us working together at night. He wanted me to get some information on you. He threatened to bring an immigration officer to the building. He said he needed you for something so I figured a tape of us together would be harmless. It was a massage, there was nothing to it. I liked you, I thought you liked me. He could try to use it, but I figured, what would you care?"

Meena no longer blocked her way, she had dropped her hands to her side and begun to lean against the door. "Does he make you do this with other people?"

"Sure."

"Who?"

"Whoever he wants to find something out about, or use in some way." Petra dropped the wet tissue into the toilet.

"And you let him do this?"

"What other choice to do I have? That's why I was helping you for god's sake. Any damage I can do is my little piece of resistance."

"So that's your secret?"

"Yeah, I'm sorry Meena."

"I don't know who to believe anymore. This place is a fucking nightmare."

. . .

Meena watched Petra, expecting reprisals. But none came. The office was the same as it ever was, people worked in cubicles, managers went in and out of offices, computers beeped, phones rang, and no one came to haul her away. She and Petra kept a distance, singed by their interactions, each wary of the other.

Meena still needed to find information. She felt there must be something within Magma, a company that big couldn't hide all the evidence surrounding the affairs of what happened in Guatemala. She'd gotten access to the company database, she was searching through files and records like a lost whale searching the Pacific for a forgotten beach. It was the Friday at the start of a long weekend, all of the staff had gone home, even those who normally stayed late finishing up extra work, vying for promotions or surfing porn. It was a good time for sleuthing.

Meena heard a commotion in the foyer, and she watched as Scott Liddle entered Tyrell's office. She dreaded what might transpire. After what she had told Tyrell, she feared for Liddle's safety.

She went to the photocopy room, as it offered a view to Tyrell's door. Not long after entering, Scott came out of the office whistling, heading to the elevators with a skip to his step. Meena pulled her head back from sight as Tyrell headed in her direction.

She heard him stop at Petra's desk. "Petra my dear, thanks for waiting." Meena watched him bend down, past the top of the cubicle.

Tyrell and Petra emerged from behind the buffer and she watched as he led her to the entrance of the offices and point to where Scott was tapping his foot as he waited for the elevator, oblivious to his onlookers.

Meena crept closer, bouncing in and out of cubicles so as not to be noticed. Tyrell said, "You see that man?" Petra nodded, her face devoid of emotion, moving as though encased in metal. "His name is Scott Liddle. I'd like you to see what kind of man he is and let me know anything interesting you find out." He smiled at her.

Petra grimaced, a smile and a glare fighting on her face. "I can't James."

Meena slipped into the cubicle opposite the entrance and crouched low to overhear the conversation, she watched them from her vantage place on the floor, using an office chair as camouflage.

"Oh yes, you can, my little dancing friend. You can and you will." Meena didn't like how he held Petra's arm, how his eyes, were unaccustomed to being challenged, blazed.

"No James, I can't."

"Listen, you little Russian tart. You will do as I say. When I say jump, you will jump. When I say fuck, you will fuck. I do hope you understand."

He glared at Petra. He cupped one of her breasts in his hand, moving his thumb towards the centre. The offices were quiet but for the hum of sleeping electronics.

Meena scrambled out from behind the chair, grabbed some papers and hustled towards them feigning preoccupation with some files. Petra had tried to shift away from him, but he held her, gripping her arm.

Meena interrupted, as if she came upon them in surprise, keeping her eyes on their faces pretending not to have seen what Tyrell was doing. "Oh Petra, great, I found you. We better get going, or we'll miss the first act."

Tyrell had removed one hand, but still held Petra by the arm.

"Oh, I'm afraid Petra has some work to do with me tonight. Perhaps…" He said to her with a smile.

"Ah, I'll come in early next week and finish it Mr. Tyrell," Petra interrupted, pulling her arm away and stealing the opportunity to head to her desk to grab her jacket hanging on the back of her chair, and her purse from inside her drawer. "Yes, we don't want to miss the show."

"What are you seeing Ms. Awinyolan?" Tyrell recovered.

"*Taming of the Shrew*. The late show. Come on Petra, let's go."

They sped down the hall. Meena pushed open the doors to the stairs. "Come on." She grabbed Petra's hand and they ran down five flights, adrenaline spiriting them away. They stopped to take a breath and looked to see if Tyrell had followed them. They didn't see anyone. Their own echoes cascaded down the stairwell. "Are you okay?" Meena asked.

Petra nodded at first, up and down, and then side to side. Her eyes welled.

"Listen, you better stay at my place tonight." She gave her a hug. "But, we need to get out of this place first." She checked again to make sure the coast was clear, then she opened the door to a foyer and went to the elevators to take them the rest of the way down.

· · ·

"Charlie, this is an outrage. You get these guys off me and Maria…" Warren demanded.

Charlie approached him. "I don't know who you are or what you want," a thug gripped Warren, preventing him from moving, "but I'll find out." Charlie smacked him across the face with the back of his hand. Blood trickled down the side of his face.

Celina was squirming to get out of the other one's grip, but the oak of a man grabbed her arm and yanked it up her back, to the point it looked like it might snap. She froze, her eyes terrified.

Charlie grabbed Warren by the hair. "I will not be made fun of, nor will I be told what to do in my mine." He yanked Warren's head backward, and then let it spring forward, and punched him again with his fist. "I don't know who you are," he hit Warren in the gut, "yet." Charlie took his time while Warren struggled to breathe. The thug who held Warren yanked him up so Charlie could look him in the eye, "But we'll find out. These boys were hired for the abilities they garnered in the military. I'm sure you'll find them quite adept and professional." Charlie smirked as Warren gasped for air.

Charlie turned to Celina, eyeing her with malice. "Normally I'd begin with you." He stepped toward her, then touched her face with his finger and drew it down her neck towards her chest. Celina held herself immobile till the last minute, then broke free and went for his finger with her teeth and did a kicking backstroke to the side of the knee of the brute holding her. She aimed well in both and caught flesh in one and cartilage in the other. Warren cheered on though he was unable to free himself from the man holding him.

Charlie slapped Celina on the side of the head with his other hand and the thug recovered to use pressure points to make her let go of Charlie's finger.

Charlie held his hand to assess the damage, checking the digit and then putting it to his mouth for comfort. He removed it long enough to issue the order to spit out a command. "Tie her up." He added, "I'm going to really enjoy you; I like feisty. But first, we'll deal with this son of a bitch." He turned again to face Warren. "You try to fucking embarrass me, not good." He punched Warren again with his good hand. Warren dry heaved.

Meanwhile, Celina's thug had tied her to a chair. She struggled, but couldn't break free.

They dragged Warren to the bed and stripped him of his clothes, forcing him to lie naked on the bed. They tied his arms and feet to the bed frame and held him in supine crucifixion.

Warren was wild eyed and Celina kept trying to catch his gaze to provide him with the minimal comfort of her presence, so he would know, at least, despite what would transpire, he was not alone.

Warren tried not to gag on the blood that dripped into his mouth from his nose.

Charlie knelt by the bed to get closer to his face. He grabbed Warren's penis and Warren recoiled. "Not so much of a stud now are we? I suggest you begin telling me who you are or we'll cut off your balls, one at a time." Charlie fingered Warren's privates while the thug nearest him pulled out a machete.

"Warren, please…" Celina cried out to him.

"So it is Warren! Now, what else do I need to know?"

Just then, a piercing sound shrieked through the mine.

CHAPTER 18
Etz'nab *(sacrifice)*

miss·ing (msng) adj.

1. a. Not present; absent. b. Lost: a missing person; soldiers missing in action.
2. Lacking; wanting: *This book has 12 missing pages.*

Thesaurus Legend: Synonyms Related Words Antonyms

Adj.
1. missing - not existing; *"innovation has been sadly lacking";*
   "character development is missing from the book"
   lacking, wanting, nonexistent, absent - not in a specified place
   physically or mentally
2. missing - not able to be found; "missing in action"; "a missing person"
   lost - no longer in your possession or control; unable to be found
   or recovered; "a lost child"; "lost friends"; "his lost book"; "lost
   opportunities"

"Petra's missing."

"What do you mean?"

Meena fingered the piece of paper Warren had left with Curtis's name and number. He had told her to contact Curtis if she needed help, things got dicey, or there was any trouble.

Curtis had opened the door before she even had a chance to ring the bell. "I don't know where she is, Curtis. She was at my house last night. She said she was going to get something from her apartment this morning and call in sick to work, but she never called and there's no answer at the apartment. I called her cell—nothing. I'm really worried."

Curtis took Meena's hand and pulled her inside. "Now why don't you tell me what's going on." He closed the door, pushing sneakers and school bags out of the way. "The girls are off from school today, but I sent them next door," he said.

Meena took a deep breath. They hadn't heard from Celina and Warren, and now Petra was nowhere to be found.

"Petra and I took off from Tyrell," Meena didn't know how much Warren had told Curtis about the situation. "She's my colleague at Magma." Curtis nodded and she carried on as he directed her down the hall. "And Tyrell, he's the boss and he was trying to get her to," Meena hedged, "do some stuff." There'd been such destroying of characters and reputations that she didn't want to feed into it anymore. "We took off and he was pissed. Petra was quite scared so she stayed with me this weekend. This morning, she went back to her apartment and I went to work, she was going to call in sick to work for a few days, to let stuff settle. But she never called. So I tried to check in with her, but haven't been able to get an answer or anything. I'm worried, Curtis."

Curtis made Meena sit down in the kitchen and he gave her some tea and then cleared the breakfast dishes leftover on the table.

"Where might she be?"

"I'm not sure. I'm not sure if she has anywhere to go."

"Maybe she needed to get away for a bit," Curtis suggested.

"Sure, but why didn't she tell me?"

"I'm sure there's a perfectly good explanation."

"Maybe Ryan told them about her, or the Russian guys found her—"

"Whoa, what Russian guys?"

Meena fiddled with the tea mug, turning it in circles, around and around, while she told him Petra's background, and how Tyrell was using her, and what had happened leading up to her disappearance, trying to avoid sounding like a *Sopranos* episode.

"I need you to come with me to her apartment. I don't want to go alone."

Curtis distracted her as they drove up the Don Valley Parkway, regaling her with stories of the kids, such as the time they cut a Pop-tart into a CD replica and then stuffed it in the car stereo, curious what sound blueberries would make.

They parked outside of the apartment complex and Meena looked up, hoping they would find Petra sitting on her couch or soaking in the tub.

Curtis held open the door for a young mother with her baby carriage, while Meena resisted trying to deke around her. They rode up the elevator in silence and Curtis followed Meena as she walked up to Petra's door. Meena stood immobile, afraid to take the next step.

Curtis put his arm around her shoulders. "Let's try knocking." He tapped on the door and Meena held her breath, silently imploring padding feet to head toward them. The buzz of the building supplanted her breaths. Curtis knocked again, louder, and then tried the door. It was locked.

"I'm not sure…" he said as he looked at the lock mechanism. Meena pushed him aside. "I have a key." She had found it in Petra's desk.

"Oh, that's a whole lot easier then, isn't it?"

Meena slipped the key in the lock, turned it over, and pushed the door open. "Petra?" Meena was scared of what she might find and grabbed Curtis's hand as if squeezing it were akin to rubbing Aladdin's lamp.

"Petra, are you home?" Meena asked into the darkness. The pair of black, shiny pumps Petra had worn were lined up side by side in the hall.

Curtis found the hall lights and clicked them on, brightening the corridor and living room ahead. He flicked on more lights as he saw them and walked into the kitchen. The table was wiped clean and there was a small juice glass and plate and knife drying on the dish rack. The living room was spotless, the carpet had been vacuumed and the throw pillows were arranged on the white couch. Nothing was out of place.

Meena glanced at Curtis. "We've got to check the bedroom."

"Do you want me to go?"

"It's okay, we'll both look."

The door was ajar and Curtis pushed it open and fumbled for the lights on the wall. He flicked the switch on to reveal nothing untoward. The bed was made, the dresser neat. Meena looked in the closet to find Petra's outfits aligned on hangers.

Curtis moved to the washroom and pulled the bath curtain aside, nothing in the tub. There was a shower mat on the floor that was damp, and short red hairs clung to a towel hung by the sink. Petra had been here this morning and had taken a shower. But she wasn't here now.

Curtis kept looking around the apartment while Meena went through the dresser. She began to feel stupid, thinking that maybe there was an explanation and Petra had forgotten to call in. Curtis checked the closet by the door and found a number of spring and fall coats and a purse on the floor beside an assortment of shoes and pumps. He opened the purse and found Petra's ID, credit cards and a five-dollar bill.

"Meena I found her purse. Why would she leave without her purse?" He checked for keys. He checked the jacket pockets and went to the kitchen and looked through the drawers. He didn't find them.

"Did she have a coat?"

"Yeah, a white ski-jacket type thing." Meena came out of the bedroom. "Did you find it?"

"No." he shook his head, assessing the situation, "She took her keys and jacket. Maybe we're trespassing and she's going to barge in on us at any moment."

"Let me just check the answering machine before we go. Just to see."

She went into the living room and sat on the couch and pushed the play button. A mechanical voice was activated. "You have four new messages. First message…" Meena heard her own voice echoing back to her as she played the messages in succession.

Meena stared at Curtis. "I don't know what to think." Her gut told her something was wrong, but the apartment looked like Petra had simply stepped out and could return at any time.

Meena looked through the curtain out the window.

On the balcony there was a deck chair and dead flowers sticking out of two planting pots. Curtis investigated the concrete below. "There's nothing here. I don't know Meena, I'm not sure what more we can do."

Maybe she was wrong, maybe everything was okay with Petra, her gut and her mind were giving her different messages and she wasn't sure anymore which one to believe.

But Petra had spent the weekend at her house; she'd been there, and she had been scared.

. . .

Raita was at the table doing a crossword and Vatu had the satellite dish channelled to a cricket game when Meena and Petra came in.

"I brought a friend, Amma. Petra, this is my mother, Raita, and my father, Vatu."

Her dad lifted himself from the couch to greet them, giving a hug to his daughter and offering his hand to Petra. "Welcome, welcome to our home."

"Did you eat?" Raita asked, as was her custom.

"I don't think I could eat a thing," Petra exclaimed.

"You haven't had my mom's food," Meena said, sinking into a chair at the dining room table and gesturing to Petra to do the same.

Petra sat with her back to the wall. Vatu took the seat opposite, still in sight of the TV, which offered the option to take in the match at a glance, and still remain part of the gathering at the table.

"You are a friend of Meena's?" he asked while his eyes remained on the pitch.

Petra glanced at Meena. "We're colleagues."

"And we're friends too," Meena said, taking Petra's hand in hers and squeezing it for emphasis.

Petra crumpled with relief. She began to weep, bringing her hands to her face. In the rush out of the office, onto the streets and then hailing a cab home, they hadn't had time to process the encounter with Tyrell. Meena moved her chair closer while Vatu kept his eyes on the screen, not wanting to intrude.

"Sorry," Petra took a tissue out of her handbag and dabbed at her eyes, trying to keep her mascara from smudging. Raita appeared with steaming plates of spinach, deep fried paneer, heaps of rice and an aromatic curry which she placed in front of them. Meena associated food with celebration, mourning, calamities, and condolences. For her mother, food in the belly helped to cure any ailment.

Raita noticed the red eyes on Petra and looks of concern from her daughter. "You must eat," she told them. "Why add pain to a mind already in grief, please eat." Raita used proverbs when they suited, often adapting them to her own contexts, and they often made reference to using food to soothe the soul.

"I'm not that hungry," Petra said as she picked at the food. She brought the fork to her lips and the paneer brought a smile to her face. The food began to work its magic.

They spoke little, the cricket game proving a welcome diversion.

When they were finished, wiping up the last of the curry sauce with torn up pieces of naan, Petra and Meena excused themselves, cleared the plates into the kitchen, then went up to Meena's room. "Thank-you Meena. This means a lot to me." Petra's eyes began to well again. "This really is not like me," she said, wiping the tears away with her hands.

"It's okay, vulnerability is not a sin. I'm sorry I mistrusted you Petra."

"I deceived you."

"I won't throw stones if you don't."

"Fair enough."

"Can I stay with you tonight Meena. I mean just…"

"Of course."

Meena threw Petra a nightshirt; they changed and crawled together under the covers. Meena held Petra, rubbing her back till she went to sleep. It took Meena a long time to follow her, there was much that was whirling around in her mind, not the least of which seemed to be the fear she was holding for everyone she knew.

. . .

With the piercing sound echoing in their ears Charlie gestured to the two thugs to head for the door.

"They're not going anywhere," Charlie said, pushing them forward, oblivious to whether they understood. He turned back to the room. "Stupid Mayos probably threw up some posters on the fence or are doing some chicken sacrifice," Charlie spit out, as he glanced back at Warren, tied to the bed, and Celina, restrained in the chair. "Not to worry, this will make it all the sweeter when we return," he said leering at them. He checked the knots to make sure they were tight, and then hurried out the door.

As soon as the door slammed shut behind them, Warren strained to look over to Celina. "I'm sorry," he said, assuming responsibility and adding another to his list of failures.

"Warren, it's I who must apologize. I brought you into this mess, manipulated you into being here."

They remained apart in their thoughts, unable to escape their bounds, and unable to move past the fear of what was to become of them.

Warren didn't pray, but considered it. He thought of Meena, and he apologized to her in his head, imagining his thoughts traversing the thousands of kilometres which separated them.

In the midst of his attempts, he heard the sound of the front door opening, and he held his breath, unsure if his time was coming to an end.

But it was Juan who appeared before them. Warren was relieved, and then despondent, as he realized that Juan had been their stool pigeon, had been playing on their fears and sympathies hours before.

Warren didn't understand as Celina spoke to him in Achí. He didn't try to follow, given he might never have a chance to communicate with Meena again he put all his concentration into eliciting her image and trying to tell her how he felt about her before Charlie returned.

"Hurry, hurry." Warren was jolted out of his state to see Celina and Juan standing in front of him as they began working on the knots that held him to the bed posts.

"What's happening?"

"Juan and the community sounded the alarm when they realized Charlie knew who we were; they have made a diversion at the front gates. But we don't have much time." Warren began shaking the meditation out of his head and, once his own hands were untied, was able to scramble to get the knots pinning his ankles undone.

The final bonds shook loose and Warren sprung up and grabbed his pants and shirt. Celina was clothed and had her bag slung over her shoulder. Warren's hands and legs were numb as he fumbled to revive the limbs that had fallen asleep from the constricting ropes. He threw his pants over his nakedness, ignoring boxers and socks, and slipped his t-shirt over his head.

He snatched up his briefcase, grabbed his shoes and hurried after Celina and Juan who had scrambled out the door. They ran to the company Jeep that Juan had left running and climbed in, tearing off in the opposite direction of the front gates.

The moving Jeep afforded Warren a chance to breathe. He glanced out the window, noticing the mining fortress, with its twelve-foot-tall barbed wire and electric gates. He shared a glance with Celina, realizing they were trapped in a prison.

"There was a way into Fort Knox, there must be a way out. We're just going to have to trust Juan."

Warren knew she was trying to appear hopeful. He looked to the man who the day before he'd taken as a drunk. He wasn't sure he felt consoled by seeing him as their saviour.

They raced along the roads of the mine, passing machinery, shovel-like trucks two stories tall, used to scrape the earth from its organic layers to its mineral innards; massive dump trucks that reminded Warren of steroid scale toys. The humid heat and the harried exertion had soaked Warren, and he brushed the sweat that was dripping down the side of his head. He took the chance to put his head out the window, to catch some air to cool him down, and to look behind, to see if they were being pursued. He assumed theirs would be a short reprieve.

They passed a large pond, with huge metal pipes suspended on metre-high pillars emitting a constant flow of greyish liquid into the murky blue-green water below.

"What's that?" Warren said, distracted from their escape.

"*El fuente,*" Celina told him.

The tailings pond. It was where the cyanide and refuse from the mine was deposited. It was the place where the earth had given way, allowing the pond to drain into the river that fed Celina's family. It was the pond that had killed her sister and her village.

"We're not going in there are we?" he blurted, images of them putting on wetsuits and floating through drainage pipes like the Fugitive. He pictured them spewed out over a cliff, where they would then tumble down a waterfall.

"There's a tunnel. Juan's been working on it for years. It's one of the old underground mines the old-timers used to work with their pickaxes. Before these guys came along and ripped off the mountaintop."

The Jeep stopped at Juan's shack, the dead vines seeming to hold the structure together. They scampered out and through the creaking door which scraped along the dirt floor. Juan moved his bed aside, and pulled away a trunk that lay underneath. He grabbed a flashlight from the wall and shone it into the hole that lay under the bed. A rope ladder hung down into the darkness though the light of the lamp did not reach the bottom.

Warren shivered, he'd run away from home so he wouldn't have to go into the mines. The thought of going underground scared the bejeezus out of him, and he hesitated at the lip.

Celina looked at him, impatient. "It's this or back to the butchers. You choose." She grabbed the rope and began descending into the abyss. Juan waited, offering the lead to Warren. He could only see darkness and hear the echo of Celina's banging as she made her way further into the depths of the ground. Warren looked to Juan and back down the hole. He thought of Charlie and the two marauders, and slipped into the pit. He sucked in air and consigned his foot to the first rung of the ladder.

. . .

"We'll have to call the police and get more details, we don't know if it's her," Vatu said. "They haven't released any names." Meena knew he was covering his discomfort, not sure how to console his daughter in front of the guest. Curtis had arrived at Meena's door with the newspaper clipping in hand.

"Curtis? I need you to go to the office and get my stuff." She struggled for composure. "And Petra's too."

Meena had spoken through compressed lips, fearing that if she were to open them, screams would drown out her efforts at maintaining composure, and she would spew out anger that would cover them all.

She'd gone into the beast and thought she was strong enough to weather their strikes. She'd seen herself as someone who was going to right the wrongs, and be hailed for her sacrifice and efforts at bringing about change, Aung San Suu Kyi or Vandana Shiva.

But as it became more complicated, and

Body Found at Cherry Beach

Tatia Czernia

TORONTO – Police investigators discovered the body of a young woman on the Lake Ontario waterfront of Hanlon's Point beach yesterday. They have released few details.

dangers increased, and she became more and more compromised, it was clear she was in over her head, and always had been. And now it felt like Petra's disappearance was her fault.

"I'm done. I can't go back there."

Raita took charge. She told Vatu to go with Curtis, so he wasn't alone. "I will go with you to the police station," she said to Meena. Let the men deal with the incidentals, the women would carry the heavy load.

. . .

Warren knew he could never have done it, every day, gone into the mine. Not like this. The darkness, with its damp metallic taste and low ceilings; he thought taking his chances with Charlie and his henchmen would have been better than crawling through a blackness, where with a twitch of the earth millions of tonnes of rock would be sent down crushing him like a worm.

He crawled, one arm reaching forward, leg bent, finding purchase to push along, trailing behind Celina, following her soles, like a lumbering cargo train. He felt pieces of rock in his hand, rock that had been cracked apart with a pickaxe, piece by piece, parts of the mountain fractured into fragments. The pieces that had been left behind, he scrambled over or brushed aside they seemed to hold him, like a blanket, like a conveyer belt leading them out. And in the blackness punctuated by the bobbing light of the lantern that Juan held as he crawled behind, Warren began to feel as if he were in the mountain's womb, giving him security and nourishment to push forward, a limb at a time.

When he saw the night sky that marked the end of the tunnel, Warren hesitated, and felt around with his hand, looking for something that would fit in his palm, that had a shape and feel that was both smooth and jagged. He put the rock in his pocket then broke out of the tunnel and gulped for air.

Warren shielded his eyes from the light that was still only half way to dawn. He shook as his body reacted to the clear air and sky above. He twitched as he looked to Celina. They were out past the confines of the mine. Juan must have worked on the shaft for years, bringing up bits of the tunnel in buckets and then dropping them down the cliff below his shack. Warren looked at him with increasing admiration.

They headed down a path that had no markings, and was not worn from travel by foot or beast. Warren felt wary, he couldn't see the mine, but he knew it was close. Celina assured him, "They will not find us here."

They scurried through the brush for hours with no one speaking as the light pursued the dawn. Warren followed Celina and Juan, anxious not to lose sight of them, despite being whipped in the face by the swinging branches, stumbling over unbroken ground, and striving to wipe from his imagination the weight of the earth over his head or the pursuit by the mining thugs.

He thought about Meena as they scrabbled through brush and twisted around boulders. He remembered her eyes, large and expressive with the white accentuated by her brown pupils and milk chocolate skin. They were like dancing cocoa beans, expressing sentiments echoed by her hands, as they stormed in elation over his body. Her smile came to him as well, the place where the corners of her mouth would slide into indented dimples and then glide into her fine, sharp features and striking cheekbones.

Celina's voice roused him from his reverie. "Get down." They had scrambled up an embankment and come to a highway.

They remained hidden until Juan flagged a bus. They climbed aboard and found seats amongst the bleary-eyed travellers heading to the city to sell their wares or work in the sweatshops and factories. Warren watched the villages and towns pass them on the highway as he tried to hold her image in his memory, but he could only see what lay before him, the whipped trees browned by the dust and fumes, the street vendors setting up their baskets to take onto the buses, emaciated dogs that scrambled for scraps and whimpered when kicked, and the little children strapped to their mothers' backs in colourful woven fabric, wrapped tight and held close. Warren could only absorb what he could see, his mind was too weary to contemplate what had come before, and too wary about what might be about to come.

CHAPTER 19

K'awak (*storm*)

"*...calls for justice were lost at the mercy of the wind and human indifference.*"
—Isabel Allende, Daughter of Fortune

The embassy was located in Zona 10. Walking around these neighbourhoods, you'd never have imagined that Guatemala had ever known anything as quaint as poverty; privilege revealed itself in the surrounding splendour: immaculate office buildings with well-kept gardens and sidewalks. There were no loud, exhaust-belching buses to be found here.

What belied the universal opulence were the heavily armed security guards who were stationed at every building. Celina and Warren walked with caution, feeling vulnerable with the information they carried. They walked through the security gate and were frisked at the metal detectors as they made their way through the entrance to the building.

The embassy was on the eighth floor. The elevator whisked them upwards, and Warren was heartened and relieved to see the Canadian flag proudly displayed.

At least we're on Canadian soil, he thought. Whatever else, they would be protected by virtue of their citizenship.

"*Documentos por favor,*" said the older woman behind the plexiglass window. Warren passed over their passports and felt a kinship for no other reason than they were compatriots caught up in this difficult yet beautiful land.

The woman sized them up and spoke in English with a Quebecois accent. "Someone will be by to see you shortly." She held onto their documents and invited them to join the six or seven other people seated in the waiting room.

Mountain posters, Inuit art and pictures of polite, happy Canadians filled the wall, spreading the message that Canada was a warm, bright and friendly place to be. Celina's frown revealed her own doubts as they took up residence in the waiting queue.

After a significant amount of time, while others moved in and out of the embassy, the Canadian face for Guatemala tapped on the admissions glass beckoning them forward. "The Second Secretary will see you."

"I'm not sure a secretary will do, with all due respect," he said. "We need to see someone in authority; if we can't see the Ambassador, then someone under him, perhaps the Vice-Ambassador or whatever they are called."

"The Ambassador is a woman," she said. "Secretaries in embassies refer to high-ranking officials, and not mere receptionists as you are loathe to meet. I'm sure you are familiar with the term Secretaries of State; you can imagine a similar concept I presume? Second Secretary Peter Shoal is aptly suited to whatever issue you may have." With that, she snorted, turned her back to them and sat down to resume her duties.

"Who knew?" Warren shrugged to Celina, hoping that pissing off the gatekeeper would not forestall their meeting.

In time a pleasant, clean-cut white man emerged with an outstretched hand to greet them. Warren was surprised to see someone in a full suit, with jacket and polished shoes to boot. Formal attire was not the order of the day from whence they'd come.

"Hello, *buenos dias*. My name is Peter Shoal, and I'm the Second Secretary of Political Affairs for the embassy. How may I help you?"

The man seemed forthright, and Warren hoped he and Celina knew what they were doing as he led them through the security lock, shutting one door behind them and waiting for the next door to open to enter the airlock. Warren imagined trying to get into the Pentagon, or a Swiss vault.

Peter Shoal's office was like one they might have found in Toronto, or anywhere. His desk had a few papers, he had a leather swivel chair, and there were pictures of his family, the Queen, and the Prime Minister on the wall.

There was also a plaque behind his desk that Warren noticed as they sat down.

In gratitude to the Canadian Embassy for their efforts to support the Economic Development of San Jacinto del Quiche —Magma International.

They emerged over an hour later, and passed the scowling receptionist at the front office and collected their passports. Warren's fear and insecurity returned. They were going to get no help from the Canadian government, civilians investigating Canadian mining companies were not high on their list of priorities.

. . .

They worked first from the list of Marcos's contacts, which then led to others, building up names and organizations, resources accumulated through a maze to find the source that would lead them to someone who could exhume the bodies from the well. Celina was tireless and determined to discover her sister's resting place. Warren tried to keep up and keep watch.

It was a labyrinthine effort to get a meeting, file paperwork, find someone who could respond. They went to the Ministry of the Interior, the Department of Justice, the Ombudsman to no avail. They met with human rights and *campesino* organizations that were working through lists and lists of cases of human rights violations from before, during, and after the civil war. Theirs were added to a litany of crimes that were strewn across the country's history.

It was only after they met with the Catholic Bishops' Office on Human Rights and an intervention from Marcos to an old seminary friend that they were able to expedite an exhumation request.

It gave Warren an opportunity to become familiar with the city, moving in and out of the different zones and neighbourhoods, which once you knew the key, became code words for class. The wealthy remained in Zones 10 and 14 while Warren and Celina stuck to Zones 1 and 2 close to the heart of the capital in the old colonial section of the city.

It was late afternoon and the sun was still hot. Warren had gone down the street to buy little packages of fried yucca chips and a Fanta from the vendor on the corner. He made his way back to their lodgings—a little hostel at First Avenue and Ninth Street. Their room was simple, two beds and a table in the room, shared toilets and showers down the hall.

He was anticipating the salty crisps and sweet soda as he rang to be let into the hostel. The proprietor held open the door and handed him a thin envelope.

Warren took it and studied it. His and Celina's names were scrawled on the front. No return address, no other markings. Warren looked at the owner, who couldn't speak English, so he inquired with his hands where the letter had come from. The man pointed to the barred window, made the gesture of a little kid, who must have dropped it off. Then he smiled and moved off. Warren took it back to their room.

"Look what I got," he said and showed her the letter.

Her face went pale. "Put it down, Warren."

Warren dropped the letter on the bed and they both watched it as it lay there on the blue and white woven woollen covers that kept him warm during the cool evenings in the city.

"What are we waiting for?" he said at last, wondering if it was going to explode or a rabbit would suddenly appear.

"Open it," Celina said. "But be careful."

Warren pulled his Swiss Army knife from his pocket and slit the envelope, holding it upside down over the table. Nothing emerged, so he pried it apart and teased out the note that was inside.

The letter was simple and indelicate. "*Hijo de puta canadiense cabron y india chingada, hija de puta perra, los van a matar esta noche.* You bastard son of a bitch Canadian and your fucking Indian whore of a dog will die tonight."

The grammar was bad, and the threat felt childish, like a note you might get slipped from an enemy in the schoolyard. Warren wasn't versed in death threat language and tactics, or aware that hundreds of Guatemalans had been threatened over the years, with letters, phone messages, whispers in their ear. These methods had sent thousands fleeing because they knew those who didn't take heed ended up in the morgue. Warren didn't know that, but when he looked at Celina he saw she was backed up to the corner of the bed with her legs hunched to her chest. She knew what it meant.

· · ·

The hospital waiting room was antiseptic. They had been placed in the family room, where family members could relax while waiting for news on their loved one. There were couches, and pastoral pictures of farmland, but it was still a hospital room with fluorescent lighting. Meena suspected they had this special room set aside so that other people would not be bothered by the sight of someone else's grief.

They'd gone to the police and filed a report. The officers took careful notes but were brief. Meena felt heartened, figuring if it was Petra who was lying on a cold slab, she would have received a much greater grilling.

Unfortunately, there were enough consistent details for the officers to ask if she could identify the body. One of the officers slid a picture towards Meena. But the picture was inconclusive. The face was distorted, the state of her appearance didn't allow for identification. It was a profile shot that showed severe trauma, perhaps from an intense battering. Meena felt both doubt and certainty, and therefore could not be sure. She began to reconsider criminal law, thinking neither her stomach nor her psyche were up to the task.

They asked her about other distinguishing characteristics—tattoos, birthmarks, dental anomalies. Meena, however, could remember only Petra's conviviality, humour, and her mischievous alliances and dalliances, things that were not marked on her body but which described her life.

But of course there were features. On her left hand, the digit opposite the thumb was shortened, nearly aligned with her pinkie. Petra had told her it was because of her Russian diet, just enough to fill the tummy, but not enough to fill all the fingers and toes.

They shared the same shoe size, although Petra was a head or two taller than Meena. They'd gone shoe shopping during one of Petra's lunchtime attempts to feminize her, and back at the apartment Petra had dressed her up in pumps from the closet.

Petra had three piercings—they both had, although Petra had gotten hers when she'd come to Canada, two on the left ear, and one on the right. Meena had straight piercings, one for each ear, and one for her nose, on the left. She'd had hers since she was a baby.

She told the officer these things. Not the details, nor the stories. She stuck to the clinical features and guarded the rest close to her, she was not ready to give those away.

Some details seemed to be confirmed, others confused.

And so they sat in the family room. Raita had gone on a search for coffee and sweets, the de rigueur accompaniment for sorrow and joy. She returned a short time later with coffee and danishes. She pressed the paper coffee cup into Meena's hand, and laid the danishes on a napkin on the table in front of them.

Meena gripped the cup and felt the hot coffee against her cold hand. She clenched her teeth against the tears. "Petra was the only good thing in this whole mess," she said. She shook her head and looked at her mother. "Jesus, what were we thinking? That somehow this big company would grow a conscience? Recognize the error of its ways and convert its mining operations into benign industries, suddenly bringing harmony for humanity? Petra was right—I am so naive." The tears she'd held back threatened to spill out.

Raita pushed a danish toward her daughter. "Not naive," she said. "An idealist, yes. You've always fought for what you believed to be right, Meena. This was no different."

Meena sipped her coffee miserably.

"Eat, Meena. You must keep your strength."

Meena nibbled at the danish, then put it back on the table. "I'm not even hungry," she said.

At last, the officer returned with an attendant and they all descended to the basement, where the morgue was located, below the surface.

They entered the steel doors into a cavernous, brightly lit, sterile room. There was no mistaking the absence of life. Ultra sanitized floors, stainless steel counters all spoke to the process of dissection.

As if in a drama, the body was rolled on a gurney and the sheet removed. A piercing on the left ear, the same disfigured face. Meena searched for a marking and a memory to try to be certain, to get full marks for the right response and at the same time hoping to be wrong. The face was too disfigured to tell for certain. Bloated, bruised, bent into strange shapes. The red hair was right, it seemed the right length, the rest was too hard to tell.

The attendant looked to the officer and removed the sheet to reveal the full body of the corpse. Meena's hand jumped to her jaw. "Oh my god!" she shouted and Raita reached out to steady her. But Meena began shaking her head. "It's not her. It's not Petra. Thank god, thank god." She began to convulse and cry.

"Are you sure?" The officer asked.

"Absolutely." Meena remembered Petra had a brown mole on her left side, just below her breast. She had noticed it when they had gotten ready to go swimming. Petra wasn't as modest as Meena, and had changed in her presence, where Meena had trundled off to the bathroom to change in private. She had noticed the mole on her skin, it had been the only place she seemed to have a blemish. The poor woman lying on the gurney did not have one. Meena didn't know who she was. She felt relieved. But it was tempered, because if Petra wasn't here, where was she?

. . .

At home they were joined by Curtis and Vatu who had returned from Magma's office. Raita fixed everyone with tea and sweets, and the four of them sat around the table.

"So, what do we do now?" Curtis looked to Meena.

"I don't know," Meena said. "Did you have any trouble?"

Curtis flashed a wicked grin at Vatu. "Nah, we just walked past the receptionist and kept walking. Had a trail of nervous secretaries and other staff following these two Indian guys. They couldn't tell the difference, one north, one south, all the same to them."

Meena could picture the nervous entourage that would have followed Curtis and her father through the lair of cubicles. "How did you find our desks?"

"Well, anytime some blue-suited dude blocked our way, we figured we were going in the right direction."

"They didn't stop you?" Raita asked.

"Told them Vatu was my lawyer and we were legally entering the premises to retrieve the personal effects of Meena Awinyolan and Petra Chemenkov." Curtis began to chortle.

Vatu joined in the tale. "I grabbed a piece of paper beside a photocopier and kept waving it around saying 'I have a subpoena. I have a subpoena.'"

They all laughed, imagining Vatu assuming airs as he and Curtis marched through the offices.

"By the time we got to your desk, I felt we were like Pied Pipers, but instead of collecting children we picked up security guards, secretaries, perplexed staff assistants, and probably a legitimate lawyer or two."

"And then?" Meena savoured the image, but worried about the outcome.

Curtis pointed to the table's edge. "I made them get me a couple of plastic bags. We grabbed everything in your desk, threw it in a bag and politely inquired as to the location of Petra's desk. No one seemed to want to say, except one young suited fella with glasses. Must have been an intern or something, looked a bit like an accountant wannabe. Anyway, he kept gesturing with his eyes. We watched him and headed in the direction he told us and dragged everyone along and then piled her stuff into another bag."

"And no one stopped you?" Meena asked. She pulled out the contents of one bag, recognizing her own desk's detritus—paper clips, a favourite pen, a photo of her parents.

"It all happened pretty fast. Vatu stood guard like a lion keeper, waving the paper around. An older, white-haired guy tried to take charge. He was kind of scary looking—not goon-like, more like the kind of guy who orders bombs to be dropped."

Vatu concurred. "Definitely not a nice man."

Curtis continued. "He asked if we were quite through. I said, 'almost' and then he asked us to kindly leave the premises and turned to the security duty to tell them to escort us out of the building. Some guy tried to take Vatu's arm and lead him away. Vatu asked him, as only your father could," Curtis tried to affect Vatu's speech, "Kindly remove your arm. A physical escort would be most unnecessary as that may provoke further lawsuits due to physical harassment and undue duress." Curtis replayed the incident grabbing at Vatu's arm and the two of them laughed aloud recalling the scene.

Vatu took up where Curtis had left off. "So, we continued on with these burly men escorting us to the elevators, and then they stood guard in front of the office doors, as if we were somehow about to make a dash back inside."

Raita topped up everyone's tea. "Your dad is quite the guy, Meena," Curtis said looking at Vatu with fondness. "I don't think we stopped giggling all the way back to your house." He added some cream and sugar to his tea. "You seemed to be an old hand at this Vatu, where'd you get those moves, that little lawyer trick and all?"

At this, Meena looked up, and stopped rummaging through the plastic bag that held the contents of Petra's desk. She hadn't found anything of note anyway—paper, pens, a keychain, nothing colourful or substantive. "One thing I learned growing up, was that there is conflict everywhere," Vatu said. He looked at Curtis. "You really want to hear this story?"

"Bring it on," Curtis said.

Vatu smiled and then grew serious. "In the town we were living in back in India, there were conflicts between the Hindus and the Sikhs. Well, that was one of the conflicts anyway. In any case, this was in 1984 there were great riots and demonstrations. And there were mobs that pillaged and raped and killed many people."

Vatu took a sip of tea and continued. "And yet, my neighbour was a Sikh. They were all Sikhs on both sides of me—all around actually." He gestured around the room and Meena was taken back to India to the crowded streets where men in turbans mixed with women in saris and men in dhotis. "We were all very friendly. My neighbour, he and I would walk to the train station every day to go to work. He became a good friend of mine. Anyway, the Hindus were mad at the Sikhs, or the Sikhs were mad at the Hindus, it doesn't really matter, you see?" Vatu glanced up at Curtis, who nodded in recognition.

"And we were in the middle of all this. One day a mob arrived on our street, my friend, he spoke up, he shouted at the mob, and he pushed them away from my door. My wife and I watched this from our window."

The story had marked Meena's early childhood. It still gave her chills. She moved closer to her dad. "We watched our other neighbours next door, cowering in their house, not saying anything, not because they hated us, or wanted us out, but because they were afraid. In any case, this man spoke up. My wife and I will not forget that day, not ever." Vatu looked at Raita who gave him an extra squeeze. "And for me, I will not forget it, not because of the fear I had for my life and that of my wife and family, but because of the grace I witnessed. This man raised his voice against a mob intent on burning us in our home. That was true courage."

Curtis soaked in the story.

"The courage to raise your voice in the midst of it all is entirely under-appreciated," Vatu added.

Images of India collided with thoughts of Celina and Petra, and Meena pictured the body of the girl she had witnessed in the morgue. She looked back at the bags she had emptied on the table. "Did you hear anything of interest about Petra at the office? Anything to tell us where she might have gone, or what might have happened to her?"

Curtis glanced at Vatu, then at Meena. "No, nothing I'm afraid."

"What's happened to the poor girl, I wonder," Raita mused aloud.

• • •

That night when she was alone in bed, Meena rummaged through memories, and tried to keep fear and panic at bay. She tried to hold onto her father's talk of courage, wondering how to do it. She remembered a conversation she'd had with Warren, when the story was one that lived on light posts and not in her living room. Holding onto memories of him helped her to stay calm, remain strong.

"What do you think about death?" Meena had asked Warren as they sat in a café watching a parade of drifters, students, employed, and aim-less coffee drinkers stroll by.

"That's a hell of a question to start the day," Warren was flippant and distracted.

"I'm serious."

"Okay Serious. Why don't you start while my brain gets lubricated?" He fingered his mug and sipped his coffee.

Meena was eager for the discussion. The lamp post stories had evoked a need for clarifying, for herself, her own thoughts, her interpretation of her culture and history, her own purpose.

"As a Hindu," she began, lowering her voice, self-conscious as a university student pulled up a chair beside them. She waited for the young man to settle and open up his textbooks before she went on. "Well, we believe in re-incarnation, karma, moksha, and all those sorts of things."

"Reincarnation I got—you come back as a rat or something," Warren teased.

"That may not be as bad as you think," Meena said. "Rama, one of our gods, rides on a rat." She kept going, stumbling on her faith as if she were revealing herself to the world—but only Warren was listening, watching her. The people in the café paid them not the slightest bit of attention. "Karma represents our actions in the world, and moksha is like nirvana, or the place where we break away from the reincarnation cycles of birth and death. It's like, if we do well in this world at this time, then the next will be better, and conversely, the same is true, only it will be worse."

"Do you believe that?" Warren asked.

"Yeah, I think so." Meena wasn't sure. Her family cherry picked the elements of their faith that suited them best. Her father had been agnostic in India, but in Canada, he described himself as Hindu. It allowed him to believe whatever he wanted.

As with all faiths, it was interpretive. Guidance was embedded in ritual, stories and symbolism. Living in Toronto; one was surrounded by people who came from as many countries as religions. She was a Hindu among Christians, Muslims, Animists, Jains, atheists and Jews. Then there were Pagans and Zoroastrians, Rastafarians, and the list went on. It was different however, disclosing to someone who knew so little about her traditions, from speaking to someone from her own family or the group of Indian girlfriends she knew growing up.

She felt a wavering certainty that spoke to her in her belly, and not so much from her head.

"So, is being a lawyer part of this celestial evolution?" Warren smirked at her. "I would have thought that would be a one-way ticket to life as a slug."

"You're a bastard, you know that," she scowled at him.

"Coarse language, there you go, another rung down the ladder."

"It's a sum total game, not a 'one bad deed card' to naraka—or I think you people refer to it as hell." Meena kept it light, though she was beginning to realize the depth of her own emotion. "I think you are quite familiar with this, my sinful friend."

"I stopped believing in that shit a long time ago."

There, she'd touched him, she thought. He did have emotions and thoughts, you just had to see through the flippancy. "You mean your faith?"

"Yeah, that too."

"But did that change your beliefs?"

"Same difference."

"Not to me. Listen, what happens when you die?"

"You're dead."

"Then what?" she persisted.

"You're dead."

"What happens after you're dead?"

"I can't see that far ahead."

"Come on, that's a cop-out."

"I'm telling you I don't know."

"Fine, what do you suspect happens?"

The repartee cooled. Meena could see Warren was agitated. He did believe in something—he just wasn't telling her. She rode the silence for a while, and then began a new train of thought. "What do you think about God?"

He'd turned back to face her, brought back from whatever place he'd been. "Whose god?"

Meena rolled over. Thinking about Warren wasn't helping either. She clicked on her bedside lamp and reached for *Anne of Green Gables*. She kept it on her shelf out of fondness, beside her law texts. When the legalese got to be too much, it helped her to read about Anne's adventures. Tonight, she hoped that Anne's run-ins with Josie Pye would give her some kind of reprieve.

• • •

"Where the hell is Petra?"

"That's what I was hoping you'd tell me."

Meena stared at Tyrell, unafraid. The experience in the morgue and the discussions with Curtis and her father had steeled her. "You mean you haven't seen her?"

"Not since she mysteriously disappeared, which was curiously followed by your absence and some characters coming into our offices to clear out both your and Petra's desks." Tyrell moved from behind his chair to lean on the oak desk in a pose of innocence.

"Listen Tyrell, if you've done anything to her. I swear to you…"

Tyrell raised his hand as if swearing an oath. "We're not throwing around threats I hope Ms. Awinyolan?" He strode towards her, closing the distance between them with two swift steps.

She held her ground. "What I'm saying is that if you had anything to do with Petra's disappearance, I guarantee you, I will find out and prosecute you to the fullest extent of the law."

Tyrell lowered his arm and moved back behind his desk. "Well I can assure you that your time would be unwisely spent. I have no idea what has happened to Ms. Chemenkov and indeed we've already initiated an investigation with the police to recover the property we suspect she has taken from us."

This took Meena off guard. "Property?"

"Yes." Tyrell sat down with serene confidence. "Some files," he paused and looked at her, "have gone missing and we believe Ms. Chemenkov's absence and their disappearance may be related."

"Why did the company hide the autopsies of those children killed in Guatemala?"

Tyrell's grin dissolved at the edges. "What do you know about that?" he asked with a tone that attempted casualness but had an undercurrent of threat.

"Plenty," Meena said, willing her body not to betray her fear.

Tyrell recovered and began to smile again. "Well, that's interesting because it is precisely the files referring to our earlier time in Guatemala which we believe have gone missing."

"That's curious isn't it?"

"Quite. Now that leads me to suspect you may also have something to do with this."

"Quite."

"I see. Well, I guess we'll be extending the investigation your way as well."

"I don't think so." Meena had not moved since she'd entered the room.

"And why is that?"

"I can assure you, copies of those files are safe. As to the originals, I can only suspect what you might have done with them," Meena added, calling what she hoped was his bluff. "But I can assure you, the Securities Investment Review committee will be very curious indeed to see those documents."

"Is that a threat?"

"Is yours?"

Tyrell smiled though his eyes had grown cold. "I really don't think that's wise on your part."

"Why not?"

"I'd hate to lose two valued employees in the same week—a kind of Shakespearian tragedy. Would you like to see some video footage we'd have to release to the police investigators. Just something we found in Petra's desk?"

Tyrell fingered a DVD he'd pulled from his drawer. "It was most interesting to watch two of my valued employees rooting around in the archives after hours." He pointed a remote control at the door and Meena heard it lock behind her. She was trapped. "I lost count of the number of laws you were breaking down there."

Meena took a deep yoga breath, but failed to feel the calm it usually promised. She knew she couldn't let him see that. She walked toward his desk. "You may not have noticed this, the first few times I was in your office. Perhaps I should demonstrate."

Meena pulled an iPod from her belt.

"It records things," she said. "In fact, it records everything." She stood in front of the desk, tried to strike a casual tone. "You may recall you asked me a few times to do some things, things one could say were not exactly, well, they were rather unsavoury. Do you recall? Some things your board, the shareholders, and even the police may not look upon

233

favourably. Interestingly enough, copies of these recordings are to be delivered by a courier in—" she checked her watch—"oh, about fifteen minutes. Give or take a few, I've never really been very accurate at these things. The courier will deliver it to the Delaney Law office, you may remember them. I believe they were involved in a hostile takeover bid awhile back with one of your competitors?"

Tyrell's smile was a politician's grimace. He stood quiet for a moment, calculating. Meena held her breath.

"What do you want?"

"Where's Petra?"

Tyrell smiled. "I truly do not know."

"How do I know that?"

"You'll have to trust me I guess."

"Fat chance of that."

"What else do you want."

"A public apology for the victims of Guatemala, compensation for the families and for closure of the mine."

Tyrell laughed. "I don't think so."

"Fine, you have twelve minutes left." Meena checked her watch, barely registering the time.

Tyrell was also calculating; exactly what, Meena couldn't tell.

"What do I get?"

"You don't go to jail."

Tyrell laughed. "I hardly think that is probable. We'll simply deny the allegations, make a public apology, ask for donations to the Lalita Arayo fund and move on. So, you have nothing."

"I have the tapes and files." Damn, she thought, I don't know if that is going to be enough to get out of here. Did he really have nothing to do with Petra?

"I see. But you don't have much more than that. You have no bodies in Guatemala."

"Not yet."

"What else can I offer you?" Tyrell was negotiating, maybe things were working after all. He continued, "It's not up to me whether the mine opens or closes. That's for the board and shareholders to decide."

Meena realized that was true and re-tacked. "Fine, unlock the door. I'll give you this tape to destroy and return to you the copies, you give me the video, and we'll call it stalemate."

"It's all yours. I've already seen it," he said with a leer and pushed the video from his desk to the edge. Meena placed the iPod on the table beside the video.

They eyed one another, measuring complicity. Meena felt like she was waiting for someone to say go in a match of war.

"The door?" She said, not taking her eyes off him or the DVD.

He leaned over and pressed the button and Meena heard the tell-tale click. She wanted to grab the video and run, but implored her screaming cells programmed to flee when you couldn't fight, to move slowly.

She placed her hand on the video. Tyrell grabbed her wrist.

Trying not to rip her hand from his grip, she glanced at her watch on her left hand. "Six minutes James."

"This is not finished Ms. Awinyolan."

"No, far from it," she said, pulling her hand away and exiting his office, with sweat rolling down her back and her heart pounding in her chest. She hoped to god she got out of the building before he figured out how to work the iPod and heard the orchestral strains of Tafelmusik blaring through the earpiece.

• • •

A palette of brilliant colours dotted the landscape when they arrived, women and children shifted around the exhumation site. Purples and reds, greens and yellows framed in black silhouettes flowed on a moving canvas cast against a hue of blue sky. Kids were chasing one another, running around barefoot in the game of tag that kids played everywhere. Small fires were burning and the acrid tang of smoke reached them. Women, mostly older, with large strong wrists and faces caked in memories stirred round metal pots over the glow of open fires.

It was more like a Guatemalan picnic than a site where they hoped to unearth the bodies of Celina's sister and the other young children.

Warren and Celina were delivered with the archaeologist and anthropologists in a convoy. There were other foreigners there to observe and to deter further harm against those assembled.

The mine was neither far from their minds, nor out of sight.

The archaeologist and forensic anthropologists had already commenced their work. A large tarpaulin was strung on poles, cut from nearby acacia trees, and hung over a pit. String and lines marked the area of discovery in a field that was as innocuous as any other in this countryside. Cows roamed tethered to ropes and chickens pecked scraps from the ground.

Celina was quiet, as she had been for days. Warren had attempted to engage her, hear some anecdote of her childhood, explanation of a Guatemalan idiom, or elicit a commentary. But she'd remained quiet. Warren followed her as she made her way on the path to the well.

He stopped at the lip of the pit, held back by the string. He braced himself and then peered below.

One of the forensic team was scraping away at the levels of soil, layer by layer. The excavation into the earth was made beside the well, not in it as Warren had assumed. They followed the outer wall, opening it up as they inched down by a fraction of a centimetre at a time. The archaeologist in the pit was using a trowel, similar to what Warren had used to smooth plaster when putting up gyp rock.

A small Y-shaped pulley with a bucket attached to a rope was mounted above the pit, and the scrapings from below were brought above and carefully sifted for fragments of clothing, jewellery, bones, or sign of a life long gone.

"Nothing yet." The head of the forensic team stole up behind him. He grabbed one of the tarpaulin supports to steady himself.

"Sorry, you startled me."

She was a stocky woman who came up to his shoulders. She introduced herself as Elizabeth Larros, a Mexican anthropologist who had studied in Colombia. She spoke to him in English. Her hair was pulled back in a bun and her forearms and face had a permanent touch of sun.

Warren struggled to introduce himself. "I'm with Celina," he said simply. The woman nodded.

"Are you an accompanier?" Accompaniers, he had learned, were foreigners tasked with being present with the forensic team and the families of the victims, and to ignite their international connections if threats should appear. They were like lighthouse beacons who could signal at signs of danger.

Warren looked to the other foreigners around, the ones with uniform white t-shirts that said Peace Brigades International, they stuck close to the families. "No, not officially." He wasn't with them, but felt like he was accompanying the process, in a way, accompanying Celina.

"But you haven't found anything yet?" he asked.

"We've only gone down a bit. We expect to find the first body at eight to ten feet."

"How deep is the well?"

"According to the community, it's about thirty to forty feet deep."

"And how many..." Warren shifted looking over to the side of the excavation area.

"We think they are all here. All fifteen of them."

The diameter of the well barely exceeded the length of his arm. It looked small, far too small to fill with bodies.

The anthropologist explained to him that they usually dropped the bodies in head first, that in this case they were already dead, but in other places, during the war, the soldiers did this while the people were still alive, they'd break their necks on the way down if they were lucky and drown if they were not.

It was hard to grasp, that people would do this, were capable of this. Warren thought of wells as places you threw pennies into.

He continued to stare at the hole in the ground, at once contemplating what Elizabeth was telling him, and yet still disbelieving that someone would be able to do that to another. He turned away to look off into the distance for momentary relief, the way the eyes flee from horror, but his gaze took him to Magma's chain-link fence on the horizon. He spun around, feeling trapped by the entrails of the mine.

Trying to remove the images from his head was almost too much to bear, images of young children in their Guatemalan dress being dumped while the company continued to scrape the soil from the earth.

"How do you do this?"

"Slowly," she answered.

"I mean emotionally," he said.

"This process can mean closure for some people and hopefully justice for others."

"How many of these have you done?" he asked, averting his gaze from both the chain link fence and the mouth of the well.

"Too many. In Guatemala alone we have somewhere between four and six hundred clandestine graves we still have to exhume as a result of the civil war. It's strange working here, you look up over there and see the gold mine which removes rocks and earth and leaves huge gaping holes that can be viewed from space, and a few short metres away, they put bodies into tiny holes and cover them up, to try to keep them hidden."

• • •

"Do you actually believe in this?" Warren asked Celina as he looked towards the tip of the mountain.

"Believe what?" She'd been distracted by the huge mining trucks that were still rumbling down the roads while they sat to the side, with the others, waiting for the exhumation to reveal something.

"The spirits, your ancestors, living through the inanimate geology of this landscape." His own spiritual heritage laid out the trinity for worship, but anything beyond that was a little muddled.

"Mountains are amongst our most sacred things. They are the places which touch the heavens. We have spirits to watch over them and subsequently to watch over us. And that's where we failed." Celina sat down on a large rock and began to draw in the earth with a stick. "Through our nurturing and care they bring our message to the gods. But who was to know the nature of our humanity, that we would have the audacity to transform the majesty of these raised rocks to piles of rubble?"

They both followed the puffs of dust scattered by the wheels of the dumpsters as they wound their way down the slope, heading to the ports and out to sea.

"And your ancestors?" Warren asked.

"They are weeping."

. . .

Warren loved the food, and the colours, and the vibrancy he found in Guatemala. Pollo asado, grilled chicken, emerged as a favourite. It was served with rice and a salad of lettuce, tomatoes or avocados. He would wash down the meal with a Gallo beer, at the little *comedor*, a wooden shack with an assortment of chrome-plated tables and fifties-inspired orange and mauve chairs on a concrete floor. It was his little bit of heaven. A beer after the dusty days at the site was a respite he was happy to have.

The municipal offices formed one quarter of the town square, set off on the other side by the large white Roman Catholic Church. In the middle of the town's centre was a park, at the heart of the community, as was typical of colonial Spanish settlements.

The town square drew the life of the surrounding village towards it. Bright blue, red, and yellow buses would rumble by from the outlying regions, stuffed through the windows and emergency doors with passengers, belching exhaust and trumpeting their horns to push stray dogs or overladen carts out of their way. Occasionally a farmer would arrive with oxen, clopping along the cobblestone road carrying jute bags filled with produce to take to the central market or returning home with supplies for his family.

In the central park, replete with large palm trees and crisscrossing paths, drunks stumbled around from the effects of the night before. There were vendors selling mango, fried plantain chips, or plastic baubles like combs, barrettes, and other daily necessities. Kids would be tearing around, regardless of whether school was in or not—the poorly funded public schools having to compete with life's learnings in the centre of town.

And there were soldiers. Despite the civil war being a memory of the past, the military never strayed far from sight. The soldiers might look bored and indifferent, but their weapons were shiny.

And inevitably there was ranchero, country-style Guatemalan music not unlike the old bluegrass from the south, playing in the air. The younger folks would have Shakira or hip hop blaring from their clothing stands in the market. Warren once even heard a Latin version of a Bryan Adams song coming from someone's shop—he recognized the melody, but not the words.

On the surface, it all seemed amiable and lively. It was underneath where the tensions lay. As much as he was welcomed by the communities and those whom he saw every day at the exhumation site, there were many others who were not happy with his presence in town — or anywhere else for that matter.

• • •

The nature and frequency of the threats was escalating. The second time, Warren didn't even realize it was a threat until he shared the incident with Celina after they had returned from the exhumation site to their accommodations beside the church.

Warren had gone into town to buy a pop, to give himself something to do other than the interminable waiting and watching as the anthropologists removed the dirt, layer by microscopic layer.

He was at the door of a little kiosk that advertised itself with faded posters of snacks and the universal colours of the cola wars, when a motorcycle roared up to the curb, startling him. He was surprised to be addressed in English, though the speaker, a policeman, in dark blue uniform, was Guatemalan.

"Mr. Warren Peace?"

"Yes?" Warren said.

"Be careful," the man said, "it's not a safe country for foreigners here," and then he throttled his bike, tearing away before Warren had a chance to respond.

The policeman's presence in itself was not disconcerting, he saw police daily as they patrolled the perimeter of the site, sitting on their motorbikes under the shade of a palm or sweet gum tree. Celina had told him they were there under the auspices of protecting the site, while their real purpose, according to her, was to make observations and track the comings and goings of all those who were present.

Warren shook his head, thinking the encounter was odd, then he stepped into the shop to get what he'd come for.

When Warren recounted the incident later that evening, Celina looked stricken.

"That was a threat, Warren," she said her eyes growing fearful.

"It was just a warning, letting us know we need to be vigilant."

Celina grabbed Warren. "Sit down," she said. "These are not idle warnings about your safety in a dangerous country, Warren. He named you, spoke in English and approached you when no one else was within earshot. He wasn't just being a nice guy, that's not how things work here. We'll have to be more careful." She eyed him with concern. "Warren, the police in my country are not here to protect the citizens. They are the same ones who massacred our people during the war. A random run-in with the authorities is not to be taken lightly."

Warren had heeded the warnings, and now the anthropologist team, their international accompaniers, Celina and Warren all maintained strict security protocols. No one travelled anywhere alone; they all carried cell phones, and there were guidelines determining how they travelled and the vigilance they undertook in the evenings.

Warren's nerves frayed when he answered a call that afternoon. He'd been expecting to hear from Meena so he was surprised when a male voice said "You will die *hijo de puta*."

He understood the message all too well.

Warren wasn't sure that he had the fortitude to withstand anymore.

· · ·

He recalled a conversation he had with Meena from before, before things became complicated, before it got serious.

"You know, thug comes from Hindi, well Sanskrit, and then Hindi."

"You mean, any particular thugs?"

"No, the word thug."

"Why do you know these things?"

"Part of my complex make-up. Besides, most people who speak English have no idea of the international nature of the language; they figure Adam was cursing Eve in English before they even left the garden."

"Is this my linguistic lesson of the day?"

"Just a start my love, just a start …" She took him over to the couch and sat him down. "Now, do you want the whole story of how thugs were a group of people in India who became criminals and strangled and robbed travellers, all in the name of Kali, the Hindu goddess of destruction—"

"You have a morbid fascination with violent stories."

"Do you want to hear this or not?"

"Only the gruesome details. I think my sensitive side can only take so many fairy tales. "

Except now, it wasn't a bedtime story, and he had developed an aversion to thugs of any kind.

• • •

The old woman was there in the morning, every morning. She'd stay right through the day and into the night. Warren found out that after dark, she went back to her house and fed others and then returned again before first light.

It was both a vigil and a feeding of the spirits. The corporeal were fed with tortillas, beans, and chimol, and she fed the departed by lighting incense, murmuring prayers, and providing offerings.

Other women would come, sometimes whole families. As the anthropologists excavated the well, children ran around playing and shouting.

The exhumation team had elaborate boards arranged with pulleys on which they would sit and hang as they meticulously removed the dirt with brushes and tweezers. Anything that was excavated was placed on a large metal screen and further sifted to find evidence, a piece of cloth, or bone, or tooth. The anthropologists would work in rotating shifts for hours at a time. Warren suppressed an urge to jump down the hole and dig as he would a grave, with large shovelfuls of dirt.

They rotated turns with people maintaining vigil of the site from evening until dawn, and he had spent the night staring at the burial well.

Elizabeth, the anthropologist, came by. She told him that what appeared to be painstaking was in fact a process of mourning and reconciliation. "It prepares people," she said. "As we remove the layers of dirt, what happened here is revealed, which allows the community to lament and grieve, and hopefully heal from this tragedy."

And so Warren became accustomed to the process fascinated by the minutiae of discovery. After the seventh day, they found the first piece of clothing.

The families could identify their children by the clothes they wore that day. They remembered, even though the years had piled up, scarring over other memories. They remembered if their child had worn a hat, or left it at home, if their sandal had a hole in the left foot. They recalled each stitch and thread of the bright *huijpil* shirts they had hand-woven for the girls. They carried these memories with them, they relived the day in detail, even if at times over the years they would cry out because they thought they were losing the memory of the faces of their children.

The first evidence they found was the fragment of a shirt. It was white and blue, a boy's shirt. There were shouts and exclamations. Warren had been resting, dozing, under a ceiba tree, which had become his place to seek shelter from the sun. The commotion awoke him, and he approached the excavation. Standing at the front was Anabel Xocuc, a quiet woman whose face showed the lines of all her days, and whose hands had patted a million tortillas. Her boy Antonio had worn a blue and white shirt.

The exhumation continued. They had to turn on the lights, as the sun was now shadowed by the bodies pressing in for a better look. At first Warren didn't recognize what he was seeing. It was so different from what was found in a biology room. And it was small. He thought the skull, which was passed up and out of the well, could have fit into the outstretched palm of his hand. Antonio, the son of Anabel, was four.

As they continued to remove the dirt, you could see the skeletal form of where the body had been crouched over; as though he'd been placed to sleep on his side. Except he hadn't been placed gently. Not here, not in a well.

There was an incomprehensible sadness, disbelief, and tearing despair in seeing the bones of a child, the weight of which pulled Warren from the scene. He headed back to the surety of the tree, and great torrents of grief howled from his body. He clung to the trunk as he was flooded with images of Antonio, his own father, brother, and the family his brother took away. It was a wracking pain like nothing physical he'd ever experienced before.

In the past, his grieving he'd done in anger, an anger that brought on misfortune. It allowed him to construct a narrative that suggested he was tarnished; a genetic blemish as identifiable as a birthmark. He'd not allowed sorrow to take up residence in his losses, till now, till sorrow found him crouched down by the ceiba tree.

· · ·

It was Meena's idea to bring in journalists. She knew the story would be taken up in Canada, and she'd spoken to an old high school friend who worked at *The Globe and Mail*. A feature article in the *Globe* opened the gates and soon there were print and radio reporters and TV crews descending on this little town in the highlands of Guatemala. And after the journalists shone their light on the story, the threats subsided.

While the tension dissipated, it did not go away. Seeing the bravery and courage of the families who stood vigil over their memories, adamant they would prevail, provided him with the elixir of fortitude he needed.

· · ·

Tyrell was pissed. This "situation," he'd assured the board members, had gone away. While Magma had mitigated each crisis, he hadn't counted on anyone finding the gravesite. He'd assured board members and shareholders there was nothing to worry about.

The call he'd received from the stock exchange was not good. Yesterday, he'd left the office to a beautiful day. The crispness in the air had cheered him and he'd enjoyed a succulent dinner, wine, relaxation and release. His morning hadn't dawned nearly as well.

The company stock had fallen by three points after the clang of the opening bell of the exchange, as investors and mutual fund managers opened their papers and email messages to the news. By 10 am, Tyrell had to run interference with board members and assuage the fears of heavyweight investors. By 10:30 am, the stock had dropped another four points and he found himself in the office of the chairman.

He emerged at lunch time, confident and cocky with neither sweat on his brow nor furrow lining his eyes. He exuded control and it was enough to carry him to his office.

They'd put into motion what needed to be done. He didn't find this to be a pleasant part of his profession, but one he nonetheless accomplished with ease.

Magma Denies Any Wrongdoing

TORONTO – The CEO of Magma International, James Tyrell, denies any wrongdoing related to the recent exhumation of bodies found in San Jacinto Guatemala. Activists have accused the company of being complicit in

"What the hell happened?" Scott burst into the office, ignoring the pleas of the gatekeeper.

"I'm as surprised as you are Scott." Tyrell rose from his desk to shake Scott's hand and lead him to the sitting room used for meetings. "I had no idea. And rest assured we are conducting a full investigation."

Scott shrugged him off. "That's bullshit James. You told us things were taken care of. Now we've got an international incident. I have journalists hanging around my door, and my email, phone, Blackberry are flooded with messages from angry shareholders. This is not good enough. What the hell are we going to do?"

"Get control of yourself. Dawson's looking at the legal side, and our communications platform is almost complete. We're holding a press conference in less than an hour. The Board chair will be visiting the exhumation and we'll be offering compensation to the alleged victims with a promise to build a school near the burial site. All the while denying culpability and calling for a full investigation by the appropriate Guatemalan authorities," Tyrell added. He'd already spoken with the authorities offering them compensation and a script to follow.

"And our shareholders? What the hell are you going to do about them?"

"Scott, this is an unfortunate incident, but we've weathered these things in the past and we'll do so again. We apologize, assign blame to the local engineers and the protracted civil war, show public remorse, pay some money and make the issue go away. Then we get back to producing gold for our shareholders." Tyrell neglected to add some of the unsavoury elements that Scott didn't need to know.

He convinced Scott to sit in a black leather chair, and poured him a glass of whiskey as he outlined the process in patient detail. He managed to talk Scott down and was able after a time to lead Scott from his office. He paused for a moment and then made a call at his desk, giving explicit instructions over the phone.

He put down the receiver and shook his head, and then Tyrell affixed the earphones to his head and listened to the music as he stared out at the waves on the lake.

. . .

"I feel sick," Melanie said.

"It's not our fault," Bill said.

"How can you say that? The guy killed himself because we told them—"

"We don't know he killed himself," Chantel said.

She looked doubtful. "Does it matter? He's dead. The paper said he had two young children."

"Magma did this. They were responsible," Chantel said.

"Do you really feel like we had no role in this?" Melanie stood up, her legs quivering. "We're not supposed to be like them. We're supposed to be different, remember?" She twisted her hands together and looked wildly around at the faces of her fellow activists, looking for one who felt the same way. Meena

Magma CEO Laments Tragic Death

TORONTO – The CEO of Magma International released a statement today lamenting the tragic death of former Director Scott Liddle. Tyrell noted that Mr. Liddle had recently been relieved of his position as Director upon learning of his role in water contamination which led to the death of 13 children a decade ago in Guatemala. The clandestine graves of these children was recently discovered.

Tyrell indicated that Magma had not been aware of the circumstances of this situation, and they have initiated a full investigation and offered compensation to the affected community. Police spokeswoman, Rhetta Zhang stated Mr. Liddle died of carbon monoxide poisoning, his car was found

246

wanted to meet her eyes, but she knew she was guiltier than any of them. She stared at her own hand, lying uselessly in her lap.

"I know Melanie. And I am sorry. I really am. I'm sorry if I sounded like I didn't care what had happened to him. I do." Bill spoke softly. "I'm not sure what to do about this or what to say. Scott didn't deserve to die, any more than any of Celina's family or community members. And now, we're all going to have to figure out how to live with that."

"Thanks Bill, but I'm done here," Melanie said. She picked up her coat and her canvas shoulder bag. "I'm sorry this happened, and I'm sorry for my role in it. Goodbye everyone." She stuffed her scarf and notebook in the bag and offered a quick wave then she closed the door and walked down the steps and up the road.

. . .

Warren had been sick, vomiting, haunted by seeing the skeleton of the boy. He'd been weakened and embarrassed by his display of grief; more so knowing that those around him had far more to grieve than he.

That evening, as the night began to fall and shadows appeared darker than they ever had before, a figure approached Warren as he crouched under the boughs of a large acacia tree. Maria spoke no English, and Warren spoke little Spanish, but she grabbed his hand and looked into his face and Warren was oddly comforted. He understood *"gracias"* and the clarity expressed in her stoic, strong, and reddened eyes. He was being thanked, not because he'd done anything, but because he reacted, where over the years so many others had not. His revulsion toward the acts against their children was an affirmation that it had been wrong, something that so many others had dismissed or denied.

. . .

At first, he'd been attracted to the excitement—that somehow his involvement was the maturation of his unfocused struggles as a teen. A part of him was also lured by danger and his attraction to Celina and her cause. In the course of time, as he'd witnessed the commitment of the families in Guatemala, he'd become connected to the people, their lives and what happened to them; like the woman who worked with Doña Isabel, who had two pronounced gold teeth and spoke no English, nor Spanish, but smiled at him every morning as she stirred a large pot of mosh, and filled his cup with cornmeal each morning; or the quiet, dignified older couple who staked their place under a tree a short distance from the old well and awaited the recovery of the fragments of their lives.

He thought about the chatter and play of the kids. Warren and the other foreigners were a novelty, one that seemed not to wear, as the young kids in flip flops, little girls in brightly woven dresses, grins lighting their faces, would try to get him to play games or give them donkey rides. Warren had once made the mistake of carrying one little fella on his back and soon an unending, unyielding parade of kids clamoured to be the next to ride the wild Canadian stallion, until he nearly collapsed under their weight.

And there was little Xochil, who grabbed his heart, and became one of his favourites. Her large eyes had stared at him in wonder the first time they'd met. She must have imagined him to be a giant as he stood a couple of heads taller than most of the Maya men and women who inhabited her world.

This little girl stared at him, long and hard, and then she took his hand and held it for the whole day while she toured him around with a never-ending monologue in Achi, not concerned in the least that Warren understood not a word. Every day he was at the site from that point forward, she'd grab his hand for part of the morning and resume the conversation she'd begun the day before. Warren responded in English, answering words in between her pauses, until over time Warren imagined they'd fashioned together a dialogue. Warren knew that somehow they understood one another.

These were the reasons he didn't flee, despite the fact that every part of his body was rigid with fear, and only the tender part of his heart convinced his rational brain not to go.

. . .

Meena had searched for Petra with the same dedication and diligence she had applied to her research of mining companies when she and Warren had first begun to read Celina's story on the light posts.

She found a Russian translator who helped her make calls to Vladivostok, the town in eastern Russia where Petra was from. No family, nor relatives, nor former friends had heard from her for many years, despite the fact that their names remained in the notebook of important numbers she had found in Petra's apartment.

Meena went to every Russian store, from Latvian to Albanian, with posters with Petra's picture bookended with the title Missing on top and Lost down below. Meena had dithered over which was more accurate. She visited all the restaurants from the Melody in Thornhill to the Barmalay Samovar along Mount Pleasant, hoping someone from the Russian diaspora would know something about Petra. She placed an ad in the *Nasha*, a Russian newspaper distributed throughout Toronto. She even went to some of the exotic clubs along Yonge Street, taking Chantel with her to those, as much for support as for protection.

The only calls she received were ones inquiring if she was available for something other than what was displayed on the poster.

· · ·

The little statue held a trident in its hand, had a rosary around its neck, a snake across the body, a third eye, and three horizontal lines across his forehead. He sat on a tiger. Meena hadn't performed *puja* since she had travelled through India and been schooled in the practices with her aunties and grandmother. She emerged from the ritual bath, robed and stood before the shrine with Shiva, the Lord of Destruction present in front of her. She invoked his name and offered a plate of fruit, water, a candle and lit a stick of cardamom incense. And then chanted a prayer of offering.

Lord Shiva was one of the forms of Brahman, known as the Supreme Being. He created and he destroyed, and he was known to protect others from evil. Meena prayed for Petra. That she find solace if she was living and be reincarnated into a better life if she was gone.

Meena reported her disappearance again to the police, and to Nellie's women shelter on Queen Street. There was no sign, she had received no message, there were no leads. It was nerve wracking and soul depleting to remain in a place of uncertainty. But after several weeks, she realized there was nothing more she could do.

She was told women went missing. For some it was deliberate, it was a way to erase one's identity and construct a new life. For others it was malevolent. In the past forty years, Meena found out, more than six-hundred aboriginal women alone had gone missing in Canada. And Petra, an illegal immigrant, was another missing woman added to another list.

So Meena made offers to Shiva, and prayed for her soul.

• • •

They were taken to a hillock. It was shaped like an overturned funnel and stood out in the landscape, out of place amongst the plains around it.

They climbed over rock walls covered in grass, the remnants of old buildings, or fortresses; the remaining ruins of a long-ago abandoned Maya community.

At the bottom of the hill was a path that wound around the mound, twirling up like a cone. They proceeded in a line as the heat of the day was upon them and brought moisture to coat their skin.

There was a canopy at the top of hill, open to the four directions, with the light from a smouldering fire inside. The wind resisted them, bringing them clouds of smoke which burnt their eyes and singed their lungs. Warren sputtered as he tried to both catch his breath from the hike and wave breathable air into his face.

A Maya priest spoke prayers, incanting the rituals that had been performed on this temple mount for thousands of years. Several older women sat around him, in a perimeter delineated by a circle of rocks. They chewed in the smoke that was tinged with an herbal incense, a type of sage or sweet grass that purified the air and called forth the spirits.

Warren and Celina joined the women in a circle, sitting down where generations had sat before them, and watched the priest as he spoke alternately aloud and in silence, adding bits to the flames, and gesturing to things both outside and around them—what could be seen, and what was imagined. Celina came to pray for her sister, and for herself, and Warren came to join her, in an act of solidarity. The prayers weren't in his language, and the rituals were not ones he understood, but he could see it help Celina and hoped some of that spirit might infuse him too.

CHAPTER 20

Awah *(ancestors)*

Stones are pieces of rocks, which can be fragments
of a mountain.
—Wikipedia

Bones were all that was left of her body.

Celina had told them about Lalita, shared her vivaciousness, the spirit that had enveloped her. And what they had left to show for it were bones taken out of a well.

Warren watched as they removed the skull, the clavicle, the femur. He watched as the anthropologist used a small brush and dusted off the dirt that clung to the digits of her hand. As each body was taken out of the well, the family to whom it belonged was allowed to witness it being taken from the earth and put upon a blanket, like a shroud. The pieces of bone put back together again, positioned into the shape of the skeleton of the person it had once been.

She had come out last. They'd waited for days, anticipating each body as it emerged from the ground. It became increasingly tense, as each remaining family was uncertain if they were going to find another one buried below. As the days lengthened, Celina became quieter, reserving her energy and strength to receive her sister.

Twelve days after they had begun the exhumation, and many years after the river had been poisoned, they retrieved Lalita's necklace. It was a simple cross affixed around her thoracic vertebrae.

Warren stood by Celina as the sun beat upon their heads, as the wind licked the perspiration from their brows, and their feet stood upon the ground. They stood side by side and watched Lalita being taken from the land, her bones raised from the earth, Lalita's cross grasped tightly in Celina's hand.

. . .

The first thing that struck Warren as the procession entered the church was the size of the fifteen coffins. The remains of clothing, bone and skeletons retrieved from the well barely filled a box the size of a small suitcase.

They were brought into the expansive basilica, with its huge portico columns, faded fresco depictions of the life and death of Christ and his disciples, and a liberal assortment of mounted saints interspersed between.

Wooden pews filled only a third of the cavernous space. Amidst the Catholic veneer, there were touches of Maya spiritual life, with remnants of candles and melted wax overflowing in front of small altars, and incense rife in the air settling over chicken feathers and an assortment of offerings placed before the saints and goddesses situated between each column.

As soon as the procession arrived, led by a priest adorned in a white robe with a red stole draped over his shoulders, Warren's attention turned from the immensity of the structure engulfing them to the intensity of the march through the enormous wooden doors.

Celina was near the front, each family carrying a simple wooden coffin, not more than three feet in length.

Warren held his breath as the coffins and the families that bore them flowed past. The cameras remained outside, and many of the journalists, out of respect, remained at the back. The faces of the aggrieved had been held in check all these years. Warren noted the permanent haunting of the processioners' eyes. Deep-etched lines marked the faces of the elders. Warren drew his attention back to the front, as he followed the rituals of kneeling and praying.

Warren chose to take communion for the first time in more than fifteen years. He took the chalice from the priest and brought the wine to his lips and the wafer to his tongue, the body and blood of Christ symbolized in the lives of all of those who'd struggled before and were there in this church, in Guatemala, and within him. It brought a kind of solace.

The service finished and the processioners, the family members, the teenagers, the parents, the grandparents, the neighbours, and all the friends of San Jacinto, lifted the coffins once more above their shoulders and left the sacred space.

Warren joined the forensic team and the foreign accompaniers at the back as the group descended the steps of the church and began their march through the town to the cemetery.

If it weren't for the occasion it would have appeared as a parade, as the town came out of their stores and faded-and-peeling plastered, pastel-coloured homes, to watch in silence as they walked the dusty streets. Even the chickens, stray dogs and animals seemed to respect the silence as the mourners passed them by.

It was a kilometre to the cemetery.

Warren arrived to find the ground replete with graves. The mourners surrounded a large trench. Each coffin was gently placed on the ground. A priest said the final invocations, sprinkling the coffins with a spray of holy water, and a Maya spiritual leader incanted prayers while waving incense and making offerings to the Creator. Each victim's name was spoken aloud as the body was lowered into the earth.

Celina spoke her sister's name, Lalita, and laid her to rest, as her brother Carlos stood at her back.

The trench was refilled and holy water sprinkled on the ground. Some families left gifts and mementos on top of the tomb; others simply turned, praying they had finally brought peace to the deceased. Celina joined the mourners as they stepped around the sorrow of the tombs and trenches of graves that dotted the land.

. . .

Warren returned alone. The night felt fresh and cool, but required no more than a sweater. Even that seemed a burden as the walk from town caused him to perspire.

He had been haunted since the ceremony at the church. He felt he had to return to the cemetery before he left in the morning, for the city, and then home. He thought about Meena waiting for him, her eyes sparkling in excitement at his return. He gathered the air that surrounded him, air that circulated from one part of the globe to the other and he infused it with his presence, his energy, and his love and released it to the wind.

Almost every night since he'd been in Guatemala, he'd been wracked by a sense of fear and panic, fomented at first by the harried streets of the capital. Experiences in the mine, and death threats, and the excavation of the bodies had cemented the sentiment.

Yet tonight, Warren walked in a state of wonder. The deserted streets no longer hid pouncing thieves in darkened doorways; scurrying cats no longer threatened pursuit by gangs and assassins. He walked with purpose.

The crypts and monuments loomed in the partial light of the moon. The spirit dance was in its glory as the wind whistled through the earthbound offerings of candles and flowers and gifts for the departed. Warren wove through them, guided by memory to the newly covered trench. Temporary placards and makeshift markers were placed where the loved ones had been buried. Warren made his way to where Lalita Arayo had been placed.

Warren kneeled to the ground, touching the mound of dirt that covered the wooden casket. He began with apologies, to her, and to the others. There was no order, nor form, to his confessions, simply a whispering of words and expression of emotions that he relayed to the spirits. He conjured forth the images of his life in a display of pictures of his hometown, time in Toronto, and all that led him to Guatemala, to this grave.

He thanked her for the journey, and he released her, setting her free from the race she had sent them on. He had caught up, and she could go home.

Warren sat by the grave, to keep her company until the dawn sent its emissary of light to the horizon. He raked his fingers over small stones as he sat and said goodbye. As he stood, he palmed them in his hand then dropped them into his pocket. He stretched his arms out and breathed in the dawn air, and fingered the pebbles as he walked back to the hostel.

. . .

"So, that's it, it's over?"

"For now."

"But the company is still operating, the mine's still open."

"Warren, you have to know that there is not going to be any 'big' victory, no resolution to solve all these problems. That's the thing about Westerners, you want the big solution, as if somehow there is an answer to everything. There isn't. Maybe my children's children will see an end to this."

"And so we have to be satisfied with that?"

"It's closure for the families, and certainly for me." Celina said. "Finding a resting place to honour Lalita and the others will allow us to work on other things. We're not finished here—the struggles will go on. Our ancestors began this process and we will continue it."

Warren contemplated this. He wondered whether the little victories were the ones worth struggling for after all, and wondered if he would ever be satisfied by that.

"Why me in all of this?"

"Why not you?"

"I'm just a normal regular person."

"Aren't we all?"

"What are you going to do?" Warren asked Celina as they waited outside the departure lounge. He knew he wasn't her bodyguard, but felt protective after everything they had experienced.

It was foolish. He wasn't a hero, and she never expected him to be.

"I'm going to spend time with my brother, my aunts, uncles, nieces, and nephews. I was so focused on doing something for my sister, I never thought about what would happen afterward."

Throngs of Guatemalans were moving past the security or hanging around the glass gates, trying to get a last look at loved ones who were moving on, going away.

Warren was reluctant to move towards the door. He didn't feel satisfied. They had done what they had come to do, to find her sister, to lay her to rest. They had done that. It should have felt like a success, but Warren felt deflated, almost empty.

"Are you going to come back to Canada?"

"I don't know," Celina said. Her voice was heavy with sorrow and uncertainty. "I'm not sure what to do."

He stretched his arms out to her and she stepped toward him, snaking her own arms around his body.

She whispered *"gracias"* in his ear, then let him go and Warren glanced back and watched Celina following him through the glass as he made his way to the departure gate.

. . .

Rusted machinery was strewn behind a rickety chain-link fence. The mining entrances had been cemented shut to keep out the curious, amorous, and carousers.

Warren kicked at the padlocked gate while Meena scrambled up and over the fence, scraping her hand and then wiping the blood on her pants. She held the gate open, while Warren squeezed through.

Magma Sold to Baron's Gold

TORONTO – Magma International, the besieged gold company was sold today to Baron's Gold, a South African corporation, making it the largest gold producer in the world. James Tyrell, CEO of Magma hailed the buyout declaring it would be a boon for investors. Tyrell is expected to remain on

They ambled around the site, not saying much, kicking at turned-over, rusted barrels, pushing at the concrete barriers, testing their strength as many kids had done many times before. They still held.

Warren grabbed one of the empty bottles scattered on the ground from forgotten teenage parties. He whipped it at a tipsy three-legged conveyor belt and watched the bottle shatter. Meena grabbed another and yelped in frustration as it bounced off an eroded rubber buffer. She rushed forward and smashed it on top of the contraption.

They took turns smashing bottles and spraying the ground with glass fragments until they both tired. Warren slumped down on a grassy mound, set apart from the broken concrete. Meena laid down beside him, close enough to touch fingers, and splayed out staring at the sky, like angels. They watched the clouds roll by in silence. Warren moved his arms as if he were in a pile of snow, scraping away some of the surface and uncovering pieces of coal.

He didn't add any of these to the collection he had jingling in his pocket.

. . .

The small cemetery held none of the grandeur of Toronto, nor the grief of Guatemala. The ghosts here were older.

The graves displayed simple, plain markers, one much like another. Yet, the site was maintained, with clipped lawns. There were no weeds crawling up the gates, though some of the gravestones listed sideways, playing tag with gravity.

Warren didn't speak, but headed through the rows while Meena followed. She noticed names that were repetitions of the ones before, grouped into sections. She saw MacDonnells and MacDonalds, Ettingers and the occasional Leblanc. At the back corner of the cemetery, they came to the Peaces, and Warren stayed at the foot.

Meena noted Dillon Peace, his elder brother, rested beside Richard (Rick) Peace, his father. Warren deposited a stone beside each grave, stones he had carried with him since the death of his grandfather, a collection added to from those cast aside in a desecration of Jewish graves, and from the lip of a well and the scrapings of a Guatemalan mountaintop. Meena watched as Warren bent to his brother's grave and carefully pried loose a rock that had been nestled next to his brother's gravestone and replaced it with some stones from his pocket.

They retraced their steps, hand in hand, from the local cemetery. "What now?" Meena said.

"Wanna meet my mom?"

. . .

They watched Tyrell creep along his driveway into the three-car garage. The beam of his SUV succumbing to the darkness as the automatic door closed behind them, shutting them out. They sat motionless and

258

observed as he moved about the house, lighting up the hallway, a living area and kitchen.

They didn't see any sensors on the lawn, but had noticed the security signs displayed near the gateway and marked on the door. They stole across the grass, along the pruned hedges, following the edging of the ornamental gardens. They crouched together under a maple. Neither emitted a sound as they waited for the alarm bells or growling Dobermans. They'd talked about what they were going to do if they were caught on the grounds. They had an elaborate ruse established in anticipation of a confrontation, so the silence had taken them off guard.

The night was quiet, still. A light appeared in a window and they saw Tyrell's silhouette settle in at a desk.

Justice hadn't been done in Guatemala, not fully, not completely, not in a way that made you believe in it, or in the systems for the rule of law, or compensation to the victims, or in any way that felt the least bit satisfactory.

The recognition of wrong-doing and the burials were all important processes. But James Tyrell still sat in his comfortable chair at home, and went to work in the newly merged Magma, got manicures and massages, and received new interns in his office. He'd faced no charges, paid no costs, no restitution.

And that was not right, not for Warren.

The Association was going to continue, the solidarity movement marched onward. And Meena felt there were still legal avenues to pursue, a court case had been initiated. There was negligence, a cover-up, corporate culpability.

But Warren needed an accounting that didn't wait for solidarity encounters or legal restitution.

He felt in his pocket for the three stones he had remaining. He looked up to the window and saw that Tyrell hadn't moved. He closed his palm around one. They'd been polished over time from his holding them, jangling them in his pocket or fingering them like prayer beads. He knew their contours, their shape, their colours.

The stone from his hometown, from his brother's gravesite, he placed near the left side of the house. He placed it under a hedge, where it would get neither moved nor noticed.

He had a small red stone with purple veins, no bigger than an avocado pit, from Guatemala. This stone he took to the back of the house, and he placed it beside the St. Francis of Assisi lawn ornament that stood in front of a large rose bush and overlooked the whole property.

Meena waited for Warren at the front of the house, and he returned to her, crouching low. He took the last stone from his pocket. This was his stone—one that had been with him a long time, grafted with his memories. It was grey, pockmarked with tiny depressions on its surface, and was weighty, dense, as if holding more in its space than its size should allow. It was oblong, like a Second World War grenade, and it fit into his hand naturally like a baseball. Tyrell was encircled, Warren had placed the stones as the foundations to a larger monument to ensure the dead would not be forgotten.

Warren walked to the middle of the property, towards the window. The automatic security lights were triggered and the glare momentarily blinded him. He shielded his eyes, and then looked up at the same moment Tyrell stood up to to see what was out on his lawn. Warren stared into his eyes and imagined the sound of glass breaking the silence as he threw the stone into the air. Instead, he smiled up at the window, squeezed the rock one last time, then he tossed the stone onto Tyrell's entranceway, and watched it roll up to the front door. Then Warren turned away from the house, joined up with Meena, and walked away.

ACKNOWLEDGEMENTS

This book began in the kale patch in our garden and grew out of a journey of the last twenty-five years. It would not have been possible without the love and dedication of my partner, Evelyn Jones, who embodies everything I believe, and does it all so much better than I; and my kids, Mady and Jade, who ask for "stories from your mind."

A big shout out to my writing group crew, led by the indomitable Gwen Davies, who painstakingly punctuated an earlier draft; and include Mary Clancy, Mary Evelyn Ternan, Dennis Earle, Nancy Newcomb, Cathy MacDonald, Kathleen Swan, Beaty Popercu, Nancy Hunter and Elinor Reynolds. I'm super grateful to the cast of characters who read my drafts, gently guided me, and didn't send me fleeing back to the weeding—Corrie Melanson, Jackie McVicar and Jen Graham. Also thanks to my old cubbyhole-mate in Calgary at the Arusha Centre, Terry Gibbs and her partner, Garry Leech who told me, "it was great," which helped me to start to believe it almost might be good enough.

And I'm super-thankful to my editor, Stephanie Domet for telling me when it sucked and when it glowed. If this books works in any way, it's because she helped to make it so.

Known as Paati and Thaaththa to my kids, it was in the gentle warm kitchen of Kausie and SG (Loko) Lokanathan where I was able to imagine a South Indian Canadian family—though any errors or cultural misrepresentations are my own.

I appreciate Beverley Rach, at Roseway Publishing, who stuck through this process, as I learned what it meant to write a novel. I'm also grateful to the Community of Writers program at the Tatamagouche Centre, with Sue Goyette, and Writers in Exile, with Shani Mootoo.

Everything I know about strategy, campaigns, and passionate commitment to justice I lay at the feet of Bill Fairbairn, Kathy Price and Kathryn Anderson.

This book would not have been possible without the culture of words instilled by my parents, Barb and Ron Law.

Finally, this book really comes out of my experiences of solidarity with Tools for Peace, Maritimes—Guatemala Breaking the Silence Network, SalvAide, Izalco Cultural Group, Radio Farabundo Marti, CORDES, and Peace Brigades International in Nova Scotia, Toronto, Colombia, El Salvador and Guatemala. I am grateful to all of the *compas* from the journey. *Que viva!*